The Fall of America

AIRBORNE

Book 7

WR BENTON

LOOSE CANNON ENTERPRISES
Paradise, CA

Ingram Edition
ISBN 978-1-944476-61-8

Cover Image © Deposit Photos, by license.
Author Photo © Copyright 2016, by W. R. Benton, LLC
© Cover layout and other images Copyright 2018 by WR Benton, LLC
Edited by: Daniel Williams, Bobbie La Cour, and Kay King
Logo fonts [*Shortcut, Dirty Ego*] by Eduardo Recife,
misprintedtype.com

www.loose-cannon.com

Sci-Fi Books by W. R. Benton

Eagle People, Snake People

Eagle People, The Year 2414

The New World Order, 666, Cold Lifeless Hands, Volume 3

The New World Order, 666, California Invasion, Volume 2

The New World Order, 666, Mark of the Beast, Volume 1

The Fall of America, Book 7, Airborne

The Fall of America, Book 6, Call Sign Copperhead

The Fall of America, Book 5, Fallout

The Fall of America, Book 4, Winter Ops

The Fall of America, Book 3, Enemy Within — Also available as Audio Edition

The Fall of America, Book 2, Fatal Encounters — Also available as Audio Edition

The Fall of America: Book 1, Premonition of Death — Also available as Audio Edition

Visit http://www.amazon.com/author/wrbenton/
for more WR Benton titles.

DEDICATIONS

To all veterans and other Americans who stand and place their hands over their hearts when the flag is raised or when they hear our national anthem. You are true Americans and understand the sacrifices of those who have been maimed or killed in the service of our nation.

To my Vietnam Veteran buddy Bill Bodeker, cancer is a hard battle, and my prayers are with you. May God make you healthy again.

What is the series "The Fall of America" about?

It started with the biggest stock market crash in history. Banks closed down under the weight of their bogus investments, and the financial sector failed. People looked to the government to make it all better. However, they couldn't. Hyper-inflation, mass unemployment and infrastructure started to breakdown. The food trucks didn't show up at the stores, and the shelves went empty.

Things turned ugly fast when there was no power for long parts of the day—then forever. Cops, doctors, and trash collectors just stopped showing up for work when the paychecks were delayed too often, or never came. Things started falling apart quickly after that. Whole regions declared a "State of Emergency" in an effort to maintain order and civility, but it wasn't always enough. Starvation, looting and murder became the norm. Then, our American civilization collapsed completely.

The Fall of America, Book 1: Premonition of Death is the beginning of a new series, about an average man whose life goes downhill fast once society breaks down. Set in the rural south, a scorched-earth showdown with some local thugs leaves John and his wife homeless and on the run. He encounters a member of a survivalist group, made up of former military personnel, and joining them may be his only hope. Just basic survival becomes vicious and resistance is at any cost, as the devastated country comes under a new siege—invading Russian troops.

The Fall of America, Book 2: Fatal Encounters is the continuing saga of the fall. John and his friends come face to face with Russian troops, but unlike the first book, this time they're ready and able to offer much more resistance. Russian invaders try to pacify the areas of the South under their control. The American resistance groups divide their forces into small cells to better operate effectively behind enemy lines. But as their efforts begin to gain ground, the Russians respond with harsh reprisals; mass executions become the norm and prison camps soon spring up in remote small towns. "Fear brings compliance," is their motto. The battle for control of Mississippi gets hot, and a violent world gets even more ugly.

The Fall of America, Book 3: Enemy Within. Things are
turning more organized by the partisans and with this organization comes larger attacks on Russian targets, which results in
more Americans killed in reprisals. As the partisans become better organized, the Russians become more sadistic. The Americans are now attacking gulags and air bases when the opportunity arises and Russian casualties mount, but there is at least one
traitor or more within the partisans. Can the Americans discover
the enemy within?

The Fall of America, Book 4: Winter Operations. The partisans turn mean after ambushing a Russian convoy and discover-
ing cases of the 9K32 Strela-2M missiles, or as the Russians call
them, arrows. The missiles soon change how the partisans operate; they are a portable, shoulder-fired, low-altitude surface-to-air
missile system with a highly explosive warhead. They have an infrared guidance system. Soon the partisans are attacking Air
Bases and shooting down random helicopters using the missiles
and Moscow is not pleased. However, it is the discovery of two
nuclear weapons, called suitcase bombs, by the Russians, that is
about to change this war in ways that have never been considered. Which side will use the nuclear weapons first?

The Fall of America, Book 5: Fallout. First they used chemi-
cal weapons on the Americans, then the Russians set off a tacti-
cal nuclear bomb in an effort to destroy a suitcase nuke captured
by the rebels. Deadly radioactive fallout now adds to the already
fierce battle to reclaim the U.S.A. and the partisans have even
less to lose. Now the rebels must decide whether to strike back
in kind—an eye for an eye? In what may be a one-way mission,
John's partisan team volunteers to pick up the gauntlet. Armed
with a stolen suitcase nuke, the partisans try to carry the device
deep inside enemy controlled land to reach their target. At first
they don't realize that to strike the Russians they'll need to va-
porize thousands of Americans too. Is this something he can do
for the cause with a clear conscience, and then live with the con-
sequences?

BOOK 7

AIRBORNE

CHAPTER 1

The room was filled with loud chatter as men and women, in twos and threes, carried on individual conversations. They were here for a meeting which had not started yet. The First Sergeant was near the door waiting for the commander, Brigadier General Thomas A. Hickey, to arrive. Suddenly the General and his staff rounded the corner of the hall, and when he was in full view, the Sergeant stepped into the room.

"Ten—hooouut!" He called out in a loud voice, the sound coming from deep inside of his diaphragm, right at the deepest pit. To a civilian, the sound might have been described as a loud double syllable grunt.

Instantly the talking ceased and the roomful of men and women stood at attention as one.

The General entered with his staff trailing.

"At ease, ladies and gentlemen." the commander said, his tone pleasant, as he neared the podium.

"Be seated." he said and then added, "This meeting is classified top secret and if you do not have at least that security clearance, please leave this room immediately." He paused for a minute or two as a couple of young officers left the room.

"I am the Commander here, and for those of you who have never met me, I am Brigadier General Thomas A. Hickey. This is a pre-mission brief and each of you in this room is being reassigned as part of our mission. I will now turn this presentation over to Colonel Mike Parker, my Intelligence Chief. Please remain in the room at the conclusion of the briefing so my medical personnel can administer inoculations as individually needed for deployment to your Area of Operations."

A thin Colonel stood, moved closer to the podium, cleared his throat and said, "Over the next seven days, each of you will be delivered to a new partisan group in occupied territory. The delivery systems or methods used will depend on your qualifications and available resources at the time. Some of you will use parachutes, others choppers, and then some will be delivered by the Chinese version of our C-130. You are to assist these partisans in becoming better organized and teach them how to get the most from their limited resources. I'll soon turn the briefing over to Colonel Wert, our Chief of Tactics."

An attack siren suddenly blared and Chinese antiaircraft guns were heard firing in the distance and then right outside the window.

Suddenly the north wall erupted in a solid sheet of dust, flames and flying debris. Men and women were heard screaming. I felt something peppering me, almost like hand-thrown rice, and then something struck my head, hard. I was knocked to my knees and then the force of the explosion knocked me to the floor. I might have been there two minutes or an hour, I don't know, only I felt no pain but could not move my legs or arms. Off in the far distance I could hear hideous screams of pain and shouts for help, but I could help no one, not even myself. My world slowly faded from full light through various shades of gray, and I felt blood running down my face. As I lost consciousness, I smelled a scent I knew well, death. The overpowering smell of blood, cordite, and human waste filled the destroyed room. I closed my eyes to rest them a second and my world turned black.

I awoke in a tent being use as a hospital. A man wearing a white coat stood at the end of my bed writing in a metal clipboard of some kind. I assumed he was a doctor, because I saw he was a Captain and wearing a white lab coat. My vision was not clear and I had a ringing in both of my ears.

"What happened, Doctor?"

"Key spots on the base were hit by a flight of drones, each carrying a Russian version of our Mark 82, 500 pound bomb. We have over 100 injured and almost that many killed. Now, you have shrapnel in your face, chest and neck, as well as a possible concussion from the bomb. You'll be in here at least a week, Colonel."

"The General and his staff?"

"All dead, including General Hickey. His replacement is enroute, but I have no idea who he is or where he's coming from."

I nodded, my head hurting. A decision like that was way above my pay grade.

"How's your pain level?" he asked as he placed my chart on a hook at the foot of my bed.

"A bit rough."

"I'll have a nurse give you something for your pain. You rest, Colonel, and by the end of the week you'll be out of here, but on limited duty."

"Yes sir." I said, knowing I outranked him, but he was a doctor. I was raised to respect those in positions of authority like police, doctors, judges, teachers, and clergy.

He left and an attractive nurse gave me a shot of something, using my IV line, and I drifted off to sleep. I guessed correctly, I discovered later, it was morphine. Just before I fell asleep, I remember thinking how clean the nurse and doctor looked compared to a partisan. They both looked crisp and smelled fresh, almost like a field of wild flowers.

I awoke at night, late night, I suspected. Most of the medical staff was sitting near a desk in the center of the tent. Some were smoking, while others were drinking what I assumed was coffee. All looked tired and sleepy. Two were seen stretched out between two chairs, obviously trying to catnap. I was in deep pain again, my shoulder felt like it was on fire.

"Nurse!" I yelled out louder than I intended.

"Yes, sir?" A man I'd not seen was standing beside me.

"My pain, my pain is getting to be rough."

"I'll help you in just a few minutes, Colonel. I have a Major here that lost a leg and is in a bit more pain than you. As soon as I kill his pain, I'll see to your needs."

"That's fine." I spoke much louder than I thought I would again. "You do what needs done and I'll wait." *I can't hear well*, I thought, *which is why I'm speaking so loud.*

"Thank you, sir. We started a major offensive against the Russians, so we have those wounded and then you folks from the drone attack. We only have 100 beds and the drone attack alone filled most of those. We're using folding cots now, just to keep the wounded off the ground. Since the drone attack, we're all working 14 – 16 hours a day, with no days off yet. They're coming, but not for a while. On a scale with 1 being the least and 10 being the worst, what would you say your pain level is right now?" He stood and then moved to my side.

"I think about an 8.5. My neck, back and head are killing me."

Looking at my chart, he mumbled something, glanced at his watch and said, "I can give you more morphine, but it'll make you sleep."

"As long as it kills my pain, I don't care if I sleep or not. What time is it?"

"Zero two hundred, sir." the nurse replied, and then yawned.

"I should be sleeping anyway, so the shot will be fine."

Minutes later I drifted off to sleep, feeling no pain.

The next day I heard from a nurse, who'd heard it from a doctor, that three men and a woman assigned to the base were executed for giving details to the Russians on where things were on the base to cause maximum damage when the drones flew overhead. They knew of General Hickey's briefing, too, and they died because they had brought death to visit us, a simple law we had. Sort of like a tooth for a tooth in the Bible. They killed the General, so we killed them. Besides, traitors and spies were always executed.

The war was dragging on, even with protesters in Russia raising hell, but there was no noticeable slow down by either side. The Chinese were more aggressive, but still did not take an active roll in combat except for flying. They constantly bombed the Russians and were very good at dropping supplies to forward partisans, using parachutes or LAPES. For the first time since the war started, most units were fairly well supplied, too.

It was also well known they dropped agents and spies into Russian controlled areas. I'd found them good brave men; they used no women in combat roles, but the language was a problem for all of us. In the field, I never knew when radioing an aircraft how limited the pilot's English might be. At times I'd get a pilot with almost fluent English and the next one might be able to say yes, maybe. Of course, those with limited command of the English language were of little use to most partisans. It was a good way to get killed, if an aircrew made the slightest mistake.

Ten days after I'd entered the hospital I was released. The first night, I gave thought to my life up to this point and while I was lucky to be alive, I didn't feel that way. I spent the first evening out of the hospital sitting in my quarters drinking bourbon, thinking, and feeling sorry for myself. I'd had three women, good women, I'd loved killed in this war. My first and second wife and my latest lover, Carol, who I'd planned to marry just a little over a year ago. We'd been wounded together during her last combat action. Since she was pregnant with my child, she was to be removed and stationed at the Chinese base. When our small forward operating base was overrun, we'd tried to relocate to a safer location but ended up in a firefight with Russian Special Forces, Spetsnaz. I recovered from my wounds, but she died of hers, of course taking my unborn child with her. I drank whiskey until I grew sleepy, then went to bed.

After five days of recovery time given by the hospital, I was sent to see a Full Bull Colonel one afternoon near 1600. It was sprinkling rain, but had rained hard overnight so there was a lot of mud and mud holes. I did my best to keep my boots free of mud, but it wasn't to be. When I entered his office area, I had large chunks of mud clinging to my boots. I cleaned off what I could, and thought, *What the hell, I see no mat*, and entered. I told the Sergeant I was there to see the Colonel.

"I'll see if he's available, sir." she said as she stood, knocked on his door, waited for his response, and then entered. She could have knocked on his door without getting up; the offices for Colonels and below were that small. I'm sure, like me, this Colonel slept in his office, too.

A few minutes later she came out of his office and said, "You may enter now, sir."

I entered and before I could come to attention, I heard the Colonel say, "At ease, Colonel, and have a seat. You'll have to sit on the edge of my cot, but what I have to tell you won't take long, John."

I sat as he pulled what I assumed were my records from his drawer and waited as he looked things over. *Watch it, because he used your first name*, I thought and almost laughed aloud.

Finally, he said, "I must say, I'm impressed with your record, and think you're just the man to command my units up north."

"Uh, how far up north, sir?"

"Oregon, Idaho and Washington state regions. All three need a commander and I don't have enough Colonels to go around. I have good men or women running the states now, but they've little experience, really. None have been in the business as long as you have."

"Okay, but that's a lot of real estate to be responsible for, sir, and I'm just one man. When did they assign a full bull to your position, sir? I thought a General officer did Senior officer assignments."

"I have been selected for my first star."

"Congratulations on your promotion, sir, and may you have many more. I'm not sure I want to be reassigned."

He gave me a dry smile and said, "I realize that, but it's where you're needed. I see you are prior army and ran a security business prior to the fall. I assume you know weapons used on both sides well by now, right?"

"My weapon of choice is a Russian Bison, sir."

"Let's do away with the formal bullshit, John. From here on out, I'm Bill and you're John, okay? I hate this rank stuff, because the way people die around here a man can go from Private to Full Colonel in a year. The Bison is a good weapon. Do you have all your field gear on hand?"

"Uh, when do I leave? I have all or most of it, I think, but I've been in the hospital for almost two weeks. It sounds like you needed me there yesterday."

He laughed and said, "I did, but I plan to have you dropped in tomorrow night, around midnight or so. Now, these people I'm sending you to are unorganized, under armed, and needing gear. If you think back to your first year with the resistance, well, you have the idea what you'll find. Go over your gear tonight and let me know what you need first thing in the morning."

"Crude, huh? I learned a lot over the years, but not as much as I did the first year as a partisan."

"I can imagine. I need you to toughen these people up and make them want to fight, even if they lack the means to do so. I suspect there are some moles or spies mixed in with them, so separate the wheat from the chaff. This will not be an easy job, but Headquarters said if you do a good job of this, you'll be wearing a star when you return."

I laughed and said, "I don't give a rat's ass about rank in the partisans. I just want to stay alive and, believe it or not, longevity has gotten me promoted to Full Colonel. Most everyone I served with at first are maimed or dead now."

"You'll have absolute power and control of those three states, so use it wisely. The Chinese rarely go that far north since there are fewer Russians, but when they do, they always drop supplies. The areas have been clear of any Russian Special Forces, but as you know, that means little."

"I've fought Spetsnaz and they're a pain in the ass but good soldiers. I'd say they're better than our Green Berets, but not as good as our SEALS were prior to the fall."

"They're good, then. Now, you'll be jumping tomorrow night, weather permitting, at 20,000 feet where you'll free fall to 1,000 feet. At that point your parachute will open and you'll be met on the ground by partisans. The password and counter password are Chuck -Wagon. The man you'll meet is Lieutenant Colonel Bill West."

"Will my jump gear be on the bird when I board?"

"Yep, along with three pallets of beans, bullets and explosives. After you are dropped, the aircraft will make a good dozen fake insertions and in the middle of all that mess a real supply drop will be made. If you have any questions between now and then, let me know."

"Sounds easy on this end, and I suspect it's much more difficult on the other. Any concerns you have I need to work on?"

"Just get them to pulling their fair share and all will be fine. Right now they lack good leadership and a strong leader, so that's where you come into play. Promote anyone you want and demote anyone you want. This would be an assignment a man with a big ego would love, because you're totally the main man in charge."

"My ego is small and so are my desires and needs. I'm a simple man who tries my best on any job I'm assigned. Is that it?"

Standing, Bill said, "If you need me, raise me on the horn but remember the time change. I'll help you all I can, but that won't be much, I'm afraid."

I stood from his bed, saluted, and said, "Bill, it'll be nice working for you."

A little after midnight, I sat on the orange nylon seats aboard a Chinese C-130 that obviously was purchased prior to the fall. We were flying right at 30,000 feet and the skies were rough that evening. I was bumped all around, but I was the only passenger. I was dressed warmly because it's cold at that altitude, and once I left the aircraft, I'd have no heater.

I was also wearing an oxygen mask, jump helmet, parachute harness, and two parachutes. One of the parachutes was worn on my back and it was my main chute, 28 feet in diameter, nylon, while the second was attached to me in front, almost at my nipples. It was my emergency, or reserve, parachute. There was a green steel "bottle" of 100% oxygen to allow me to breathe as I fell to opening altitude. A canvas bag filled with gear I'd need for my new job was attached to my harness as well, and once my chute opened, I'd pull a lanyard and let the bag fall below me. It would be the first part of me to touch the ground.

The pilot on the trip spoke excellent English, and he was discussing the latest weather with me and explained the ground winds were gusting where I was to jump, so he might land the plane and allow me to walk off the rear ramp. It didn't matter to me, no matter how I get on the ground.

"We have reports of some Russians in the area, but not many. I have radio contact with the partisans and they report all quiet near them. If the wind gusts grow to high, I'll land, push the pallets down the aircraft rails and onto the ground as you walk off. However, I really don't expect that to happen."

"It doesn't matter to me, but keep me informed so I know what is going on."

"Roger, I'll do that. Our flight time to your jump zone is five hours, so you can eat or sleep if you want, sir."

"Understand, but I'm a bit too excited to do either right now."

"I understand, and I'll let you know when we're lining up to approach the jump zone."

"Copy."

As I sat on the seat and gave thought to my jump, I realized it would be my first parachute jump since I was on active duty and that was a couple of years before the fall of America. I was always nervous prior to a jump and felt any sane person should be. I felt there was a difference between being nervous and having a fear of jumping. I respected jumping and knew many things could go wrong, but usually didn't. I allowed my mind to relax and soon fell sleep.

"Cobra One." I heard my call sign and woke immediately. I was still on the aircraft, so it had not been a dream after all.

"Go, Eagle One."

"We're about 30 minutes out, sir. The winds are now mild, with no high gusts. The jump is a go, I repeat, you will jump. After dropping you, I will circle around, report your condition and then LAPES the three pallets. You will land on a large field, but recover from your PLF quickly and enter the woods. The partisans will meet you on the west side of the open area."

"Copy, they'll meet me on the west side of the field."

"Roger that, and now please move to the rear of the aircraft. Once I give you the green light, simply walk off the open ramp. I am lowering the ramp now, too."

I heard the ramp opening and it suddenly grew colder. My ears popped as we lost cabin pressure and I could see nothing but darkness outside the ramp. With the help of a loadmaster, I stood and made my way to the wide open ramp.

Minutes later, the light turned to green. I heard the pilot say, "Go, go, go."

I disconnected my communications cable, pulled the little green ball near my hip to activate my portable oxygen, and disconnected from the aircraft oxygen system. I then stepped off into the air.

CHAPTER 2

Russian Colonel Senkin Yakovich was squatting on a trail a good two miles from the drop zone, cursing because they'd lost the partisans they'd been following.

"Do you hear that, sir?" Senior Sergeant Uvarov Victorovich asked, his tone barely more than a whisper.

"Aircraft! I would guess a good 3 kilometers to our west. You?"

"Yes, sir, about that distance."

"Vadimovna, I want you on point, and head due west quickly. Maybe, if they drop supplies, we can catch them unloading the pallets."

"Yes, sir." the Private said, and took off at a pace just a little faster than a walk. He still had to look for mines and while wearing NVGs, that was hard to do while moving fast.

They were on a trail which both sides traveled a great deal and where few mines were ever planted, by either side, in the conflict so far. The Russians had only been active in the three states for a couple of years and they rarely left their bases. The Russian Colonel was hoping to leave America with a line number for General. Most of the enlisted men just wanted to leave alive and healthy.

The first two kilometers were covered quickly and the aircraft engines were still heard. They continued at a fast pace. Then, suddenly, there was a huge explosion, a sheet of narrow flame moved for the sky and Private Vadimovna simply disappeared, replaced by a red mist of blood.

"Mine!" the Senior Sergeant yelled. As he glanced around, all he could see of the Private was part of one foot laying beside a shallow hole in the trail. Smoke filled the air.

"Private Igorievna, take point."

"Y . . . yes, sir." The Private moved forward because the order was lawful and he wouldn't dare speak his thoughts. He was sure if the Colonel knew how crazy he thought the point job was, he'd shoot the big Private.

Igorievna was six feet and six inches tall, 220 pounds of solid muscle, and his closely cropped hair was brown. He was cleanly shaven and an intelligent young man, with a year at a university behind him in Engineering. His pale blue eyes reflected his intelligence and his white even teeth were seen often in a big friendly smile.

He wasn't currently smiling, but sweating, as he marked three more mines. He was nearing a field now and expected to run into the partisans at any second. He'd not been on point an hour yet and his nerves were shot. He noticed he was shaking as he took his Bison into his hands and stopped cradling it. *By God, I may die, but I will take some Americans with me*, he thought as he spotted movement ahead. He held his right hand up, his fist balled, to indicate danger.

The Senior Sergeant was quickly by his side. A minute or so later, the Sergeant motioned for the Colonel to come up.

The Colonel appeared, looked the area over, and then returned to the unit.

"Radio." the man whispered.

As the radioman moved forward, the Colonel pulled out a poncho and flashlight. Pulling out his maps, the Colonel covered his head with the poncho, turned the flashlight on underneath it and, using the radio, reported the Americans position. Once the position coordinates were repeated, he requested artillery be fired at the Americans. His request was granted with the first round being white phosphorus to help him see where the explosives were falling.

The first round was was too short and fell behind the Russian Company, bringing murmurs of anger and prayer. They adjusted and fired once more.

This time the round landed right in the middle of the field so the Colonel moved the next rounds to the west a bit and then said, "Fire for effect."

The loud cracks and whistles of falling artillery was loud and most of the men were on the ground, as flat as they could get, because in training they always had a faulty shell land short. This time was no different and it just barely missed the Russian company as it exploded, sending rocks and dirt high into the air.

"Medic!" someone in the group screamed, and their tone was of fear.

"I am coming." 'Doc' Yakovna, a Junior Sergeant and their medic, yelled to be heard over the shells.

When Doc neared, a Private was seen through his NVGs on the ground and his chest was covered in blood. His whole body was shivering as if cold and the temperature was near 21.1 Celsius.

The Private kept saying over and over, "I do not want to die."

"You are in no danger of dying, unless you do not lay still and let me bandage you. Keep moving like a fish out of water and I might kill you out of frustration. Now, be still."

The medic quickly administered morphine and after a few seconds, the shaking slowed and then stopped. Using a permanent marker, he placed a huge M with the date and time on the patient's forehead. He then cut the front of his bloody shirt open, saw a single jagged puncture wound and rolling the man over, saw the exit wound. He pulled out his pea green bandages and gauze that he'd use to slow the bleeding.

Minutes later, the medic stood, walked to the Colonel and said, "Sir, we have one man wounded by the artillery, but it is not life threatening."

"Can he move?"

"Yes, sir, but not under his own power. Struck in the left side of the chest and missed his lungs. He is not hurt as badly as he thinks he is and if he were a stronger man, mentally, he could get up and walk."

"Sergeant, prepare the men to attack the pallets just as soon as the shelling stops."

"Yes, sir." He left to inform the drawn out line behind them.

Once they were informed, he'd move them into position, and have them ready to attack as soon as the last shell struck. He knew many were frightened since it would be their first combat, but he thought this would be a limited and quick engagement. The partisans would run, as usual, and the Russians would claim what was still on the pallets as their own. Two hours from now he'd be back in his tent drinking vodka.

"Three more rounds will fall, Senior Sergeant." the Colonel said, and then pulled his pistol from his holster. He made sure a round was in the chamber and then smiled. Fighting the resistance was like fighting kids, or so he thought. However, in the past they'd not had the gear or supplies for a sustained fight so the Russians had only experienced hit and run. Soon, the length of the fights would change.

"One more shell." Yakovich said as he looked at his watch, 0100 hours.

The last shell struck and lit up the night as it exploded. When the noise of the shelling ceased, it became surprisingly quiet and still. Using his NVGs the Colonel saw the partisans on the field and yelled, "Attack, now! Onto the field!"

Almost 100 Russians attacked less than thirty American partisans and this time the resistance wasn't going to leave until the pallets were clean.

A machine gun began a tat-tat-tat from the woods and Russians fell. Then another one opened up on the opposite side of the field with deadly accuracy. Explosions followed with screams and rifle shots as the stillness of the night was shattered by full blown combat. A Russian RPG zipped through the air, struck close to the machine gun in the woods sending the dead crew tumbling, and it grew quiet. Minutes later, with a new gang in place, the gun started once more.

"Uh, Base, this is Tolstoy One Actual and I am currently pinned down by an unknown number of Americans. What do you have to assist me at this time?"

"Wait Tolstoy."

"Roger."

A minute later, "Colonel, this is Base Actual, what is going on? Did you run into some boy scouts tonight?" The man at base heard the firing but didn't believe it. Usually partisans ran.

"Sir, I am losing men and we are pinned down. If nothing else, drop some smoke by artillery and I will withdraw."

"Smoke on the way, and I want to see you immediately when you return. Do you understand me?"

"I fully understand and look forward to the meeting."

"Six smoke shells on the way, uh, now!"

"Copy and Tolstoy out."

"Senior Sergeant!" He yelled to be heard over two machine guns and who knew how many small arms firing.

"Yo!"

"When the first shell hits, we pull back into the woods and return to base."

"What? Just like that, sir?"

"Those are our orders."

"Yes, sir."

When the smoke shell hit, the Russians fought an orderly retreat to the woods, and then gave first aid to their troops. Once the injured were treated, they started the long walk back to the highway where trucks waited for them. Unless the trucks were attacked; then they had a long walk home.

As they moved, the Sergeant said, "Sir, we have ten dead, twelve wounded, three seriously enough they are on stretchers."

"Headquarters did not believe the partisans were fighting for a change. In the past, they have always avoided contact."

"There must have been something on the pallets they wanted badly, sir. But what?"

"I have no idea, Senior Sergeant, but I suspect our enemy has changed and is more aggressive. Something they got their hands on tonight has changed how we fight a war here from now on and we can expect wounded and dead. I have been here six months and never had ten men killed in one mission before."

"If the trucks are gone, you will have more dead, sir. Those on the stretchers are seriously wounded."

The Colonel shrugged and kept walking.

They found the trucks waiting and they were never in any danger. They'd heard the firefight and knew their comrades were in combat, but they were guards and drivers, not infantry men. Some of their eyes grew large when the ten bodies were placed in the back of a truck and the stretchers with the seriously wounded were loaded. Even the walking wounded attracted attention, because it was unusual for a Russian unit to experience a bloodying as these men and women had. It made most of the drivers realize a person could get killed in this country.

The ride to base was sober and quiet as each man and woman gave thought to how they still remained alive, while others were dead. Even the badly wounded, if conscious, gave the subject thought. Some wondered if taking the bonus money to serve in the infantry was worth the amount now that killing had actually started.

Senior Sergeant Victorovich thought, *I spent all of my last tour here and was never fired upon the whole year, and now they have started fighting half-way through with my second tour. I am lucky though, I could be in New York City or some other large place and have a fight every damned night. Ivan said in his last letter that the partisans in the city ambush Russian soldiers using attractive women offering free sex as bait. That would lure most of my boys, and even some of my girls, too.*

"Sergeant, when we return, get the troops cleaned up, hot food and double ration of vodka for each man and woman. If you have any problems, let me know. The dining facility might not want to cook so take leftovers as long as the food is served hot."

"Yes, sir. Do you want me to go with you to see the Colonel?"

"No, he and I go way back and he knows I hit something hard out there this evening, but he has no idea of the fire power we encountered. He may think I have grown soft and think the partisans popped a few bullets at us and I wasted the money of the people in unnecessary artillery."

"It was needed and if he wants to talk to me, I will speak with him. I served with him twice before when we both had less rank than we do now. I have been here 18 months, this is my fourth tour and never have they stood and fought like tonight, sir."

"It may be a peek of what is to come."

"Maybe, or they may have needed what was on the pallets too. I noticed they kept unloading them as we fought. With the two machine guns they had us in a murderous crossfire."

The trucks rolled through the front gate without even slowing down, which meant they were expected and the Colonel would be waiting.

"I will handle Colonel Slava, so take good care of our men and women. I want them cared for and once that is done, I suggest you go to your quarters and get some rest. We will do nothing tomorrow, but we may be out tomorrow night, I have no idea."

When the trucks stopped and unloaded, a Junior Sergeant neared and said, "Colonel, I am to take you to the Commander's quarters now, sir."

"Very well, Sergeant, lead the way to your car."

"I am telling you, Slava, the partisans were ready to dance this evening, but what has caused this change? They showed they are smart by establishing the crossfire too. If they had not fired so early I would have had half my troops slaughtered. I say from this point on, things have changed and those units out in the brush need to keep their eyes open. Hell, I lost my first man to a mine and I have never seen one in this country."

"Senkin, perhaps their headquarters have given them more aggressive and direct orders. Have you considered that?" He pulled a bottle from his desk drawer, "Drink?"

"No, no drink in case I go on a mission tomorrow. Look, this situation, well, it surprised me is all. When do we go back out?"

"Tonight, and you are to hit a farm house that we think has partisans using it as a safe house. No prisoners, military or civilian, are to be taken. Check with intelligence, because the house is not used all the time. If they want to play rough, they will find we can do that. I know you may think it is too early for your troops to go back out, but like being bucked off a horse, the best thing to do is to climb back on."

"We will be ready. Is there any way of getting air support up here?"

"I do not think so, not with the few contacts we have had with the resistance. The aircraft will stay where the heavy fighting is, and right now, that is not here."

"Okay, then keep the guns ready. Where do you want us to be this evening, other than the house?"

"Check with Intel and see where the resistance has been moving the most."

"Okay, and what time do you want us in place?"

"I do not care. Look, get with Intel, find out what you need to know and then go kill some partisans. Moscow has been on my ass lately for not getting results." the Colonel said and then picked up some papers; the conversation was over.

"I will do what I can, Slava."

"Good, and I know you will, Senkin. Good hunting."

It was dark as the trucks, which had their lights off, pulled off the side of the road and parked. The drivers had been driving using NVGs and they loved it and considered it fun. No, they didn't park on the highway, but drove a short distance into the forest. The Russian troops dismounted and tonight the Colonel only had fifty troops and he was to try to ambush supplies moving up and down a road. It was suspected old trucks or bicycles were being used. Satellite photos, taken on three different nights, all showed both. The house was suspected of being empty and was no longer a target.

"Men, the partisans usually come through near 0300 and we will hit them as soon as their point man passes by us. Now, once in place, 50% alert until 0300, then 100%. If for some reason you get separated, just move south and you will come to the highway. Continue south until you see the tracks where the trucks left the road. I will leave one hour after sunup, with or without you. Any questions?"

Silence, except for a cough.

"Private Igorievna, you are my point man and Junior Sergeant Plavovna, you are my drag. Both of you stay where you can see me at all times." the Colonel ordered.

They began to move.

After about a half a kilometer the Colonel said, "They are bunching up and too close. Get them spread out more, Senior Sergeant."

"Yes, sir." He stopped and as the troops neared him, he had them spread out more.

Once at the ambush location, they placed an L shaped ambush, and each line of the letter had command detonating mines pointed toward the gravel road. The most experienced troops held the clackers. Then, they settled in and attempted to get comfortable and relax.

Yakovna, the medic, wondered how some men could sleep on ambush, knowing killing could start any second. *I can never sleep out here. I feel the enemy moving around and I worry about his sneaking into our site and cutting my throat. No, sir, I will stay awake and keep my eyes open, thank you.*

Near 0300, closer to 90% of his troops were asleep, not fifty percent. It got so bad he could hear snores, so he sent the Sergeant around to wake all the men and women. It was then he heard an old engine moving toward him.

He soon identified it visually as tractors, and each was pulling two flatbed trailers loaded down with supplies and gear. He spotted a man on each tractor, the driver, and a man on each trailer. Behind them walked a good 200 partisans loaded down with boxes and supplies. They even had bicycles loaded down, and packing a load that would be hard to believe if he wasn't looking at them. The ambush was on a gently sloping hillside and the road he was watching was in the narrow valley below. The resistance was coming through the valley and moving for the hill. He had a clear view of most of the partisans. They, and the rest of the world, looked pea soup green to him through his goggles.

The Colonel elbowed his radioman, who handed the handset to him.

"Base, Tolstoy 1." he whispered.

"Go."

"I have a target and will spring my ambush shortly. I will call you once the fight is finished."

"Copy, and good luck."

When the partisans neared, he saw only the lead troops had NVGs so he knew the others would be lost once combat started. All they'd see once the fight started is the light from muzzle blasts as the weapons fired.

The point man for the partisans walked right past them and never knew he was being watched by almost 50 Russians. Yakovich felt his stomach tighten as the main group entered the kill zone and then smiled just before he squeezed two mine clackers. He knew he was setting Russian military history in the three state area by most resistance fighters killed in one battle.

The explosions were loud, as were the screams that followed, and bodies fell. Maimed and dying men and women rolled in the dirt and on the grasses as they tried to stop the flow of blood or find detached limbs. Then the Russian machine guns opened up and stitched the road up and down a good half dozen times. Clods of dirt were thrown high in the air as the big bullets struck the dirt roadway. Explosions were heard as additional mines were detonated and then the small arms fire started.

A small squad sized unit attempted to attack the Russians which is what the military teaches in case of ambush, but they were blown away in seconds. The sniper beside the First Sergeant was sending bullet after bullet into the folks at the rear of the group, creating pure chaos for the Americans. Then suddenly, all was quiet.

Low moans were heard, prayers, and even one man calling for his mother. The Russians remained in place. They were to move only when the Colonel ordered them to move. He'd wait a while and let the injured bleed a bit. Those seriously injured would die and the others would grow weak from blood loss.

An hour after the last shot, Colonel Senkin Yakovich of the Russian Army stood and said, "Let us see what we caught in our trap. Junior Sergeant, you and your people check the trail for wounded. Just a reminder, we are to take no prisoners, so any survivors are to be executed. Be sure to destroy or take any undamaged gear or supplies. Let us hurry, because I want to be back at the trucks in less than an hour."

Junior Sergeant Plavovna and his troops moved for the trail.

CHAPTER 3

The air was cold as I stepped from the ramp of the C-130 and the slip stream of the aircraft was almost freezing. I ran through a mental checklist as I fell. My oxygen was working fine, so I tried my communications. "Cobra 1 to Eagle 1, over."

"Go, Eagle 1." the C-130 answered.

"Radio check."

"Read you five by five, over."

"Copy, Cobra 1 out." I closed communications and checked my altimeter, and found I still had a long fall in front of me.

I was spread eagle, with my back slightly arched and falling stable. The ground below was nothing but a black pit, but I could see a new sun wanting to peak over the eastern horizon, only it would still be a good hour. Stars were twinkling overhead, and a predawn grayness was covering the land like a veil. Before long, the sun would appear.

The closer to the earth I got, the warmer it became. I was watching my altimeter as I passed through a thousand feet and I felt my parachute deploy. I'd been watching so I could pull my reserve chute if I had problems. I felt the pilot chute tap me on the helmet a couple of times and then I heard a loud grunt as it filled with air, pulling the rest of my chute out behind me. A second later, I was hanging in my harness.

I quickly checked that I wasn't spinning or coming down too rapidly, and I glanced upward to find my chute fully inflated with air. I reached down with my right hand and released my gear bag, allowing the almost hundred pound bag on a lanyard to fall a good twenty feet below me. Ideally it would hit first and then I'd land, but it didn't always happen that way.

I relaxed, saw I was to land in an open field, and then slightly bent my knees and waited for landing impact. I was moving forward at a slow rate of speed so I wasn't worried about hitting hard or being dragged once on the ground. I'd do a parachute landing fall (PLF) and then disconnect from the harness to continue my mission. I'd have the olive drab nylon parachute brought back to camp with me to be used in a number of different ways. It always made a great lightweight shelter and at 28 feet in diameter, it was a big shelter too.

I hit softly, let my body relax, and rolled with the flow. I stopped on my back, disconnected the two J-1 canopy releases, and saw the chute collapse behind me. I stood, removed my oxygen mask, unbuckled my harness, and tossed it on the canopy. I flipped my Bison off safety and looked the area over closely, but saw no one.

I heard a male voice say, "Chuck!"

I replied, "Wagon!"

A dark form moved toward me from the trees.

"How was your jump, sir?" I heard a woman ask as she neared.

"As smooth as silk. I'm the guest you're to pick up this evening."

"Good, I'll have some troops gather the chute, harness and your equipment bag. We have to move and quickly, because the Russian bear is out this evening. Follow me."

As I walked behind her, she was giving orders and people were moving quickly. She gave some hand signs and we moved out in single file to the other side of the field. We didn't cut across the field like some folks would be tempted to do, but walked along the edge, remaining in the trees.

Once in position, I heard her speak, "Eagle 1, Echo three over."

"Go, Echo."

"Ready for your eggs, over."

"Roger, ready for the eggs. I am lining up now, so expect delivery in less than five minutes. Copy?"

"Uh, copy loud and clear."

I heard the four engines of the C-130 and saw no lights in the air. Scanning the skies I finally picked the aircraft up in my night vision goggles. The sky and aircraft were a pale green.

The bird lowered until the wheels were just a foot off the ground and as it flew like this, I saw a parachute inflate behind the aircraft and then watched as the chute pulled three pallets of gear and equipment off the ramp. The pallets hit hard and the chute collapsed a second later. The aircraft gathered more speed, the ramp began to close, and the wheels rotated back into the wheel wells. I saw the nose go up and the bird began to climb for more altitude.

Tracers flew through the air as Russians shot at the C-130, but none came close. In a matter of a few minutes the aircraft was too high to be hit by ground fire and I lost it to view. The enemy ground fire alerted us to the Russians in the area and we had a good idea where they were too. Two machine guns were quickly positioned and the rest of the group began to unload the pallets.

Instead of taking the time to unbuckle the straps on the supplies, knife blades flashed and nylon straps were cut. As quickly as possible, boxes were handed out and we began to move the supplies into the trees, where others picked up the boxes and moved toward home base.

Minutes later the Russians hit us in what they might have called an attack, but it was poorly done, with half the troops not even firing their weapons at us. We returned fire and the machine guns began their tat-tat-tat.

The woman yelled orders and everyone left the pallets, and we all moved under the cover of the trees.

"Artillery in a few minutes. It happens every time."

"No aircraft support?"

"No, not yet."

I heard the loud crack and scream of the first round as it struck near the woods, way off target.

A minute later, after correcting the big guns, the next next few rounds were closer, but not actually on target and the pallets were not being destroyed, if that was the target. We calmly waited and were in little danger, unless a round fell short.

The battle might have seemed to have taken a long time for the Russians; being under fire from two machine guns is hard on the nerves, but it was all over in much less than 15 minutes. The enemy was seen moving toward the gravel road and we moved off to cut cross country to our base camp. As we moved, I saw no attempt to mine or booby trap our trail and I'd bring it up to the commander when I spoke with him. It was near noon before we entered a small clearing in a dense part of the forest.

I was asked to wait by the female leader, who I discovered was a Captain, and waited under a huge tree for the Commander to appear. As I waited, I looked the troops over and none had that hungry dog-assed tired look of Southern partisans. Maybe the war here had been less blood and contact rare, and if so, I'd soon change that.

"Colonel, I'm Major James Hall and I'm the overall commander here. We're not much, just a company of mixed partisans. I understand you've been assigned as the three state commander and we are directly under your control."

I shook his hand and said, "I'm actually glad to be here. I'd like for you to arrange a meeting with some of the commanders of other units in the three states, so I only have to cover my information once. I expect to make some changes, some of which may be liked and others that will not be liked. Today, in about an hour, call all of your line Sergeants and above together and I want to speak with them."

"I can do that, sir. In the meantime, come with me and I'll show you where your quarters are, where we eat and where some of the more important parts of our organization are located."

"Do you have showers?"

"Our showers are 55 gallon drums, sir, with one for males and the other females. Holes are punched in the bottom of the drums and as water enters, it sprays out overhead. No water is heated and our living facilities are tents, which is much better than some units. Our toilets are outhouses about 200 feet behind the tents. Again, some for males and others for females."

My quarters were nice and I shouldn't have complained, but I did, "Too big. Cut my space in half and give someone who will work for me the other half. If I have a clerk typist, give the area to them."

"Yes, sir." Then, glancing at his watch, Hall said, "Time for your meeting with my NCOs and officers."

The meeting room was a huge tent, and I wondered how they could live in tents if they were actively after the Russians. It seemed to me neither side was pressing a war home here.

I arrived in the tent right to the minute and made my way to the front as everyone stood at attention. I suspected a few were late, because I was starting to have some bad feelings about this whole region.

At the podium, I said, "Be seated."

Two junior officers then entered the tent and I said, "Excuse me, but both of you officers are late. When I call a 1300 meeting, I expect you in your seats before that time, and not for you to arrive around that time. Now, please leave the briefing and be on time for the next one. If this gets to be a habit, I'll be speaking to each of you."

I heard some mumbling, so I knew those in seats were listening to me closely. Over the next ten minutes I covered who I was, why I was there and then I start explaining what I expected out of the unit. I could see some were shocked and others happy with my words.

"From now on, you will engage the enemy at all times you think you can win a battle. If you encounter a tank on a mission take it out, if you can do so with little loss to your unit. Always weigh your possible losses before any fight you start, and then decide. The idea is to bleed the Russians dry with seemingly small fights that eat up troops, supplies, and resources in the long run. Tanks, choppers, aircraft, and other high cost items should be attacked if found isolated or vulnerable. Make your presence known when you can. If you don't and I hear you passed up the chance to do so, I will have your ass replaced. I want fighters in this unit and if you have a problem with what I want, see me after this meeting."

I met the eyes of every man and woman in the place and then said, "I want my intelligence folks working 24/7 looking for targets, and I want us out daily looking around and stirring up trouble with the Russians. I want snipers sent to areas near the Russian bases and I want them to start killing. I want hits on rail lines, airports, convoys, and even Russian bases. I want us to keep the Russians on their toes wondering where and when we'll hit next. I want strikes on isolated roadblocks, supply depots, and other places where just a few men would be assigned. I want to instill a great fear in our enemy and to the point they are afraid of the dark and to be left alone. If you feel you can't do this, then I don't want you in our unit. Any questions?"

"When is this to start, sir?"

"Right this minute."

Silence.

I said, "Dismissed."

A Sergeant Major yelled out, "Ten-hooouuut!"

"As you were." I said as I left the room.

I was in my quarters a few hours later after supper, when I heard a knock on a tent pole. I walked to the door flap, opened it and found a middle aged Sergeant Major.

"Evenin', Sergeant Major." I said.

"Evening, sir. I think I know you, but cannot remember from where." he said.

"Come on in then, because I have a quart of good bourbon that will likely help you remember."

He laughed and entered.

"Let me pour the drinks, Sergeant Major, as you take the only chair. I'll sit on my bed."

Extending his hand, the man said, "I'm Gordon N. Byrd, Sergeant Major, and I'm your senior ranking enlisted man. I know you, but can't put your face to a place or date."

Grinning, I said, "Come on Birdie, you can still jump from a perfectly good airplane, can't you?" I remembered Private 'Birdie' Byrd from Fort Benning, Georgia, and Jump school.

He smiled and said, "Sumbitch, jump school! I didn't have any officers in my class."

"I was an E4 at the time. I'm a mustang and I tend to run things with an enlisted flair, which means either shit or get off the pot. I'm looking for men and women who want and will do any job assigned to them, or at least make an effort."

"Damn me, are you the same John that ran with Mark Jones and his men?"

"The same. Look, that was a lot of years ago and both of us are older now, but when with me privately, drop the formal bullshit and I'm just John. Life is rough enough and I'm sure after a few weeks, I'll have few friends here. It looks to me like nothing is being done to hurt the Russians."

I handed him a bourbon and he took a sip. He met my eyes and said, "I brought this up over three years ago and everyone told me to sit down and stop rocking the boat. You'll find few of our officers have any real backbone."

"Then, I'll get rid of them, one at time. Did they expect the rest of the states to do all the fighting for them? If we can tie the Russians up all over the states, they'll be hard pressed to handle it all that well."

"John, they were waiting for it to end, but I know as well as you do the end is not even close."

"Well, I had a female Captain bring me here, and she's good. I don't know about how mean she is or if she's command material, but she damned sure had her troops under tight control."

"That had to be Captain Cynthia Morgan, and she's good. I'd rate her right behind Carla Simmons and she's the best we have, male or female. Both are go-getters and run their commands as professionals. As a matter of fact, Morgan was just chewed out for taking on a Russian road block and killing four of them. Hall told her she was taking excessive risks."

I took a gulp of my drink, enjoyed the way it burned all the way to my stomach, and then asked, "What was her response?"

"She told him bullshit, and it was in the middle of the night and all the Russians were sleeping on guard. She said only a fool would have passed it up. Hall then made it a requirement for all attacks to be requested by radio first. I can tell you right now, not a single request has been approved since then."

"I'll soon change that. Birdie, I want you to take over the other half of my quarters and set your office up in there. From now on, you are the Command Sergeant Major and work only for me. I'll keep your ass busy, too. I think in the morning, at stand up, I'll turn honest on Major Hall and see how well he handles a good old fashioned ass chewing."

"He's a good man, really, but a poor leader. Don't be surprised in the morning if he doesn't start crying."

I took another gulp of my drink and said, "If he does, I'll remove him immediately. I want a list of those officers you think we should watch for promotions to leadership roles and those who aren't worth a shit. We'll play this by ear and give each man or woman an even chance. But, to be clear, I'm looking for men and women who'll be aggressive and maybe fit the old airborne mold we had."

"I hear you, sir."

"In the meantime, find me a person who is not medically qualified to go into the field to be my admin Sergeant. I want all able bodies in the field. If you can find me a trooper with a permanent disability that would be best, because I don't want them rotating in and out of here every few months."

"I'll do that. Listen, I need to make my rounds and inform Major Hall I am not long to be his to work with. He'll have no idea that you and I have known each other for years and let's keep it that way."

I tossed the remainder of the bottle to him and said, "Enjoy. I'll see you in the morning for stand up and pass the word, I want everyone there and on time. Remind them, it starts at 0800, not at 0801."

He laughed and left after a quick salute.

At 0800 the next morning, Birdie called the room to attention and I entered. The tent was full this time, so I had an inner chuckle. The word was out that I played few games.

"Be seated." I said as I walked to the table near the west side of the tent. I sat in the head chair and said, "Who is first?"

When all were done, I had a basic understanding of how well we were operating, our personnel status, and any supply issues we might be facing. Out of the blue, I asked, "How many missions did the three states run last night, Major Hall?"

The meeting was called stand up, because when the boss asked a question you stood up to answer him. Hall stood and I could see he was at a loss for words.

"Well?" I asked, "How many?"

"Uh, none, sir."

"None!" I shouted, "And why not? Give me one good reason no missions were ran?"

"No orders, sir."

I actually laughed, but didn't mean to respond at all. Once I was sober again, I said, "By God, Major, I want missions scheduled around the clock seven days a week. Allow down time for the troops, but otherwise, keep them all gainfully employed. No more sitting on your asses as others in the United States fight and die for us. We will, from this moment on, contribute our fair share of dead Russians. Am I making myself perfectly clear to you, Major?"

The man lowered his head and nodded. He actually nodded in response.

"By God, I asked you a question, Major, and you will answer me."

I heard a meek, "Yes, sir."

"I can't hear you!"

"Yes, sir." he said, and it was still not loud enough.

"Major, do you think you can do your job?"

"Yes, sir." Same tone as before.

"Then answer me like a man and shout it out like a proper soldier."

His face turned crimson and I caught him looking at his boots.

I stood, looked around the room and said, "Major Hall, you are hereby relieved of all duties and responsibilities until I can order a thorough investigation into the lack of military effort by this unit. If warranted, a court martial will be held. You are confined to your quarters until further notice and Captain Cynthia Morgan is your replacement. If Captain Morgan cannot do the job, I'll fire her too."

You could have heard a pin drop in that tent.

After a minute or two I said, "Sergeant Major, please find three sergeants to escort the Major to his quarters. They'll remain there and guard him. He will be allowed all we can provide that is guaranteed under the UCMJ. He will be addressed as sir, Major, or Major Hall. He will not be addressed as prisoner because he has not been convicted. At this time he is considered innocent of any charges I may bring against him in the future. Until a court martial conviction he is still a Major in the United States Partisans."

After Hall left, I looked around the room and said, "I will deal harshly with cowards or those who fail to take the initiative against our enemy. We are not here to duck out of the war. We are here to kill our country's invaders and by God, kill them we will do."

I stood and said, "Dismissed."

I met Birdie's eyes and saw the humor. At the cost of one man with no spine, I now had me a unit I could form into something. Exactly what remained to be seen, but it was a damned good start and I was pleased.

CHAPTER 4

The Russians spent some time looking at satellite images of the area and overlooked the partisan camouflaged tents a number of times. As a result, they called in a few artillery strikes deep in the forest and called in bogus body counts. Calls were made, recommendations for medals sent forward, promotions handed out, and all was well in the tri-state area.

Full Colonel Igor Romanovna 's work day was done and he looked forward to an evening with his American mistress and a bottle of premium vodka. He worked as one of the many Full Colonels at the headquarters building and his job was the chief of partisan re-education. In reality, he ran the almost empty gulags for Mother Russia in all three states. Since the Americans had not resisted the Russian invasion much, not in the northwest anyway, little action was taken by the military against civilians. The resistance was a joke so things were quiet, and the Colonel loved his assignment. Besides his lover, he did a lot of trout fishing in the mountains.

He stepped outside and, just as he put his hat on, he felt a hard blow to his chest, center mass. Looking down as he fell, he saw blood on his jacket and knew he'd just been shot, but who would shoot him? He hit the concrete steps hard and the air was knocked out of him.

A Major neared, squatted and asked, "Are you okay, sir? I see blood on your tunic. Were you hurt when you fell, sir?"

Folks began to gather around as the Colonel laid whimpering in pain. Before anyone else could speak, four more people fell, all over the rank of Captain. The Major was the last to fall and he was struck by the sniper right between the eyes and at 500 yards. His spotter thought it was a fluke shot and whispered as much.

Finally, a Russian Sergeant on his third tour in war torn America yelled, "Sniper!"

Three more officers fell screaming and bleeding before they fully understood they were in danger. Folks scattered, and a couple of squads of Russian infantry moved from the base looking for a lone sniper.

Colonel Yakovich was briefed and exploded in rage.

"You mean to stand there, Major, as my chief of security and tell me eight Russian officers were killed, four more were so severely injured they are being returned to Russia, and two had light injuries and not one American died? How did this happen!"

"A sniper."

"Sniper? Surely you jest? This is one of the oldest Russian air bases in the United States and we have never been under sniper fire before!"

"Well, we were today. Our people were so lax, they thought the first few victims were clumsy and tripped on the steps to headquarters. It was a sharp eyed veteran Sergeant that brought the sniper to our attention."

"This sniper is dead now, right?"

"Uh, no sir. No American died."

"And, why not?"

"Uh, he has not been found yet, sir, but we will get him."

"We must make an example of him."

"I fully understand, sir, and we will."

Less than a mile from the conversation in the colonel's office, Senior Sergeant Victorovich was cursing as he made his way in a run between trees. As he moved, the man beside him suddenly jerked to the left and fell, the hole in his back big enough to stick a hand in. The sniper had been located but was in no way boxed in or trapped. He already had four dead and two wounded.

Pulling the handset for the radio, the Sergeant said, "Mission support, I am requesting artillery."

"Wait one, Blue Three."

A good minute passed and then, "Uh, Blue Three, you are after a sniper, correct?"

"Affirmative."

"Uh, Blue Three, Guns Five denied the mission. He will not spend the money the shells cost to take out a sniper."

"I have people dying out here! Get your damned junior grade officer on this radio and do the job now!"

"Copy, Uh, Blue Three, wait one."

Sergeant Yurievich neared and said, "Cancel the fire mission."

"Cancel? Why?"

"The sniper is gone."

"How do you know this?"

"I am standing beside you and in the open, right? Cancel the fire mission."

"Uh, Guns, cancel the mission."

"Roger that, mission request canceled."

"The old man is going to be so pissed the sniper got away." Sergeant Yurievich said.

"I have been here 18 months and this was the first time I have heard a shot fired in anger on the base. He has little to complain about."

"Let us load up our dead and wounded and return to the base." the Senior Sergeant said. He was tired and frustrated. His troops lacked good training, most had no idea how to remove a sniper, and while they tried, they lacked the knowledge. Some of that was his fault, because like everyone else, he never expected snipers to shoot at the base. They'd been living with a false sense of security and now that feeling was gone, replaced by fear.

The walk back to the base, carrying the dead on stretchers, was a sober affair and when they crossed onto the base at the entry control point, everyone knew the sniper was not under one of those ponchos. The walk to the unit was short, but once there he had the dead on a truck so Sergeant Yurievich could take the bodies to Mortuary Affairs, as he went to speak with the old man.

Walking down the hallway he caught sight of himself in the mirrors at times and he was filthy, covered with dirt, stains and blood. He wondered if he should shower first, and then decided to hell with it and made his way into the Commander's office. The receptionist looked up, twisted her nose and asked, "How may I help you?"

Not in the mood to play, Victorovich met her eyes and said, "How may I help you, Senior Sergeant Victorovich? You know who I am."

He continued to stare until she said, "How may I help you, Senior Sergeant Victorovich?"

"I wish to report my after mission results to the Commander. See if he has time for me and do the job now, Junior Sergeant." he said and thought, *I bet you think you are special because you sleep with the old man once in a while. Hell, the whole base knows. I am surprised he has not promoted you to Master Sergeant by now.*

She got up, left the room, and then returned a few minutes later and said, "You may go in now, Senior Sergeant."

He walked to about three feet in front of the Colonel's desk, snapped to attention, saluted and said, "Senior Sergeant Victorovich reporting, sir. The sniper was not killed, but I did suffer four more dead. Additionally, I have some wounded, but they will all recover. My troops are hardly trained, sir, and part of that problem is mine."

"You mean to stand there and tell me one sniper, just one man, a peasant American farmer or cowboy, killed over fourteen Russian soldiers and sent even more to the hospital? One man did all of this?"

"No, sir, there were two Americans. One was the sniper and other man was his spotter."

"Seven lives per man is good, huh? And, they still are free to kill again in the morning."

"Starting tomorrow I will begin to train my people to be smarter and deadlier in the field, sir. Something has changed here, sir. I am not sure why, but I feel our days are about to take a turn and they will be rougher in the future."

The Colonel waved his hand as if the man was crazy and then asked, "Why should today be different that yesterday?"

"I have no idea, sir, but check with your intelligence section. Surely they must have had some hint a sniper was near, or some kind of attack was due, or was he sent out just to get us stirred up? Sort of a lone wolf attack."

"I think if there is one team of snipers, then there are others as well." He picked up the phone, dialed the number to his police and said, "Ivan, Senkin here. Fine. Listen, starting tonight, I want patrols inside and outside the base at all times. I realize it will stretch your manpower, but we took a good dozen or more dead today from a lone sniper. If needed, round up some cooks and bakers to man the gates and other places on base. I do not want my personnel on base too scared to leave their quarters to walk to work."

The Colonel listened for a minute and then said, "Consider it an order and make it happen. I have bodies now and Moscow will have questions. Cover your ass, Colonel, and get people in the field, and do the damned job now. Goodbye."

"Sergeant, give me my Intel Section." He yelled out.

"Yes, sir." the receptionist replied.

Glancing at the Senior Sergeant, the Commander said, "That will be all, Sergeant. You are dismissed."

The Senior Sergeant left the building and noticed the blood had not even been washed away by the fire department and was still staining the steps. He'd call them and have the job done tonight, so it would not be there in the morning to remind others of the deaths.

He walked into his tent quarters and removed his boots, shirt, and trousers. Just wearing his underwear, he pulled out a bottle of vodka, and took a long pull. His mind was full of information and running so fast he needed the drink to slow him down. After the third long drink, he made his way to the community shower and washed. He also shaved, intending to be in the field in the morning way before dawn, and he'd have his people with him. It was time to teach them how to stay alive in combat.

At morning stand up, Colonel Romanovna, Chief of Base Intelligence, stood and said, "Our reports indicate the overall commander for the three state region of Washington, Idaho and Oregon has changed. Actually, for the first time, one has been assigned. We know little of the man, except I have initial reports he was a senior leader in an old partisan group called the Aces. Let us hope that part of the information is false, or more Russians will start to die here, and quickly. The Aces alone killed thousands of our troops and at the cost of only a handful of theirs in return. The group was cold, calculating and professional in all ways. We have reports this new man wants operations stepped up and for blood to flow."

The Commander asked, "Do you have any information on the man at all?"

"Not on paper. I was assigned to the Mississippi Delta area four years ago, sir, and know a great deal about the man, from personal and professional experience, and he's deadly. I suggest our threat level be elevated and steps taken to better secure the whole base. Entry control points, remote areas, and supply storage areas must be made more secure, and our people must realize this is a war zone and not a holiday assignment. I have seen what the Aces did to our people."

The Commander thought for a few minutes and then asked, "Colonel, do you have time to stay after the meeting and speak with me privately?"

"Yes, of course I do, sir. I work for you."

"Good, now weather. I suspect you are going to forecast more drizzling rain, right?" The Commander tried to joke and, while all laughed, his attempt was hardly funny. No one at the table wanted to laugh now. All wondered if they'd still be alive at the end of their one year tour.

After the group left, the two Colonels sat in plush chairs in the Commander's office as they discussed the new partisan Commander.

Colonel Romanovna said, "Do not take this new American lightly, Senkin, or you will be returned to Moscow and placed against a wall and shot. The man is deadly. That is, if he is the same Colonel John Williamson that was part of Aces."

"You make the man sound like a superman or someone that cannot be killed. If he pisses me off, I will bring Spetsnaz in to clean his clock. More vodka?"

"Yes, but only half a glass this time. Uh, he has fought Spetsnaz before and while he lost a few battles, he won a few too. Spetsnaz would not scare the man and I think he would be happy just to tie up some of our valuable special forces resources to come after him. I do know he would end up killing some of them."

"That tough, huh?"

"Professional is what he is. We once tied five Americans to a fence and poured petrol on them. We then burned them alive to scare the partisans into leaving us alone. The man had ten Russians burned alive, but tied to trees near the base so everyone could see the flames and hear the screams."

"He sounds like a damned animal."

"No, he is human, and at times even compassionate with our wounded. But, do you not see? For every one of his to die a horrible death, two Russians died the same way. We soon stopped the executions of American soldiers."

"By God's holy name, the bastards are not soldiers, but ignorant peasants!"

"Do you really believe that, Senkin? Do you know that the average American partisan over the age of thirty has a college degree? About a third of them have an advanced degree. Does that sound like a peasant to you? Hell, most of our troops are farmers and kids off the streets of some large Russian city. If anything, we are the peasants. Remember the first rule of combat, know your enemy." He gulped down about half of his vodka and smiled.

"Why the goofy smile?"

"When I faced the man years ago, I often wondered how I would deal with him in combat if I had been in charge of the fight in those days. I will soon find out, if this John Williamson is the same man. Time, just a short time too, will soon show who he is. If he was a part of the Aces, order more coffins and replacement troops. In the meantime, I will check with Moscow and Saint Louis to see what we have on the man. I think, I really do, that he is the same man. I will give you an updated briefing as soon as I get the information."

"Damn me. I am close to retiring too. Good night, Colonel."

"Good night, Senkin, and if you are a praying man, pray this Williamson is not the same." Colonel Romanovna downed the rest of his drink, gave his friend a half assed salute and left the room.

Two days later at the Russian stand up, Romanovna stood and said, "I have some information to share on the new three state Commander, Colonel John Williamson. Approximately one week ago the Colonel was sent here by parachute to take command of operations against us. Gentlemen and ladies, things are about to turn extremely rough for our side.

Here is just a little about Williamson. Our DOD files, captured intact when we invaded, tell me he was a ten year army veteran, airborne qualified, HALO qualified, scuba qualified, he earned Thai jump wings, has Philippine jump wings, and is Ranger qualified. Now, he got out of the army, went to college and earned both a bachelors and masters degree in criminology. He started his own business in security and was financially well off when this country fell. There are a couple of years after the fall that we lost all information on him. I mean we have nothing. Then, he suddenly turns up in our records as the assistant to a prior special forces Captain named Willie Williams, who is now deceased."

"So, is he a special forces type?" someone asked from the back of the room.

"*No*, but he is considered smart and damned dangerous. Williams was a man who understood the Russian mind and was raised by Russian parents. Williams taught Williamson a great deal about us, which makes him even more dangerous. Then, add all the years he has survived in the resistance, and he becomes one of the most valuable men the partisans have."

"Okay. What has he done with the resistance?"

"Some of the information I am about to tell you has not been validated by more than one source, which means, plainly, it may be bullshit. We suspect, highly, he was responsible for the success of the nuclear suitcase bombing of Jackson, Mississippi. We have confirmation he was in the area at the time. We know he and Williams led the Aces for at least two years and maybe more. He is more than partly responsible for the loss of a detachment of Spetsnaz shortly after two of our suitcase nukes were taken from an ambushed train. He is a master at making booby traps and other explosive devices that kill Russians and he will scatter them to hell and back. We know he hates us because we killed his second wife. His first wife was raped and killed shortly after the fall. And, here he is. This photo was taken slightly over a year ago. While it is grainy, it is the best photo of him we have that is age appropriate. All the other images are at least 20 years old."

Colonel Yakovich gave a dry laugh and asked, "So, see, he is no superman, because I see no cape on him."

"Sir, if he decides to come here and fight, you will wonder why he is not wearing his cape in the photo. No, he is just a man, but a well trained one and one with nothing to live for. We just have word that his girlfriend, who was pregnant, was killed a while back in a battle with Spetsnaz. So, as I said before, our special forces do not scare the man and he will face them any time we want to send them."

"You have told me much about his man and his skills, but what are we, us here, going to do to stop him? How do we keep our losses low? If a total no quarter given war has come to the region, how do we win this battles?" Yakovich asked.

"That, Colonel, I do not have yet, but I am working on an answer. One mistake and it will all blow up in our faces. Patience, sir, and I will provide you with a plan."

CHAPTER 5

I stood in the shower and let the crud from two days in the field wash from my body. I was in a good mood because earlier in the week my sniper teams had returned and their reports were excellent. I also had good word from Oregon and Idaho on sniper teams working there. I'd finally made Major Hall a Corporal and assigned him duties with the Security Troops as a guardhouse guard. He'll spend the rest of this war guarding others. I felt it was a waste of a good mind because he was intelligent, but he lacked guts and I needed some brave people working with me.

"Sir, I thought I might find you here. I have an important message from Headquarters for you." Birdie said.

"What does it say, Top?"

"There are cases of smallpox popping up down south, making Russians and Americans ill. Deaths have been recorded on both sides. So far the Chinese have stayed clean, but their shots are up to date before they deploy here. We currently have vaccines being flown in by the Chinese, and I'm sure the Russians are doing the same."

"Try to get some of the medicines sent to us. It's easier to avoid the disease than it is to treat it later. Also, see if some of the clothing from a victim can be sent here. If so, we'll introduce the Russians here to smallpox through some very simple germ warfare."

"John, Smallpox is a horrible way to die. Are you sure you want to do this?"

"If it kills Russians, we can use it. Now, you and I both need some rest, because in the morning, we're off to mine some roads and ambush a train. The troops have the knowledge of how to do the job, now is the time to let them do it. We'll go with Major Cynthia Morgan's unit."

"Yes, sir, I'll be ready."

The next morning was cool, but not cold, with a slight warm wind from the west. It was an excellent day to be in the field. It was warm enough not to need a jacket, but chilly enough to not sweat excessively while carrying a 60 pound pack. Most folks don't realize the typical member of the infantry carries at least half their body weight in their backpacks. Clothing, food, ammunition, explosives and weapons are all carried. No wonder most of us have bad backs.

Thanks to the pallets that dropped with me, we had better gear, and for the first time had NVGs, grenades, and other individual gear. Individual weapons, Russian, Chinese, and American, were available for use, but most of us didn't trust the Chinese weapons as much as American or Russian models. I stuck with the Russian Bison.

Morgan gave a detailed briefing before we left and as we started walking, she said, "Walker, you're my point and Johnson, you bring up the rear. Keep an eye out for mines and watch for trip lines across the trail."

While few areas were mined now, soon I hoped to have them all over all three states. Why? Mines kill Russians. I knew once we started hurting them with injuries and deaths, the Russian Bear would come for us.

About every mile, or maybe a little less, mines and homemade toe poppers were planted. Toe poppers were usually shotgun shells in small wooden holders with the shell primer sitting on a nail. The shell protruded about a quarter inch above the wood. A person stepped on the shell, pushed it down and the nail set off the primer, sending pellets into the victim. Usually the groin area or a leg was severely mangled with a toe popper. They were cheap to make, too, and any gauge shell could be used in a bind.

By evening we'd covered some miles, but this day was really a test and dry run. To place the anti-personnel mines where they'd cause the most damage we had to get closer to the Russian bases, on the road and trails around them. That would come with time. After eating and relaxing a bit, we moved to the railroad tracks and prepared to take a train out of action.

Claymore mines were placed facing the tracks and some C-4 under one rail. When the time was right the C-4 would blow and the mines were there to take out any Russians on or in the cars. I had two Russian machine guns brought along and they had inter-locking fields of fire, so they'd be deadly once they opened up. I could see one bright eye heading for us and had everyone get into position. The train was cooking as he came out the mountains and was on level ground, knowing home was right around the bend and then about twenty more miles.

I knew the trains were engineered by civilians, but they knew the risk when they took a job with our enemies. I've killed more than one railroad employee and I was about to kill even more this evening. There was a good chance anyone with the engineer would be killed when the engine left the track this evening. I was in a war and I'd not avoid destroying a train just because a civilian might be killed; after all, I did consider them traitors. They either lived or died, depending on God's will, not mine. I think anyone who offers their skills to the Russians should be shot.

Major Morgan was to blow the C-4 just before the engine reached it and that meant waiting until the last second. Blow too early and the train would just stop on the tracks, or blow too late and the engine would go to the next city and call the Russians. Timing was important. I moved to her side and watched the big beast move toward me.

Just as the train neared the C-4, maybe 20 feet away, I yelled, "Now!"

A narrow wall of fire appeared on the tracks and I saw a rail, broken, pointing toward the skies. The engine hit the open space and continued to roll forward even when the tracks gave a gentle turn to the right. The engineer was attempting to stop the train, but that wouldn't happen now because the engine was off the tracks. It moved forward about 50 feet then leaned to the right and fell over on its side. I heard a horrible scream and knew the engineer was crushed by his heavy engine. The noise all this made was thunderous and loud. Steam, smoke, and debris filled the air. The second car held troops and it struck the rear of the engine, and then the Claymore mines went off.

Screams, yells, and shouts were heard as hundreds of small steel ball bearings filled the air, striking the Russians hard. Men fell and body parts were blown from torsos. A mist of crimson hung over the car as the troops fell, many to never get up again. Then the rat-tat-tat of the machine guns were heard as the gunners racked the length of the train and back again. More screams were heard and I knew men and women were dying. This was a killing field and this day it was the Russians dying; tomorrow it might be my troops.

There was little resistance and soon we swarmed the train, shooting and looting the passenger cars as the infantry tried to fight us off. We'd fire a few rounds through the wooden sides of the cars and then lob in a grenade. Within ten minutes the battle was over.

A search of the supply cars provided us with Russian rations, called a Green Frog by them, RPGs, ammunition, two more machine guns, NVGs, bayonets, and all sorts of various clothing. We took all we could carry and then I'd have someone return later to pick up what we hid. I did find five cases of vodka and one of bourbon, a fine Kentucky sipping whiskey, and took it all for our wounded. Medical supplies were a priority and that's all one car had, medications, needles, gauze and other supplies. I destroyed any medical machines, because we had no electrical power.

"Colonel," the Major said, "I think our first train robbery was a great success. I'd like for you to take a bottle of the bourbon and my medical team will take the vodka. Think of it as a celebration of passing our first skills test. The rest of the bourbon will be kept for your use, sir."

"By God, I'll do that." I said with a smile. "Have half of the dead Russians bodies booby trapped and lay mines and toe poppers all over the place. Any injured Russians that are still alive should be given medical care and left here. We do not have a POW camp, yet." I then found a young, but very dead Russian Captain and placed an ace of spades card in his open mouth.

"Yes, sir." she replied.

"See to this now, Major, because I want to leave in ten minutes."

She smiled, proud of herself and her troops and said, "Yes, sir."

Ten minutes later a dozen bikes were loaded down with supplies, every troop carried a box of something and it was almost a walk in the park to get back home. I knew this would be the last trip we'd get away so cleanly, because we'd just brought war to the three state area. While we hit this train, the other two states were to hit trains too. Three trains in one night, one in each state, would alert the Russians that things were forever changed and war had come to stay.

Once back in camp and after a mission debrief, which would always be done, everyone settled down to shower, eat, and then get some sleep. It was near 0200 before I was in bed. I did have one small glass of the bourbon and must say, it was smooth. I placed the other bottles under my cot.

Morning dawned cool with gray clouds low in the sky and a distant sound was heard right after daybreak.

"Chopper, and I've never heard or seen one out here." a male Lieutenant I didn't know said.

"Searching for us, most likely. Hitting a train like we did last night cost them big time, and they're pissed now. Have everyone get in the tents and under the camouflaged netting. Let's pray they don't come back this evening with one equipped with infrared radar. All they'd have to do is shoot at the running red images on their screens like a video game. We'll discuss those helicopters this morning, once this one completes his search grids. In the meantime, Lieutenant, have some RPGs brought out and LAWs if you have them. I don't suspect you have any SAMs do you?"

"No, sir, no SAMs. I'll see to the RPGs and LAWs."

I stood in place watching the chopper look for us and when about a quarter of a mile away, he broke out of pattern and flew south. I knew then we'd been lucky.

I walked into my quarters, gave what I'd just seen some thought and then called out, "Radio!"

"Yo!"

"Get your ass in here, Thomas, and get Headquarters on the phone."

"Yes, sir."

I smiled when the Sergeant entered my living space and began his phone chatter.

"And the nature of our call, sir?"

"I have a shopping list. Tell them we'll send it in code within a few minutes. It is essential I get everything on this list. Tell them things are heating up and quickly."

Smiling, the young man said, "Yes, sir."

A few minutes later he said, "Let me pull out my code book, sir, and we can start."

The next night, three pallets of gear arrived, along with some Russian shoulder launched missiles and enough NVGs and batteries for all of us, along with 5,000 spare batteries. More anti-personnel mines and C-4 was sent too. Soon, within this week, I'd start to send my squads out hunting Russians. I'd soon have Mother Russia crimson with rage, but I was unaware of this. Seems I came along and spoiled the perfect war zone assignment in America for the Russian troops. Now, they knew they had a war going on.

Four nights later, I saddled up and moved into a line led by newly promoted Major Carla Simmons. She was short, with red hair, green eyes and even white teeth. Just by looking at her smile, I knew someone had paid thousands for dental work, because it was perfect. She was even tempered, unless angered, and untested in combat. I found her intelligent and motivated to be a good leader. This mission would change her, one way or the other.

About four miles from us was a roadblock with a huge Russian tank, T-90, at 46 tons, and it was armed for bear. I wanted to see if my people could take it out of action. The entire mission was hers, from the planning through the execution. As we moved, we left booby traps behind us and used every trick in the book.

We planted pressure mines on the dirt trail, toe poppers, fulcrum booby traps with sharpened spikes that would hit a person at chest level, trip mines with all kinds of surprises, and even a line across the trail that would pull a grenade from a can. The pin on the grenade was pulled, the grenade was slid into a can but the sides of the can kept the handle down, and then a line was attached to the grenade. A line was stretched across the trail and secured. It was about 4 inches above the walkway. An unsuspecting Russian would hit the line, pull the grenade from the can, the spoon would fly off, and the explosive was then armed. A timer allowed the explosive a zero to five second delay before exploding.

When we were about 150 yards from the tank, Simmons had her team stop and then sent a single man forward to scout.

When he returned the man said, "There's a Russian T-90 tank and a machine gun nest in the middle of the road, but I saw only three men moving around. No one was near the machine gun and all three men were sitting on the tank. I suspect they're the tank crew. I saw men sleeping under a tarp that made a crude lean-to. The canvas was attached to the side of the tank and angled downward with rocks holding it in place. I'm guessing maybe four men in the shelter. I know some were sleeping, because I heard them snoring."

"We'll launch a three sided attack against the tank. I want you, Sergeant, to attack toward the rear, I'll attack the front and Corporal Jones will attack the left side. Crawl forward as close as you can and then wait. At some point, my flamethrower will open for business. At that point, try to kill the three men on the tank, they probably are the crew, and get a couple of grenades down a hatch.

Everyone needs to lower their night vision goggles and let's move." Morgan said.

It sounded too easy to me. Something would go wrong because it usually does, and I'd watch how she handled the stress.

"Pike, since you're my sniper, hang back and kill any that seem to see us or that move for the machine gun."

"Will do."

Pike was short, five feet and three inches, and maybe twenty pounds overweight, or he may have been big boned. Due to our poor rations, we rarely had anyone overweight and no obesity at all. His hair was brown, his face cleanly shaven, and his teeth in poor shape. He had eyes like a wolf and they were constantly moving and scanning. Now, he moved off to get a good position.

"We crawl to the tank." Morgan said and then began to move.

About twenty feet from the big beast, I heard a long burst of gunfire, followed almost immediately by a loud swoosh. The first burst of flame from the flamethrower hit the canvas the Russians were sleeping under and the second hit the top of the tank.

The three Russians on the tank were engulfed in flames and each of the men in the tent had some of the jellied gas on them. As the three staggered on the tank, the screams were hideous and made the hairs on my neck stand out.

"Shoot the men on the tank!" Morgan screamed.

I heard three shots and all of the men dancing in the flames dropped. I saw one of our troops approach the tank and toss two grenades into both open hatches. One grenade was thrown right back out of the hatch and exploded just as it left the hatch. I saw the driver try to leave by his hatch, only he waited too long.

The blast inside the tank was loud, and it knocked one of the burning bodies to the grasses. Guns were blasting away at the Russians who'd been in the tent. I suspected most were severely burned. Grenades exploded and men fell. The woman carrying our flamethrower ran forward and climbed up on the tank and sent two longs squirts of flames into the driver's open hatch. Surprisingly, even as she jumped down and ran for cover, a loud scream was heard, followed by an explosion.

Suddenly the tank blew and the turret was thrown a good one hundred feet into the air when the fuel went up. Now secondary explosions were heard. We stayed back and under cover as the compressed air tanks and ammunition cooked off, and black oily smoke joined the greasy flames as they rolled inside of each other as they rose.

Once the flames died down a little we rushed forward, and rifle shots followed by screams were heard as more Russians died. We reached the machine gun, found it in perfect shape and so was the ammo, so we took the gun, making three of the guns for us on this trip. One of the burnt men was still burning from the waist down, and his face was a black melted mess as I slipped an Aces card into his mouth and then pushed it closed. Now they'd know they were up against professionals once again.

We even found a mortar and cases of ammo, which explained why we'd killed over a dozen men. You can figure 2 or 3 men for the machine gun, 3 for the tank and about 4 for the mortar. I'm sure a few were assigned there because they were infantry and the roadblock needed guards.

"Don't forget to booby trap about half the bodies and remember to replace some of the ammo with our super-duper ammo filled with C-4." We'd taken about 40 cartridges back in camp and replaced the powder with C-4 plastic explosive. I knew from experience it'd ruin someone's day if fired.

"Rogers, see the Russian wounded cared for. Wrap them up and give each of the seriously wounded a shot of morphine. Alright, I want everyone ready to leave in five minutes, so take what gear we need and let's get ready to move."

Ten minutes later, as we moved down the trail, we heard a chopper. I prayed they had no infrared on board or we were dead meat. I knew sooner or later we'd run into some that did and when that happened, we'd have folks die.

"Looking in grids, so they're looking for us." I noticed a front with gray clouds moving in and suspected rain.

"The second one flew by us, so it must be headed to the tank." Morgan said.

"Stop and crawl up close to a tree." I ordered and moved toward a giant pine. I watched the others move to trees as well.

A spotlight came on, but they were in front of us and not close. As they worked a grid, I removed a Chinese Ground-to-Air missile and waited. I was the only one on the team that had ever downed an aircraft with a missile and I'd hit jet planes and choppers. It's fairly easy if you can remain somewhat in the open long enough to sight them in, but that is difficult to do at times.

The aircraft moved closer and I locked onto the target, unsure if my lock on caused any alarm systems to respond on the aircraft or not. I saw no evasive action taken. I then squeezed the trigger and saw my missile strike the aircraft in the engine and explode.

There was no huge fireball, but the aircraft immediately sounded different and after an instant, it began to spin horizontally as the pilot attempted to put the bird on the ground. He was on fire and, when he was about twenty feet from the ground, the blades struck the trees and down he went to land almost dead center on our trail. When he struck the ground, rear first, the fuel tanks must have ruptured because a huge fireball made for the sky. There came a loud explosion and oily black smoke rose for the low gray clouds. Two men ran from the aircraft in flames and the co-pilot opened his door and stepped out. The flames from burning fuel had not reached him yet.

Seeing one of us, the co-pilot raised his pistol to aim, but it was his last act on earth. We opened up on him and the burning men, dropping all in seconds in a hailstorm of lead.

"Move, move! Go around the aircraft!" I screamed before the second bird arrived. As we moved, I heard the aircraft nearing. I saw it fly overhead, but it didn't even slow down. It banked and returned. Two spotlights came on, most likely mounted on machine guns and they quickly located the trail.

"Off the trail and now!" Morgan screamed.

Shit, she's seen something, I thought and a second later, one of the big guns began to fire. By the light of the spotlight, I saw clumps of soil thrown six feet in the air as a Type 67 machine gun fired. I watched in shock as it continued to hit off the trail and then blood, gore and bones replaced the clumps of dirt. One of us had just been killed. The aircraft hovered a few minutes and then I heard Morgan yell, "Fire!"

Everyone but me fired, and I was trying to remember who had the other Chinese surface to air missile, but I gave up. It would take time for me to remember names and faces in a new group. The aircraft rocked and began to smoke. When the firing stopped, I heard two lone shots by us and figured the sniper was trying his luck. The bird suddenly nosed down and began to move forward as it gained speed. I knew then it was going to gain altitude, but I had no idea if anyone on the thing was dead or wounded. Slowly it got higher than the trees and then limped south, still smoking.

"Check our people, Sergeant." Morgan said as she walked toward me.

"I screwed that up, huh?"

"Not really, but an experienced crew working with jets would have pulled up with the first shots fired at him and called in the fast movers to kill us. I think he was new to combat, so running into us was as much of a surprise to him as to us. He reacted slowly, and poorly too. We both made mistakes. Now, lets move and return to base camp. Be sure to booby trap the trail as we travel."

Of the three troops hit by the Type 67 machine gun, the 7.62 rounds tore them to pieces, and all were dead. Even with three dead I considered it a very good night, and the price paid for destroying a heavy piece of armor and chopper as light. I didn't realize how cold I was getting to be and I now thought of the price we paid for everything; human life was slowly losing it's value to me. Three of us were now dead and I didn't even ask for their names.

CHAPTER 6

Colonel Yakovich paced in front of the table during his morning staff meeting. He was livid. He'd lost a valuable chopper, four crew members, and then a T-90 along with two squads of infantry and a machine gun nest. He'd messaged Moscow, as directives said he should, and now he waited for the ass chewing he'd get via message or phone call. The returning chopper, which was badly damaged, had reported three or four dead partisans but he had yet to confirm anything. He had a company of infantry inbound on helicopters now and would soon have a radio report.

The hospital commander stepped in and took his empty chair.

"Well?" the Commander asked.

"Of the two wounded from the damaged helicopter, the aircraft commander just died from a single round to the head. The door gunner will live, but his dancing days are over unless he learns to dance with only one leg. I took it off at the knee. We were able to save his left eye, but the right one he will never see out of again. I've booked him on the next flight to Moscow."

"Intelligence, you are sure the terrorists were only at a squad level?"

"It was no larger, sir. I got a report just before this meeting that showed less than 12 troops. Something has stirred them up, and I think it is Williamson."

"I dread a call from Moscow because the General ate me alive over the damned train we lost, and here it is just days later and I have lost a tank, chopper, machine gun nest, and no idea how many troops. He may have me shot."

"No, trust me, your losses are small compared to the rest of America. They may not even call you or mention it. However, we need to turn aggressive and go on the attack. Now, we found two of these cards in the mouths of dead men." He tossed two bloody Aces of Spades onto the table and said, "Your biggest nightmare is indeed here, Colonel, and in the flesh. It seems to me, Aces as a partisan unit has relocated here, or Williamson is starting a new group. In any case, we will soon be up to our asses in partisans. I suggest we get all available troops out in the bush and let the hunt begin. I think that is what Moscow will want too, so beat them to the punch and do it on your own."

"Yes, of course, and see it is done immediately. I want all aircraft ready to respond in a moments notice and I want some jet aircraft assigned to us. Base operations, you make the assignment of jets happen. I want our ground troops to work with our aircraft and let us make things come about."

"When do you want the infantry out into the field, sir?"

"Within two hours. In the meantime, Base Ops, get me a helicopter so I can go see our downed aircraft and destroyed tank."

"Yes sir, and when do you want to leave?"

"Ten minutes, so I can arrive while my troops are still on the ground. This meeting is dismissed, and Base Ops, use the phone in here to get me some aircraft."

"Uh, yes sir."

An hour later, the Commander stood by the shell of a tank, met the eyes of a doctor who'd flown out earlier and asked, "Are you sure the resistance bandaged our wounded and administered morphine to those in pain?"

"Positive, sir. I think our enemy is suggesting we fight a humane fight, sir. I tend to agree with him."

"I am not sure what to think, except my enemy is an exceptionally intelligent man or else he has been around a great deal. War here can turn savage, or so I have heard, like it did in Mississippi, with no quarter given or expected."

The doctor watched the Colonel's face closely and prayed the man was not vicious and bloodthirsty like some commanders or more Russian boys and girls would go home in an aluminum box.

"It is savage enough on its best days, sir." the Chaplain said.

Yakovich wore no rank, no one saluted and, as a result, anyone watching wouldn't know him from a private soldier.

Pike, the sniper, was high in a pine tree a thousand yards out, looking for someone to slip up and show him the ranking man or woman. He'd been there all morning and most of the afternoon, waiting to take that one important shot. So far, he had no idea who was in charge.

What's this? he thought. This young man snapped to attention while speaking to that older man. He lined his cross hairs up on the older man's back, took a deep breath, and as he released the air from his lungs, the rifle fired. The shot was loud and everyone went to ground.

Master Sergeant Rykov Adam Yegorovich took the 30.06 bullet high, just above his breast. It hit his shoulder and he felt a burning poker go through his body. He was knocked on his ass in the mud and lay still, knowing any movement would bring a killing shot.

"Medic!" Someone screamed, and no sooner had the man knelt beside the Sergeant than a bullet struck him in the middle of the chest. He dropped without a shudder or movement, dead. Two more men tried for the Master Sergeant and both died. Finally, seeing men searching for him, Pike left the tree and moved silently deeper into the woods.

Movement was seen, shots were fired, but the sniper got away.

The Master Sergeant finally stood on his own power and began shouting orders.

"Sergeant, that is enough, I have a helicopter coming for you now. Doctor, see our Master Sergeant gets morphine for his pain and I want you to return with him. I will spend the night out here with our troops."

"Yes, sir."

Near dark, the Russians dug in and began to eat their supper. The Colonel had stew, liver pate, cheese, crackers and two additional meat and vegetable dishes from his Green Frog ration. For dessert he had a chocolate spread, walnut spread, and a cup of lukewarm tea. He could have had his meal hot, but with a sniper around a fire wasn't a good idea. He knew it would give him indigestion, because the old rations always did. He could have had his meal flown out, but he wanted his troops to see he could eat and do what they did in the field.

"Fifty percent alert. Half sleep while the other half guard." a Captain yelled out. "If I catch both of you asleep, I will kill you. Now, buddy up, and goodnight."

The Colonel went to sleep near the radioman.

It was near 0300 hours when the radio operator woke him and said, "Someone is getting their asses creamed, sir, listen."

Using the headset, Yakovich heard a fierce battle taking place.

"Hello any aircraft, hello any aircraft, this is Oscar One and I am under attack by a good two companies of partisans," It would later show less than a full company of partisans had attacked, "and they are attempting to blow the dam."

"Oscar One, this is Base One, and you are to hold at all costs. If the dam goes, you had better hope the resistance kills you, because if they do not, I will. Protect that dam!" Then he turned to the radioman and said, "Get me base operations on this thing, and now."

A minute later, the soldier handed the handset to the Colonel who said, "Igor, Senkin here, and I want everything that can get in the air north and over the dam. It is currently under attack and if it goes, so does the base and any number of towns and villages down stream."

"Sir, do you realize the time?"

"Get them up and get their asses in the air! Do it now, and this is a direct order."

"Yes, sir! I will also put the base on standby in the event the dam goes."

"Get a move on, because the dam is about to be overrun by the resistance!"

Less than 30 minutes later aircraft were hitting the partisans, who'd managed to crack the base of the dam using explosives but it was in no danger of bursting. The more effective aircraft were those loaded with machine guns, cannon, or 20 mm rounds. The damn was saved, but it was close. Once the resistance broke and ran, three fixed wing aircraft had a field day dropping napalm, 500 pound bombs, and hitting them with Gatling gun fire and cannons.

Colonel Senkin Yakovich returned to base with the first helicopter, thinking rightly that he'd be needed more on the base.

He'd no sooner walked in his office and poured a cup of tea, than his receptionist said, "Colonel, Moscow on line two, sir. It is a General Yurkov Rustem Geogiy, sir."

Growing nervous, the Colonel opened his top right drawer, pulled out a half-pint of vodka and broke the seal to open it. He then downed the whole bottle and tossed the empty in his trash can. He picked up the phone and said, "Colonel Senkin Yakovich speaking, sir."

"Senkin! Good to hear your voice again. We were just talking about you at a staff meeting earlier, and everyone was wondering why your quiet little place in the woods was suddenly seeing combat and experiencing losses. I explained that it was very likely you had turned on the resistance and were taking the battle to them. We all knew the area was passive and none of our commanders assigned there in the past had been aggressive. I told them it was about time the place entered the war and it was a shame none of the previous commanders had done anything. I am proud of you, and you will have a place on my staff when you return home. Try to keep your losses low, but go get them, tiger!"

"Uh, oh, thank you, sir. It took me a while to find them, but I decided it was time an assignment here was no longer a vacation. From now on, you can count on us to be an active part of our war."

"You keep this up and there will be a star for you when you leave there, understood?"

"Yes, sir. I just got back from an attack site where one of our roadblocks was destroyed. Some of our forces are inexperienced and we lost a tank and a helicopter. While there, the partisans attacked a hydro-dam and so far our body count is over 100 members of the resistance killed. We only killed around a dozen when the roadblock was attacked."

"When small outposts are attacked we rarely win, because they overrun our troops or catch them sleeping. But, see, when they attack us in mass, they die by the dozens. You have made them pay just by their number of dead at the dam. Excellent work, Senkin."

"Thank you, sir." The Colonel was overwhelmed and had fully expected an ass-chewing. *I am very surprised they think I started the killing here. That is good if it will get me a star before I retire. A General is treated very well in Moscow, even a junior one.*

"I know you will need more of most things now that you have taken the war to the Americans, so have your supply and manpower folks send in requests for what you need."

"Sir, I desperately need some air support for my ground troops."

"I will see all your bases have at least a squadron of fighter jets and a squadron of attack helicopters. Then I will add some search and rescue helicopters for you and your base, and I will see you get some bombers as well. Finally, someone got off their asses up north and took the fight to the enemy! I will see to a medal or two for you immediately, Senkin, and a well deserved one. You are proving to be the kind of man I always thought you were. I have another meeting now, but expect the aircraft to start arriving at your bases any day after today. I will get all you need to you as quickly as I can. Good bye and take care."

The line went dead.

Unknowingly the Colonel was smiling, so he picked up the phone and said, "Sergeant, I think it is time you wrote a couple of messages for me to headquarters. Do you feel up to it this fine day? If so, come to my office now."

His secretary smiled, because writing messages was a code they used to have sex. When he wanted her, he needed a message written. When she wanted him, she asked if he had any messages he needed written. Their affair was normal in most Russian units, and it assured her of a very fast promotion, and kept the Commander in a good mood. Besides that, she enjoyed it and it helped her assignment pass smoother and quicker.

Master Sergeant Asmik Yeva ran bent over from the helicopter to the edge of the trees, where he squatted and scanned the countryside. He saw nothing out of place. He was soon joined by eleven other men and women in the forest. Once all were together, he used hand signals to get them up and moving west, toward their intended target. The helicopter would fake a good half dozen more insertions and then return home.

Yeva had a man on point and a woman bringing up the rear on drag. His unit was made of all combat veterans, none with less that five years of service, two combat tours behind them, and most spoke some English. Speaking English was optional but speaking the language assured the soldier a spot on the team.

They moved until darkness, seeing nothing and hearing even less. The people on point and drag changed every hour to allow fresh eyes to blaze the way. While he'd not encountered it here yet, not in Washington state, most partisans areas were heavily mined. So far they'd seen no mines, except back at the dam where most bodies were booby trapped. His primary task right now was to discover the tracks of those who'd attacked the dam and then follow them back to their base camp. From there, he would get air support.

"Base, Tiger One." Yeva spoke into his radio.

"Go, Tiger One."

"We are stopped for the night. We had a quiet day with no contact. We are located . . ." as he spoke his people dropped their heavy packs, most weighed well over 20 kilos, and rubbed sore muscles. When they did get to sleep this day, they'd sleep well. After packing a heavy pack all day, no one had insomnia.

Green frogs were opened and meals consumed. Yeva smiled as he watched his people trade parts of the rations they didn't like with others. Some disliked the jellies, others the pate, and some the small tins of sardines. Most disliked the small fish because they added a strong scent to any temporary camp or location. The smell of fish was overpowering at times. The fools, Yeva had once said, making the foods never realized troops could also be smelled. He personally avoided the fish, but most of the meal was satisfactory. He usually tossed the tins of sardines or gave them to someone else. He liked the cheese and crackers, along with the tins of soup or stew. The goulash was tasty as well, if eaten with a few crackers.

"Corporal Afanasievich, after you eat, see some mines ring us and place a command detonated mine near the trail. Then, relieve a guard so he can eat. We will sleep back to back this evening and in a circle. Have your NVGs on and wear them as you sleep. Questions?"

Silence.

"Good, once you eat, see to your gear and equipment."

The evening passed quickly, but at 2000 hours they all moved to the sleeping circle. Guard would be pulled from the circle and no one, for any reason, would leave or break the circle. If they had to pee or poop, they stayed in the circle. Each of them had peed their pants rather than break the circle in the past and they'd do it again. They were on fifty percent watch, which meant every other person in the circle was awake at all times. Unlike other units, his people stayed awake. They knew if he caught them sleeping they'd, at the least, end up with a court martial, and sleeping in a combat zone could get a soldier shot for not following orders. The biggest reason they didn't sleep was because sleeping was a good way to get killed.

Near midnight, an elbow touched Yeva and he opened his eyes without moving. A lone partisan was seen approaching and, while he was good, it's almost impossible to spot someone sitting absolutely still while wearing camouflage from head to toe. He walked by them. The circle broke after the point man passed, with each troop now laid out in a line, facing the trail.

Minutes later a squad of ten was seen by the pale green light moving down the trail toward them. Yeva waited until the group was right in front of the command detonating mine and then squeezed the clacker. A huge explosion filled the cool night air and loud screams followed the blast. All of the Americans were down and none seemed to be well enough to stand or offer any resistance, so now they'd wait.

Ten minutes later the point man was seen returning and Yeva thought, *You had a chance to live, but now we will kill you. Why did you return to your comrades? Now you will die.*

The Master Sergeant swung his Bison toward the man and squeezed the trigger. Bullets went through him and zinged off into space as they struck rocks, trees and other objects at an angle. The sub-machine gun stitched the poor point man right down the middle of his body and he was dead before he struck the ground.

Again they waited. Finally, they moved back into a circle and waited for daylight.

Morning was cold, but not overly so, and they moved forward as a team to check last nights kill. The mine had torn off limbs and blown ball bearing sized steel balls through meat and bone. All were dead, but one was found where he had crawled to some brush and bled to death. The man shot by Master Sergeant Yeva was torn to pieces and laying in a pool of blood.

Taking the radio, he said, "Base, Tiger One, over."

"Go Tiger."

"I have fourteen partisan KIA. Repeat, one-four, killed-in-action partisans. No casualties on my side, over."

"Copy, partisans 14 and the Russians zero."

"Affirmative, Base. I am continuing my mission, over."

"Copy. Base out."

He clicked the mic button twice to let them know he got their last message.

"Eat, and we need to be moving. Sooner or later, someone will miss this squad of Americans."

The day grew warm after the sun was up fully and by noon they were sweating under the weight of their packs. They were deep in the forests now and very much alone. At times the radio wouldn't work and each knew it was the mountains and atmosphere that caused the problems. On they moved.

More than once they heard aircraft near and usually it was a helicopter. Once a jet said hello on the radio and then left them. Birds were chirping and all the day sounds were there.

"Do you hear that noise?" Junior Sergeant Irisa Pavla asked near dusk.

"No, what do you hear?" Yeva asked.

"Someone is chopping wood."

"Which direction from here?"

"Uh, north by west." Private Lerka said. He'd once been a Senior Sergeant but the Russian army disliked when he'd get drunk and wanted to fight. Most of the time he was a quiet man, unless full of drink; then he wanted to fight.

"How far do you think? I still cannot hear it."

Lerka and Pavla looked at each other and then the Sergeant said, "Hard to say, but maybe a half a kilometer, but that is a wild guess."

"Let us go and find this man who chops wood and see what we have."

Less than two kilometers later, a member of the resistance was seen chopping wood in a small densely wooded area. It was almost choked by underbrush and tall grasses. Off a short distance a lone log cabin was seen. As one man worked on the wood, two others stood guard.

The small Russian team melted into the woods to spend the next day watching the partisans, if they could survive the night. Once again they formed a circle after they'd eaten. The night passed slowly, but partisans were seen and heard moving through all night. One large group, made up of over 40 men and women, passed a couple of hours before dawn and they were seen moving supplies and gear. This gear was being moved on animals, bicycles, and small two wheeled carts, using wheels from damaged bicycles.

Yeva picked up the radio and called his position in. At first the base wanted to use artillery, but the Sergeant didn't like the idea because then the partisans would know someone was in the area watching them, and correcting fire. Instead, anything that could fly would strike the area, then artillery would be used, after the aircraft left.

CHAPTER 7

I was up before dawn and my squad was out of the house before sunup. The house was a huge barn turned into a hunting lodge the partisans now used as a supply storage facility and safe house. It had never been attacked since the war started. We'd spent the night there, sleeping on cots. We were about a hundred yards away, filling our canteens with treated water from a huge metal container. Ten minutes later as we discussed the days mission, a loud scream of a diving jet was heard, two missiles were fired and the country cottage went up in flames. It was a flight of three and each struck near the house with missiles.

Each aircraft banked softly to the left after striking the house so by the time the second aircraft banked, I had a Russian missile out and was tracking the last aircraft. As the plane went into his gentle turn, I squeezed the trigger. One of the other aircraft must have seen my missile or the aircraft warning system lit up, because the aircraft went into a steep nose up and power was applied. The missile adjusted accordingly and was seen closing in on the jet. Chaff was dispensed, and I must admit, it looked beautiful as all the burning munitions fell from the ass of the aircraft to act as a decoy, but it didn't work. The missile flew right up the tailpipe of the jet and then exploded.

A parachute was seen to fully blossom and begin a gentle floating drift to the ground as a sebaceous fireball fell into the trees. Partisans were seen running in all directions and I knew why. The two surviving aircraft were lining up for another pass. I prayed the pilots didn't have napalm, but as I watched, a container fell from the two, who were attacking side by side this time. The containers tumbled through the air and when they hit the ground, the entire house was struck by the burning flames. I knew anyone inside was dead.

Small arms were heard firing and the last jet began to smoke a little and pulled up. Then, going around, they both made one more attack using cannons this time. Small secondary explosions were heard and then as the aircraft left the area, the crackling and popping of the flames were clearly heard. The screams of the injured filled the early morning air and I could see hundreds of dead resistance fighters. I immediately sent my medic to gather up folks to help him gather the wounded and establish a triage so the most seriously wounded could be treated first. Those with no hope, would be given morphine and set aside.

Three partisans appeared with the captured Russian pilot.

He looked like hell, and getting out of the aircraft had caused him some injury. His left arm was broken, he had a cut down his left thigh, and his eyes were red from the g-forces he used to try and lose the missile and his high speed ejection.

I called for Igor, our Russian speaking partisan and a medic. As we waited I had him checked for weapons and all they found, since they'd already taken his pistol, was a pocket knife. I motioned for him to sit on a huge rock.

Huge reddish black fireballs were reaching for the sky near the barn and behind it. There must have been some fuel and munitions stored there. As the fire raged, blasts were heard as one thing or the other exploded. The fireballs would roll inside themselves with each new explosion.

The medic and Igor arrived at the same time, so as the man was treated the medic asked questions through our man. The cut to his left thigh was deep and while the medic wanted to treat him now, I made him wait.

"Bandage him for now and you can sew him up in a bit."

I turned to Igor and said, "Ask him his name and rank."

I heard the words thrown around but they meant nothing to me.

"He is Junior Lieutenant Damir Sasha Joravitch and he demands he be given medical treatment."

"He will be, once he's answered a few questions."

"Tell him I am Colonel John Williamson and I am the senior officer for the partisans. It would not be smart for him to piss me off."

"He agrees, but he is in pain."

"I understand. Tell him, we do not have a prison for him or a gulag, so . . ." I pulled my pistol.

"Wait, he will answer all your questions."

An hour later I knew more than I'd asked. He was willing to talk so I turned him over to a Major Smyth that ran my intelligence section with the words, "If he gets killed escaping, or if you execute him, I'll see all of you hang for murder. I think we can trade him for some of our people."

"Now, Colonel, do you think we're killers?"

"You heard me, Smyth, and I mean it. I want him fed the same exact food you eat and the same amount. When you drink water, I want water available to him too. I don't want to hear he's being mistreated."

"Where am I to lock him up?"

"Lock him to a tree if you have to do the job, but you'll eventually find a place to keep him. If it looks like the Russians are about to overrun your position, then and only then do you have my permission to kill him. They must not get him back, unless they trade with me."

"John, you know me better than this. I'll follow orders as given."

"See your men do as well. Sometimes pilots get treated rougher than most."

"Well, you can't bomb someone and not expect them to be pissed off when you bail out over them and land in their lap. Of course the fliers are often murdered on the spot." he replied and then rattled off some Russian to the pilot. Smiling, Smyth said, "I told him to come with me, I had him a new home and treatment for his leg. You know how to reach me if you need me, sir."

"Did he know anything we needed?" Sergeant Cummings asked.

"No, not really. He's just a Junior Lieutenant so I don't expect him to know much and nothing of importance. Smyth will try talking to him in the coming days and if nothing else, we'll get general information about the base that might come in handy."

The Sergeant nodded.

Sergeant Major Bob Hall neared and said, "I heard you were here. How are you, sir?" He extended his hand and we shook.

"I'm doin' fine, Bob, any idea how many dead we have?"

"No, not yet, but I suspect we suffered a good 60% loss of all personnel. We lost over a thousand gallons of Mogas[1] and two bunkers full of munitions. None of that stuff should have been stored so close to the house. They're new and they're learning."

"When did you get here?"

"I jumped in last night with a detachment of weather folks."

"Do you know Sergeant Major Gordon Byrd? He's my assigned Top Sergeant."

"I know Birdie, and he's a damned fine top soldier, sir. I'm assigned to your weather shop, if I can find what's left of it. I'm to work weather and was to be the top dog over this supply point, but I'm out of a job now."

"Reform it all, if need be. Let me know how many people you need and I'll see replacements are sent in. It won't be fast, but you'll soon get back up to strength."

"Thank you, sir. I need to find the commander, if I can, or at least discover if she's alive or not."

"Do you have a working radio?"

"I have no idea. Right now, well, you see what a mess it is. I need to see about moving these people too, before the Russians return."

"I was going to suggest that. I have a spare radio, but it has some range problems. However, that's better than nothing. Once you're in a new position, if you have to, send a squad to me with your location and I'll see the Chinese drop you some gear. Wilkerson!"

"Yo!"

"Give the Sergeant Major our spare radio and let's get ready to move. Sergeant, in a couple of hours I'll contact you and we'll

---

1 Motor gas, slang for gasoline.

check the radio out. Take care, and get these folks relocated as soon as possible." I suddenly smelled burnt bodies, blood, guts, human waste, and cordite. I needed to move before I turned sick.

"I'll do just that, sir." Of course he didn't salute me, especially out in the field.

"Simmons, contact base and let them know this place is no longer operational. Tell them I'll send them a coded message when we stop for the night with as much information as I can provide them. Saddle up, folks, and Major Morgan, please take control of your formation."

"Thank you, sir."

As we moved toward our home base, I gave consideration to moving it too. I had no idea how long we'd been there and who knew about us. I could see now my activities had the Russians as mad as hornets in a fruit jar.

When we stopped for the night, Simmons sent a long coded message and I learned in return that none of the Russian choppers in the three states had IR^2 capability. With all the rain this area gets, the Russians didn't think it'd do them much good since rain greatly impacts the results of the imaging. However, Headquarters seemed to think that would change now that we were active in my region.

We were cutting cross country to get home quicker and for the first time since I got here, I felt safe.

As I sat eating a dessert from my rations, Major Morgan neared and asked, "May I join you, sir?"

"Have a seat."

"Thank you. How do you cope with all the death and destruction you've seen?" she asked.

"I really don't know and I have no answer, except I turn it off mentally while it's happening. I often finish a battle and cannot remember a single thing I did *during* the battle. My orders and commands are automatic and come natural for me."

"I can't do that, or don't think I can. Why isn't a man like you married?" she asked and then lowered her head.

------

2 Infrared/Thermal imaging camera

"I have been, twice, and was almost married a third time when the Russians killed her and my unborn child. I'm starting to think a relationship is not possible in a war like this, but people need each other now more than ever."

"Did your first two wives die in the war too?"

"No, not really, not the first one. I was gone trading one day from my home, right after the fall, and some thugs broke in and killed my family. I returned to find my wife raped and kids dead. It took me years to get over that."

"Hell, I'd guess so. I was married to a Marine and we lived on the coast then. He was a Captain and I was a stay at home wife. We had no children and a medical examination showed his sperm count was too low. If you want to hurt a big bad-ass Marine, tell him his testosterone is low or his sperm count is off. Just when the medicine was working well, he was killed when a flight of Russian jets caught him and his Marines out in an open field one night. They dropped napalm and my husband, lover, and best friend burned to death. That was five years ago and I've not seen another man that interested me; then you showed up."

I chuckled and said, "I am your senior officer."

"That's true, but we're just talking and I need to be honest with you. If this war has taught me nothing else, it's to be 100% honest at all times. I may never get another chance to speak with that person again in this life. We might both be dead by morning, and you know it as well as I do."

"Well, don't tell me you love me or I'll laugh." I said and then chuckled.

"No, not even close. I can say I respect you, find you ruggedly handsome, and a very distinguished older gentleman. I'd just like to know you better is all."

"Well, that's honest enough, I guess. I'd not thought of you really, not with all I have on my mind and all. As a matter of fact, I'd noticed none of the women in the unit." I was speaking the truth and meant every word. I didn't go around visually raping the female troops I had. I was 100% professional all the time and that meant hands off, unless like in the past, a woman told me she was interested in me.

"That's understandable and —"

"Let me close my eyes and describe you from my memory." I said.

She laughed and said, "Sure."

"Uh, you're a Major, big blue eyes, nice teeth, auburn hair, narrow waist, nice breasts, about five feet and seven inches tall, and petite. I know very little about you, since we've never talked before. Oh, and you have a nice rear."

She broke out laughing, which I had to stop quickly because of where we were, but I loved to hear her laugh. She sobered, met my eyes and then asked, "Does that mean my butt is too big?"

It was my turn to laugh and I said, "No, it's actually a compliment. I think many men are attracted to well shaped women, because I know I am."

She chuckled and said, "You, sir, are a liar. You just said you'd not noticed a single woman in the unit and some are much sexier than me. If you didn't notice them, you'd never notice me, so I had to at least speak with you about this. If you think I'm too forward, just tell me so."

"Look, let's start by being friends and see what happens, okay?"

"I wouldn't want it any other way. I'm not looking for sex, but something more to go with it. I want what I had before, a lover, mate, and best friend. Am I making sense?"

"You are to me, uh, Cynthia. I can call you that, right?"

"Of course, sir."

I laughed and said, "My first name is John."

"John I think every soul out here that is alone is a mess inside. We have no one to speak to and to share our fears with, or our dreams of the future. It's even more difficult for officers because we are fewer in number. I just thought we could be friends and take it from there."

"Let's do that."

"Tell me about you, or do you mind?"

Once back at our base, I began to see Cynthia more often and then transferred her to another commander. There was no way I'd let her still work for me and see her as much as I was. I didn't think it looked proper, but in many cases, due to our organization, it happened. I had a choice, so I had her reassigned on the base.

We'd grown closer and were sharing a great deal about each other. I discovered she'd once been a teacher, but that was before her marriage. Over time, seeing her each evening became the norm.

Then, one day she came to me crying. I asked what was wrong; she'd heard a rumor that the Marines were to move on the base and share it with us. I'd not heard that, but at times word of mouth is faster than any other method of notification. She didn't know how she'd feel seeing the Marine uniform again, and she knew it'd bring memories of her husband back.

I was honest with her and said, "If this is true, we'll deal with it when it happens. We'll do what you think it takes for you to adjust to this change. I doubt few have complete Marine uniforms, but you might catch a shirt, hat, or pair of trousers at times."

Well, two days later about 300 Marines arrived by Chinese C-130 aircraft that landed one right after the other. As soon as the Marines landed, I got them moving from the drop zone to our base. I'd have to get with their commander and have some of them assigned deeper in the woods. There were too many of us at my small base and one attack would cost us a lot of lives. Lives I didn't want to spend.

When I spoke with a Marine Top Sergeant, he said the resistance was planning to eventually establish the Army, Navy, Marines and Air Force, and assign veterans to their old service. These Marines were the first batch.

Early the next morning I had a surprise visit by a Full Colonel in the Marine Corps. He wasn't spit and shine like the old days, but getting by with what he had and could steal from the Russians.

He had a dog turd stuck in the corner of his mouth he swore was a cigar, he was in excellent shape, and he was intelligent.

"Colonel Williamson, we've too many people here and we're taxing your supply system."

"That's why I think we need to establish two more bases and have each manned by about 150 of your Marines. They can report directly to you and then you to me."

"As long, by God, as we're killin' Russians, I don't care if I report to the Devil himself."

"Russians you'll soon have, and as many as you want. My first name is John."

"I'm Bill 'Bulldog' Peppers and I retired from the Corps the week before America fell. I like the idea of two different Marine bases, because my people work best alone or with other Marines. Just see we're kept supplied and I'll call in the Russian body count daily."

"I can do that." I opened my desk, pulled out a bottle of whiskey and asked, "Drink?"

"Does a frog hop? Hell yes! And a double too."

When I handed him his drink, he threw it back and then extended his glass for more. I gave him another double and he said, "I'll sip this one. John, my Marines are different than your group and we all take pride in once a Marine always a Marine. After the country fell, I soon rounded up over 500 prior Marines and we worked alone for years. But, with the Chinese supplying us now, it's easier for them to have just one supply point."

"I'll leave you pretty much alone, but will have missions for you at times, and I'll see you have what you need to do your job. Did you bring much with you?"

"We don't need much but beans and bullets. Of course," he gave a sad smile, "some first aid items too. I love these men like my sons, that I don't have."

"I can understand that." I said and then refilled his drink. I was still on my first drink and I poured him number three.

"You prior Army with all the ropes and trashcan lids on your uniform?"

I laughed and replied, "Yep, I am at that. Tonight move your men about a thousand yards on both sides of us and bed down. In the morning you and I will take a look at a map and determine where to locate your bases. Get a sharp man for the second base commander."

"Oh, I have one in mind right now, and I'll bring him in the morning when we meet. Sir, I thank you for the whiskey, but my men need me. If you need me, just scream Bulldog and I'll come running." he stood and I realized he was taking control of our conversation, but I let him do so, this time.

There would be no second time. I allowed it this time because his troops did need him and I wanted them scattered out and away from us in case of attack. This time I didn't have an issue with it, but we'd see what the future brought.

He gave me a crisp and tight salute, so I returned his and said, "See to your men."

"Yes, sir." He replied and then he was gone.

CHAPTER 8

The Russians were confused and a bit overwhelmed by the partisan attacks. They'd show up in one area and the next day be miles away to strike again. They realized there were either more members of the resistance than they'd figured or they had transportation. Of the two, the first was more probable. They were not aware that the partisans from other states were pumping all the bodies they could to the northwest to support new efforts against the Russian Bear. If the Russians had to remove troops from other areas to protect the northwest, it would take some of the pressure off the other states. It was a battle plan like General Robert E. Lee used against Grant. In Lee's case, it bought him some time and that's all.

The Colonel was out for an evening walk when a man in a black suit walked up to him and asked, "Colonel Senkin Yakovich?|

"Yes sir, and you?"

"Who I am is not important but there are those in Moscow watching you closely. It is imperative you win this theater of the American invasion. If you do not, your return home will not be a happy one. I was sent to warn you, start making things happen over here. If you do not, then you and I will meet again, but the next time will not be so pleasant and it will not be in this country. Not six months ago there were no attacks here and now it is just like the rest of the country, infested with resistance."

"It is a damned hell hole of a country, and you damned fools had to invade the only country in the world with more guns than people. I have no explanation why this part of the country is now fighting so hard except they have a new commander."

"I am but a messenger, but you have been warned." The man in black turned and walked away. In the matter of a few seconds he was swallowed by the darkness.

Turning toward his office, a small animal seemed to come alive in his stomach, and while Senkin knew the KGB was long gone, it was obvious now something more sinister had replaced it. He fought the urge to puke a number of times before he was able to get to his desk and pour a glass of vodka. *What am I going to do? Every commander assigned to America has failed to stop the resistance, with only one man promoted to General and his plane was shot down by a SAM missile the day he was going home. I wonder why I've never thought of this before?*

Calling his vice-commander, Lieutenant Colonel Sigayev Vadim "Vadik" Gennadiyevich, he asked, "Did anyone visit you tonight, Sigayev?"

"No, sir. Was someone to come here?"

Yakovich told of his visit by the unknown man and then asked, "Who do you think he was?"

"The Federal Security Service of the Russian Federation (FSB) would be my guess. All they are is the KGB with a different name, in my view. Same people, I think. I'd take his warning seriously."

Damn, not good, he thought but said, "Okay, enjoy your evening and I'll see you in the morning."

The next day at stand up, he announced, "Starting tomorrow, I want more pressure put on the resistance than ever before. Get our teams out and find them." He said as he paced the room. All knew he was under a lot of stress, but only Colonel Gennadiyevich knew of the visitor.

"Colonel," Yakovich said to the infantry Commander, "Get all of your troops in the field and let's make this place like it used to be, quiet. Additionally, find out where Colonel Williamson is living, and I want him dead. I think a sniper team could do the job."

"First, we will have to find him and that will take some time."

"Get on it and start early in the morning. I want a briefing on the progress each day at 1600, unless I am off the base, understood?"

Snapping to attention, the Lieutenant Colonel said, "Yes, sir."

"Intelligence, I want a reward of one million dollars offered for Colonel John Williamson, partisan. Make the reward payable Dead or Alive. You will find his image in his file and I want reward posters all over the three state area. Drop them to partisans in the field too. Everyone has a price, or so the Americans say. Alright, everyone has jobs to do, so get back to them. Dismissed. Master Sergeant, do not call the room to attention when I leave."

As he walked back to his office, he turned to the sergeant and said, "Master Sergeant Asmik, I want you to accompany the first few searches for Williamson and evaluate how well you think the infantry is doing the job, and let me know after each mission."

"Yes, sir."

"Go, and prepare to leave. I suspect they will be gone before daylight in the morning."

"Yes, sir." He turned and ran for his gear.

Right at dawn the next day, as they flew slowly toward the landing zone, Asmik was puckered up because they were taking ground fire and couldn't land until the helicopter in front of them unloaded all their troops. They were moving fast enough, but with bullets striking the aircraft everything seemed to be in slow motion. *Plunk—ping*, a bullet struck the floor, passing through the cargo hold, just missing the Master Sergeant's legs, and then entered the roof where it struck only God knew what. His knuckles were white from gripping his weapons tightly.

Oil and another liquid began to drip from the newest bullet hole and when he felt the oil, it was hot to the touch. The strong scent of burning rubber filled the aircraft.

The machine gunner on the right side screamed and then fell back into the cargo area with half his face missing. His body jerked and shivered as he screeched. Blood, caught in the slip stream, was coloring a long wide red stripe down the side of the aircraft. A light gray smoke began to fill the helicopter. The wounded gunner tensed up, jerked a couple of times and lay still. His war was over.

"Base, Taxi Six, and I am taking heavy ground fire from the left side of the field."

As bullets of all sizes struck the side of the helicopter they made a loud *thunk, thunk, thunk-ping.*

"Roger that. Did you hear him, Bobcat One?"

"Copy, and I am rolling in hot now."

The woods on the left was suddenly a ball of twisting and turning flames as napalm struck. Screams could not be heard due to the battle taking place, but Asmik knew they were there. He shivered as he imagined burning to death.

"Uh, Taxi Six, this is Bobcat One, how was that?"

"Took the pressure off of me, thank you."

Master Sergeant Asmik was looking at the ground coming up when a piece of aluminum from the engine cover fell to the earth. It flew by his face and was soon lost from sight. The smoke grew darker and the pilot said, "Uh, Master Sergeant, you and your men get out now."

"Negative, sir, we have heavy packs on, and to jump from here will seriously injure some of us. We need to be closer to the ground."

Downward they continued.

"I am still here if you need me." Bobcat One said.

Just as they landed, machine gun fire struck the windshield moving from left to right. The co-pilot screamed and a bloody mist filled the cargo bay to mix with the smoke. Asmik failed to see it, because he and his troops had already cleared the aircraft and were running for cover away from the helicopters. Smoke filled the bird and the left side machine gunner started to exit the aircraft unbuckling his strap, but before he could move he took three rounds in the chest. He fell dead, right beside his big gun mounted on the helicopter. His body twisted and turned in his death throes.

The chopper was in flames now; the engine throwing pieces of hard steel of various sizes in all directions as it flew apart. The pilot, the only man left in the aircraft alive, opened the door and stepped out. He ducked and ran for the relative safety of a ditch. There were three other young soldiers in the ditch with him and two were bleeding badly. He glanced around and spotted a Bison sub-machine gun with magazines on a dead soldier to his left. He picked the weapon up and joined the fight. He would die less than two minutes later from a gunshot wound to the head.

Asmik join the rest of the troops gathering in the trees. Seeing no officer to take charge, he yelled, "Spread out and move on me. Stay alert as we flush some partisans."

Guns began to pop as partisans were encountered, but the Master Sergeant saw no one in the dense foliage and brush. Suddenly a woman stood and she was wearing a Chinese uniform, so the Sergeant fired, his bullets stitching her down the middle of her tall lean body. She fell and remained down. He moved forward once more.

That was a partisan, because she was tall enough to make two Chinese. Ummm, I love my women tall too, he thought as large bullet struck the limb by his face and clipped it from the tree. He shivered and ducked, but he kept moving forward. Soon, all resistance stopped.

"Corporal Krasimir, get me a Russian body count and number of wounded. Private Lerka, contact base and let them know the Landing Zone is now secure. I will send them our losses and the losses of our enemy once I have them. Tell them a battlefield assessment is still being done."

"Master Sergeant!" a Major called out from a ditch.

"Sir!"

"Once the body counts are finished, form the men up and let's move inland."

"Yes, sir." he replied and then thought, *Why did I not see any officers until the fighting was over? I had no idea the Major was there.*

The place smelled like a slaughter house to the old Sergeant. He looked at the burning shells of metal in the field that used to be helicopters, the smoke thinner now and not as black or dense as before. Dead and wounded men littered the whole field. Moans, groans and screams were heard as the medics worked as quickly as possible.

"Master Sergeant, we have forty dead, twenty-six injured, and the partisans lost over 200 dead. Some of the bodies were hit by bombs and napalm, so my count may be off some for both sides. I think our missing is six. As mangled as they are, it is really hard to tell. Oh, and we have two prisoners."

"Thank you and that is good enough. Private Lerka!"

"Sir?"

"Bring me the radio." A minute later he said, "Base, Whiskey Six, over."

"Go Whiskey."

"I have forty dead, twenty-six injured, and six missing. The partisans lost over 230 dead, I repeat, 230 enemy Killed in Action. We have two prisoners."

"Wait one."

"Copy." Then, turning to Corporal Krasimir he said, "Inform the Sergeants and Corporals to form up into individual squads and move away from the landing zone. They are to start their individual missions."

"Yes, Master Sergeant." The man then walked away.

Three hours later, the wounded Russians were gone, as well as the dead. It was then the whole group started their individual missions, using squads of men and women, so they could hit and run. The groups moved in every compass heading, each with a unique mission.

Asmik and his group walked beside an old trail as they moved deeper and deeper into rough mountain country. Junior Sergeant Luka was on point when he suddenly stopped and then pointed out a thin line across the path, and some toe poppers in the soil near the mine. He gave a big smile and stepped over the line.

His foot struck the ground on the other side of the line and continued down into a hole. Six steel spikes mounted on a fulcrum rotated up and stuck him hard in the center of the chest. As he jerked and screamed, his dancing set off an anti-personnel mine mounted in front of the booby trap, which took most of his left leg off at the knee. His screams filled the air.

The medic, Sergeant Tikhonov, ran forward, only to step on two toe poppers and he lost most of his left foot. He was bleeding hard and his lower belly was wide open when the Master Sergeant reached him.

Looking into the Medic's eyes, Asmik said, "You know what I have to do, right?"

Biting his lips against the intense pain, the man nodded.

Reaching into the medic's bag he pulled out two syringes of morphine and stuck both into the medic's arms. He cradled the dying man's head in his lap and sang for him in a low tone. The burly Sergeant brushed the medic's hair from his eyes and wiped his face clean as he continued to sing. By the time the song was finished, Sergeant Tikhonov was dead.

When the Master Sergeant reached Junior Sergeant Luka, he was dead, having bled to death. The sergeant shook his head and said, "Timurovna, you are our new point. Watch your ass, too, because this area is mined."

"What about our dead?" Junior Lieutenant Lada Stanislavovna asked. It was her first mission in the field, so the Master Sergeant ran the group this time. A few more missions and then she'd be in charge.

"What about them, ma'am? We cannot pack them with us, we cannot call in a chopper to remove their bodies, and I am for sure not going to bury them."

"I suppose you are correct, but it seems terrible to leave our dead when they should be honored back home."

"Ma'am, with all due respect, this is not back home and we have no other choice. Trust me when I say they do not care if we leave them or not, but I fully understand what you mean."

"It just seems wrong."

"Get used to it, because you will leave them more often than you will remove them."

"I hear you. Let us move, Sergeant."

The old Sergeant winked at her, she blushed, and they began to move. It was a good kilometer before he realized he was old enough to be her father, or maybe her grandfather.

The Colonel paced the floor as helicopters landed and began

taking hits. Soon, sitting in Base Ops, he was able to hear the men as they were hit and some were even dying as they called in for this or that. One pilot, his helicopter on fire, had the courage to say, "Sorry, comrades, but this is as far as God has decided I am to go with you."

His aircraft then crashed and exploded, killing all on board.

The Colonel heard bullets striking various aircraft, cries of pain, and the disbelieving voices of those watching a friend die. He was damned proud of his people.

The after action report was good, actually, with over 200 partisans killed, and he wanted to forward that to Moscow. He'd wait, because there were sure to be more dead and maimed on both sides.

Now, he paced as he waited for the units to give their evening reports and to have their overnight locations marked on the big map. As he waited, the Chief of Base Operations brought him a tall glass of vodka which hit the spot. He sipped his drink as he listened. Most of the units had no further contact with the enemy, one had killed two resistance fighters, and one had killed a squad of partisans. The Russian losses had been light, with three men killed, and two of those were with the Master Sergeant.

Finally the radioman shook his head, nodded, and then said, "A squad led by an experienced Captain was wiped out with no survivors. Master Sergeant Pulakov found the mangled bodies, and they are not even cold yet. They were killed by a Claymore mine. He will rest overnight after a couple of more kilometers and will radio in his location once in place. It is raining out there too."

The rest of the evening was quiet.

Junior Lieutenant Lada Stanislavovna felt uncomfortable and didn't know why. She was sitting in the nightly circle, wearing her

NVGs, and had just finished eating. She'd felt that way since well over an hour before they stopped.

Over supper, the Sergeant had said, "Ma'am, you may feel the enemy following us. Many people can do that, but I cannot. Listen to the feeling and let it guide you this night."

There was something she'd forgotten maybe? She ran all she could think of through her mind and the most important was calling in their nightly location, and she'd done that. Finally, since it was her turn, she went to sleep thinking about the Sergeant. *He is a handsome man in his own way and very dignified*, she thought, and then fell asleep.

Near 0200 the radioman nudged Master Sergeant Asmik and handed him the handset. Whispering, the Sergeant asked, "What do you have?"

"Another squad reports a two squad unit of partisans headed your way. The Colonel said take them out."

"Roger and copy. Out."

He woke everyone and few minutes later the point man walked by. Once the main body was in front of the mine, the clackers were squeezed by the Lieutenant and screams were heard before the explosion had grown quiet. Russian guns were heard as bodies were raked with gunfire. The screams died.

The sniper of the group was using a night vision scope and he very slowly moved it over the downed men, women and children. He said, "Some children with this group, Master Sergeant."

"How many?"

"About half."

"Damn me, children? You sure?"

"Take a look through the scope. Children, and they are dead, too."

"What in the hell are children doing out here?" While he was speaking at almost a whisper everyone heard his anger. "Base, Whiskey Six, are you aware that group had a bunch of children in the middle?"

"Children? No, I had no idea. Wait one."

"Roger." he said and then thought, *I did not come all the way out here to kill children.*

"Base One said to confirm the body count at sunrise and to count the children too."

"Count the children? I will if they are armed, over."

Oh, he is a man of honor too. Lieutenant Stanislavovna thought. *I like that in a man. I will have to approach him carefully and not be too fast. But,* she smiled, *I want to know more about this man. Why would children be in this group?*

CHAPTER 9

I suddenly had Russians up to my ass. Most of my units had been engaged, and many suffered mass casualties. Many of my company Commanders and smaller sized units were in a deep panic and I knew if I didn't get them to settle down and get things under control, I could lose most of my forces. I used the radio to contact most of the big units and things began to smooth out some. For many, I knew they'd be almost normal by morning. Others were cut off and for some reason could not be reached by radio.

I had the Russians scattered all over the damned place and when that happens, you plant mines. One of my units had found a napalm container that had not worked on impact and my EOD[3] people broke it open and we were able to take the nasty stuff on the inside and prepare some special mines for our use. Many of my people out in the bush had those mines with them. Within 24 hours thousands of mines were scattered to hell and back. Then my people vanished, and we waited for the Russians to return to the field to be picked up.

As we waited, we placed command detonated mines, with the napalm, near the trails. I wanted to see them explode, so I spent the night walking to the field, trailing a Russian cell. I even took Major Morgan and her squad with me. We knew we passed some Russian units, but for some reason, probably fatigue, they let us pass unharmed.

Once at the field I could see and smell death. The field looked like a cemetery for choppers, their twisted, busted and bent

---

3 Explosive Ordnance Disposal

frames all burnt black, and reminded me of markers for the deceased. The scent of death was strong, and there was a solemness to the place usually only found in large military cemeteries. I was almost afraid to speak, because I felt a deep desire to offer the place respect and whispers, not loud human voices. But, I had a job to do.

"Base One, Base One, over." The trance was broken by the radio.

"Go Base."

"Be advised we are in position, over."

Captain Morgan asked, "What makes you think they'll try to leave from the same place they landed?"

I met her eyes and said, "Absolutely nothing, but people are creatures of routines and habits. I think they will return and when they do, we'll be ready for them. Sergeant, bury what's left of the napalm in the very center of the field and attach some C-4 to it, so I can ignite it from here."

"Does it ever bother you, what we're doing?" she asked as we walked toward the woods where I'd be hiding if the Russians returned.

"It did at first, but not now. The Russians are in my home and they're interrupting my life. They will never leave unless we kill so many the Russian people say that's enough. So far, they've said very little, so I'll keep killing the sonsofbitches until they're gone."

"You're a hard and cold man."

"I see me as determined," I shrugged and continued, "but maybe I am cold and hard. I didn't invade them, so remember, they came here looking for trouble. I'm an American and no one can take my country from me as long as I'm alive."

"I see your point, but aren't you tired of war?"

"Of course I am, but I love this country and the life we had before the fall. None of us really appreciated what we had, do you know that? Now that it's gone, I'm not sure we can ever have it back, but we can have something close. I think it's worth fighting and dying for."

"John, don't speak of your death, because that would break my heart. I care . . . I care more for you . . . than you know. Hell, maybe more than I know. Only, I don't want to care about anyone, especially now, not in the middle of a damned war."

"Why is it bad to love or care now, in the war? I think it's wonderful, and a little caring or love is what all Americans need at the moment. I care about you too, but I'll not call it love, but something is growing inside of me."

"I am happy around you, love to make you laugh and enjoy just being with you."

"For right now, leave it alone and take what I offer. Let's see what happens naturally. If it's meant to be love, it will happen." I said, meaning my words.

"I guess I just don't have your faith like that."

I leaned forward, kissed her nose and said, "God will do his will. If we are meant to be together, it'll happen. If not, then no amount of wishing will make it happen."

"What do you think will happen?"

"I think, it'll happen, but over time. We don't want to rush this."

"Sir!" Sergeant Wilson said, "Base on the radio for you, and they said it's urgent."

"I'll be right there." I kissed her and walked away. I wouldn't lie to her just to crawl in bed with her and what I told her, I honestly thought and felt.

"Base, this is Badger One."

"Uh, roger, Badger, be advised eyes in Georgia saw a squadron of Russian Blackjack (Tu-160M) aircraft departing for Seattle, Washington. That was a week ago and they arrived safely. We have intercepted a message that states they will start using them as early as today."

"Copy, Base. How many other battlefields or attack missions do you have going on, besides mine here?"

"None at this time. The bomber is essentially a missile platform, but can carry 88,185 pounds of bombs. They usually fly three aircraft to a flight, so they have near 132 tons of bombs and that's a lot. They also can carry 18 rockets it fires in a rotary launcher. It comes with IR and all the bells and whistles. Base advises you not to get caught under a flight of them."

"Roger that, copy."

"That is all."

"Copy and out." I handed the headset back to Wilson.

I then gave thought to moving or staying. I finally decided to stay, but only with a company sized unit, and to move in so close to the Russians when they returned that they'd be unable to use the big Blackjack bombers on us. I'll scatter my troops all over the field too, making it harder to determine how many of us there might be. In any case, I wasn't going to let the Russians leave without a fight.

The general information I was getting from my units was our mines and booby traps were hard on the Russians, with hundreds hurt by them since the operation had started. I figured for every man down, it took between two and four men to carry him or her. A squad of 8 to 12 men and women couldn't afford to pack too many injured or they were useless, more or less, as a fighting unit.

I saw to the napalm placement and then moved deeper into the bush. I'd know when the enemy appeared because I'd left a squad to watch the field. Most American line units learned to never leave by the same place you entered. I was gambling cherry, or new Russians, would not know that yet. The reason was simple; I was planning an ambush to teach them a lesson.

Cynthia and I lacked the private time to talk now, because many of the Russian units were returning. I sent one man to keep them awake by firing random shots into the Landing Zone, so they could report it as sniper fire. This was done to keep their minds on the sniper and not have time to think about an ambush. I wanted my sniper to get close to hitting them but to not severely injure anyone. I hoped they'd not kill him, using the logic I might send in a replacement that was a better shot. Snipers are good for keeping things unorganized too.

About three hours before dark, I could see most of the landed Russians were in camp in the field, which was rather dumb. I suspected they were using bomb craters and everything from wrecked choppers to freshly dug fox holes for protection. It felt kind of strange to be using the same ambush spot I'd just used not a week ago. I ordered my troops to crawl as close as they could to the Russians because I was about to blow the planted napalm.

Cynthia was at my side when I squeezed the clacker. I happened to glance at my watch and it was full dark and 1920 hours. A mushroom cloud of black smoke mixed with fire rose about the field and the screams of men and women were heard. Two men were seen in the openness of the field stumbling around engulfed in flames, lighting the whole area for 200 feet or more. I was just adding more pressure on the Russian commander, hoping he was new and a cherry to boot. I had no idea how right I was, but he had some very experienced senior Sergeants along on this trip. Three had actually argued against returning to the same LZ to leave, but the young Russian Captain was hard headed. I then put the four snipers I had to work. Their screams were hideous and I knew the sound and sight was unnerving to my enemies, because no one wants to burn to death. I think most humans have a very natural fear of fire.

Each sniper had orders to seriously injure someone and then kill those who tried to get near the downed men or women. All of my snipers had a Russian scope with night vision and it was like shooting fish in a barrel. With each low *poot*, all the noise the silencers on the sniper rifles made, I knew a Russian was dying. Most did not die quietly either, but few men or women do when shot. To me, being shot feels like a red hot poker being pushed through my body. I get a burning sensation when struck.

Machine guns on both sides began to fire, so I gave the order to fire at will. Individual weapons now added their noises to the sounds of battle. Grenades were exploding and my mortar crew was about to add even more noise.

On the Russian side of the attack, Captain Bekhterev Petr Artemovich, was in a near panic. The napalm exploding and the two men in flames had his mind jumbled. He started to order an attack and then realized that would be foolish. Then his radioman took a hit to the head and splattered blood, bone, brains and gore all over the place, with much of it on the new Captain.

"Gator One, Base." The radio squawked, again.

"I need help, we are being butchered out here!"

"Settle down, sir. Work with me, because I have some aircraft to help keep you alive. Slow your breathing and take a few deep breaths."

"I am taking heavy fire from all the trees."

"Copy Night Hawk?" Base asked.

"Copy." Night Hawk replied and then continued, "I am a flight of three Black Shark attack helicopters out of Seattle. I am armed with a 30 mm automatic cannon, rockets, and four 250 kg (550 lb) bombs. We'll hit the north side first. Get your heads down, I am coming in hot now."

The helicopters struck the north side hard, with rockets spewing from the aircraft and spreading death on the ground below, but few deaths, or at least not nearly as many as suspected by the pilots. They then hit each side and I had my troops slow their rate of fire a great deal to appear to have been hit hard.

We waited, and my ears were still ringing from the bombs that were dropped on my side of the field. Other than make some new stumps, the bombs did little good, but my folks were dug in well and each prayed the Black Sharks were not loaded with napalm; they weren't.

Then the pickup choppers arrived.

The Black Sharks continued working with the Captain until a flight of jets took over so the helicopter could return to base to refuel and rearm. Our firing was held to a minimum until the second wave of choppers landed; then we opened up with all we had, including missiles. I had a launcher and brought a chopper into my sights, locked on and they squeezed the trigger. I watched my missile fly from the launcher, move toward the chopper, and strike the aircraft's engine housing. That was the second Russian missile fired by me and neither was sidetracked by chaff.

Bullets began peppering my position, but on we fought. Four men ran right for my position, having realized I was in charge. A machine gun beside me opened fire and cut them to pieces. I watched as the big bullets removed limbs and heads from torsos. Blood filled the air and the mutilated bodies fell without life in any of them. I heard a scream and a Russian was suddenly in our position, rolling around and around on the ground with Cynthia.

I ran to them and when he was on top, I grabbed the front of his helmet and pulled his head back as I pulled my sharp sheath knife with the twelve inch blade. I cut his throat and watched the blood spurt from him before I released his helmet. He fell to her right side and began to jerk and twist as he fought the loss of his blood. Try as hard as he might, his hands could not slow the flow of blood and he was bled dry a few minutes later. He lay still.

I helped her to her feet and then returned to the radio.

My folks were holding out well, but I knew our time was short or I might meet the bombers Headquarters warned me about. Glancing at the field, I saw another half dozen choppers on fire and a couple smoking badly. Time to light shuck out of here, as my cowboy grandpa would say all the time.

"Badger One to all units, withdraw and return home. I repeat, gather our wounded, withdraw, and return home."

One by one I got a reply and a call sign. Then we melted into the forest and disappeared.

Over the next few days we counted our losses, doctored our wounded, and rested. Deliveries, resupply really, in the form of LAPES, took place almost daily and we were glad to be resupplied. While most items were deeply appreciated, the Chinese rations left a lot to be desired and since they contained traditional Asian food, many of my folks didn't like them at all. Pickled turnip root is not one of the dishes most Americans relish with an entree.

My relationship with Cynthia grew stronger and then one evening, close to bedtime, she showed. She'd been drinking, but clearly wasn't drunk. She'd gotten her hands on a bottle of Crown Royal and dropped by to share a few drinks. We had a few glasses of the drink and then things turned hot, following one deep kiss that brought all our passion to the front, where it ignited into hot burning flames. Moments later, she stood and then led me to my cot.

"Colonel, you'll not believe what the Chinese brought us late last night." One of my Sergeants said the next morning. "I discovered four pallets of four wheel All Terrain Vehicles, with utility trailers."

"What else?"

"Two five hundred gallon bladders of fuel, along with bullets, beans and first aid supplies."

"Do not take the ATVs into direct combat. They'll help us in many different ways. With trailers we'll be able to move our wounded much faster, deliver bullets and food to battlefields, and to move people who need to get some place fast in a fight. Improves our fighting power tenfold, or so I think." I said.

Near noon I got a call that bad weather was headed our way and to recall all troops and to suspend all missions. This storm was to hit us with high winds and snow; well over 36 inches in some spots was expected. I reached all of my people, except one squad who had reported radio problems. I had them called and called, but no response.

I sent four men out on ATVs to look for them. They had extra food and emergency gear they would need if caught out in the weather. Each vehicle had a trailer with gear stacked high when they left. For some reason I was deeply concerned, and that just isn't me. I knew most missions resulted in deaths and injuries but this was no typical mission. After they left, I started worrying about them running over a mine, so I finally opened my desk drawer and fished out the whiskey bottle I kept in there. Two shots of the strong amber colored drink and my concern was less, but still there. I refused to drink more, because I didn't need a drinking problem as a commander.

Intel called on me to discuss the Russian pilot we'd captured a while back. They'd learned a great deal about him and the Russian Seattle Air Base. He knew very little of any real value, due to his low rank and position. And no military secrets to really speak of, so now we had to figure out what to do with him. Intel suggested killing him, but I was more interested in keeping him alive for a prisoner exchange. One highly trained pilot would be worth a good dozen partisans, easily, but with the Russians you never knew.

Four hours after the ATVs left, I received a call that stated the unit had been found and they were heading back to base. Mines had slowed the ATVs down to the point that a man had climbed from the trailer to walk in front of them so they could safely move forward. Since the unit had three wounded, the two worst injured would ride home. I smiled then, because nothing was more nerve-racking than having a badly injured person and having to carry them by stretcher to someplace they could be treated properly. Over time they grew heavy, and it also limited the number of eyes scanning the countryside as we moved. Each man carrying the corner of a stretcher was one more fighter out of the picture for a few hours. That was why most of my snipers injured a target instead of killing them, because it took men to care for the wounded. The ATVs allowed me to do more for my wounded, faster, and at a cost of less men. I liked them.

When they walked into camp they looked like hell, and it was just starting to snow. It reminded me of images I'd seen as a kid of American soldiers fighting in Korea in the early 50's. Cold and worn out is how they looked to me, with all needing some hot food and a night of sleep.

"What are you doing!" I heard Sergeant Major Byrd yell out and watched as he neared a man and knocked him down with a hard right.

"What's going on here?" I asked as I neared.

"He was pacing our compound, sir." Birdie said.

A quick search of the man found a crudely drawn map of our base with the paces to various tents and facilities. A man would start at an easy to locate place on a base, say a discolored tent, a tall tree, or boulder easily seen, and then pace to a series of targets. All a mortar or artillery crew needed was the map and they'd clean me out. I grinned when I saw my tent circled in red ink. I was 500 paces from our main gate.

"What do you have to say about this?" I asked as I pulled my pistol.

"T . . . the Russians have my whole family in a gulag, sir. They said they'd release them if I made a pace map for them."

Then removing another piece of paper from the man's shirt, Birdie unfolded it and gave a loud whistle. He handed it to me and I found myself looking at a photo of a much younger me on the paper and noticed I was now worth one million dollars, dead or alive. I had to smile at all those people in the past who said I'd never amount to much, because I was now worth a lot of cash money. The man Top had caught was obviously out to make a few bucks at our expense.

I never answered the man, but raised my pistol and fired twice, both rounds taking the spy in the face, killing him instantly. When he fell to the ground jerking and twitching in his death throes, I said, "He deserves and gets no trial. Once he's dead, use an ATV to move his body out about 5 miles and dump him. He deserves no burial and we'll not give him one, either."

As one of my men drove off a bit later, the dead man on a trailer, I wondered, *How much will a one million dollar reward change my life, if at all? But, I will have to be cautious.*

CHAPTER 10

The whole Russian staff was fit to be tied when intelligence reported the estimated number of partisans in the area. Early estimates, from just three years ago, thought there might be 400 or so in the state, but now they were saying 5,000 to 10,000, only how could that be? Just in the last few hard battles they'd fought against the Russians, the partisans lost over 200 people. But the Russian losses were three men shy of 500 dead, with 1200 injured and fifteen missing. The missing were all presumed dead with their bodies blown to hell and back or burned to the point they were cremated. The only known Prisoner of War (POW) was the Russian MIG jet pilot they watched being taken prisoner.

They were all seated at stand up, the main purpose of the meeting a good hour behind them. They were brainstorming now, trying to figure out how to get the upper hand with the resistance.

"Shoot hostages." Intelligence suggested.

Colonel Yakovich said, "Colonel, it won't work. In Mississippi, a part of the United States that was a once part of the Confederate States of America, they went to their deaths by the thousands and it changed not a damned thing. My cousin saw them hanging the Americans one morning. They were on a cobblestone road in town and hanging them from telephone poles. They'd toss a rope over the pole, put a noose around the person's neck, and then push them off the back of a flatbed truck. He actually saw and heard the doomed men and women pledging allegiance to their flag or singing their national anthem as the noose was placed on them. They were still pledging or singing as they were pushed off the truck. He said it gave him the chills, and he suspected then we could not win a war here."

"I know they do not fear us, no matter what we do. On my last assignment here I was stationed in part of Texas. We started executions and so did they. For every one of them we killed, 10 Russian soldiers died, and in the same manner as we killed their people. Once we put 100 people in a church and set it in flames; the next week at midnight they put 217 Russian soldiers in an old building, poured gasoline on the structure and then set it in flames. They left a letter that said the rest of them would burn to death as soon as they captured more Russians. They kept their word, and 1,000 Russian men and women eventually burned to death. No, executions we want to avoid at all costs, because they do not frighten Americans."

"Let us poison gas the bastards, then." a Captain suggested.

"That worked in Mississippi, but all we killed were civilians. The partisans had our chemical/biological protective clothing and masks, which they stole from convoys, trains or supply houses. All it did was just irritate them, as it did us. No, these people are hard when need be. I can remember years ago, I used to think all Americans were fat and soft, but those Americans are dead already. We are dealing with the lean and mean citizens now, and they are a handful of determination."

"I want all of you to know that Jackson, Mississippi even used a nuke on them three years or so back and they are still fighting there. They turned around a few months later and used a nuke on us. Now most of Mississippi is radioactive and a serious danger to anyone stationed there. We need a different approach to these people. I suggest we keep fighting as we have been, traditional warfare. We bandage their seriously wounded and leave them. If we take them as POWs we had better damned sure take good care of them. Starvation rations will bring down harsh attacks from the resistance." the Commander said. He then asked, "How many prisoners do we have of theirs?"

"Sir, we have 5,000 civilians and 326 soldiers." the commander of the gulags said.

"How many more can we keep in custody?"

"With a little crowding, we can double our current numbers. If we stop feeding them and do not care about their comfort, maybe we can house four times that many."

"Did you not hear me when I said if we take them as POWs we had better damned sure take good care of them? Starvation rations will bring down harsh attacks from the resistance? I have seen it happen too, and they eventually freed the prisoners. No, they will be treated humanely by me as long as I am the commander here. We can beat them on the battlefield, and we will. But if anyone comes up with something new, let me know. I want my infantry commanders to remain seated while the rest of you are dismissed." Colonel Yakovich said as he pulled his cigarettes from his jacket pocket. He lit one, took a deep puff, and let the smoke release from his mouth and nose. He wanted a drink of vodka, so he pulled his coat open, removed his flask, and took a drink. He was the only man to do so.

"Gentlemen, tomorrow morning at 0600, over two thousand Russian paratroopers will jump over Washington State, and then break into small ten men and women squads. We will use the paratroopers with attack helicopters to hunt partisans. The Russian units in Mississippi had great success working together, so we have high expectations, as well. Also, our total armor force will start rolling at the same time. The jumpers will land in the northern part of the state, while our armor will start in the South and move North. We will see what gets trapped between them. The name for this operation is Operation Fish Market."

"Is that all, sir?" the weather chief asked and then glanced at his watch.

"Why, do you have a hot date, Boris?" the Commander said and then laughed. He knew the meeting was double the length of his usual meetings, but he'd covered a lot of material.

"No, sir, but another storm is headed this way from the arctic and I expect heavy snows. The last I saw near noon, it was passing Alaska and dumping 76.2 to 101.6 centimeters, or 30 to 40 inches, of snow within 24 hours."

"That much, eh? I guess we can wrap this up then. Gentlemen, support Operation Fish Market in all ways. Dismissed until tomorrow."

"Colonel, if you will wait a minute, I will walk to the weather station with you. I want to see this storm of yours on radar."

"Yes, of course, sir. It is a wide storm and heading right for us. I see no other fronts between us and the storm so we will be hit, just exactly when I have no idea, but maybe 48 hours."

"Much snow? You said Alaska got a lot, but what about us?"

"I think we'll get well over 101.6 centimeters before it is over and that's within the first 24 hours. There is a second front right behind this one that looks even more menacing to me."

"Surely our paratroopers and armor are aware of this weather change? I need to warn Headquarters this evening and our troops will need skis or snowshoes. I am sure they know of this and may be using it as a cover for their attacks."

"Sir, I know little of tactics and such; I am a weather guesser, but I am a damned fine one."

"In this particular case, I hope you are incorrect, but I would not bet money on it. Headquarters does not care of the hardships of our troops, as long as they have a good body count. Weather like you are suggesting could bring temperatures that are sub-zero and frigid for those living out of doors."

"Sir, it will not be that rough on them, because it snows in Russia, and hard too. They have all been in training with the ground covered with snow and well below freezing."

"Sure, but they were prepared and had their winter gear with them. What happens if they jump and there is no gear? Infantry never carry an ounce they do not need. If they feel jackets are not needed, not a man will have one along when they jump."

"Surely Headquarters knows as much about this storm and the weather for the next few days as we do. I thought part of jumping was knowing the pending weather and conditions, especially the winds."

"They may, but then again, the equipment and gear we bring to this country often does not work properly. Or their weather man may disagree with you and think this front will do little or even move off in a different direction. They have a weather section twice as large as I have."

Again the weather man shrugged and said, "I have no idea, sir. I do know this front will hit us and I am sure within 48 hours."

They moved up the steps and entered the weather station. All sorts of computer screens were showing weather radar and they were active, meaning live. Colonel Yokovich was a bit of a nerd and loved being around computers and gadgets of all sorts. He followed the Colonel into his office. Pushing two buttons on a remote control, two TV screens were shown. One was showing downtown Anchorage and the other here. The storm was hitting the town of Anchorage hard, with snow flying all over and no one on roads. A bank in the image, across the street from the camera, registered *-60 f.*

Picking up a lone piece of paper in the center of his desk, the Colonel said, "The front will be here within 48 hours, my people think. We forecast the same for us as Anchorage is getting, with over 101.6 centimeters of snow. People do not fight long in weather like that."

When Colonel Yakovich called Headquarters they told him, more or less, to mind his business and take care of his own troops and base. The jump was still a go and nothing would change their minds, except high winds on jump day. It was a short phone call.

On jump morning, the Colonel was up early to listen to the operation on the radio. He'd warned his radio operator they would not comment but just listen in on the communications. The mission went smoothly and without the loss of a man, at least not from the jump. Radio messages for the next two hours showed a few injured on landing due to brush, trees, and one man was drug into a barbed wire fence and cut to hell and back. He was evacuated by helicopter due to extensive injuries and blood loss. There were no deaths.

The winds were high an hour later and snow began to fall. The troops quickly assembled in small squad sized cells and started their missions. Master Sergeant Tyoma Akulov had his troops moving and didn't like the snow that just started. He was experienced, having jumped all over the world and in different kinds of weather, night or day. Of all conditions, he disliked arctic the most, due to the difficulty in staying both dry and warm. However, as a man in the Army he followed orders, likes or dislikes aside.

He was also concerned about mines because the snow would make seeing them difficult and pressure mines were just as deadly under snow as not. There was one advantage of cold weather; most homemade booby traps would freeze in position. He'd once sprung a fulcrum trap in the field and due to the temperature being well below zero, everything had frozen into place and didn't work. He prayed if it had to snow, let the temperatures drop too. His folks had removed sections of their parachutes and would use the nylon to make shelters with later. It was much lighter than using issued tents or other gear, and they only took the green panels of the chute.

His thermometer showed a temperature of -22.2 Celsius and that was cold, but he had gear to survive. Someone said the bad weather was discussed during the pre-jump planning, only Headquarters thought it would pass by quickly and leave little snow. Akulov had heard close to 101 centimeters of snow would fall and that was a lot. He was starting to sweat from the weight of all the gear he was packing. He unzipped parts of his parka, to allow some of his body heat to leave the coat. If he got too hot and then stopped, the sweat would freeze and then he was in danger of dying. He had to move slowly.

He and his troops were using the white panels from the parachutes to camouflage their uniforms and gear. They even wore white face masks made of leather that had fur on the inside, against the flesh. The Russian airborne troops were almost impossible to see in the snow as they moved. He knew the partisans were likely in camp sitting by a warm fire and not moving much, so he looked for smoke and tried to smell it as well. So far, nothing was smelled or found.

He was looking at the woman on point, Junior Sergeant Irisa Vasilievna, when she disappeared in a loud explosion and wall of flames. She'd had no time to warn the others or even scream. She was simply there one minute and gone the next. Moving forward, he found her boot with the foot still inside of it and the footwear was still laced up. He shivered and dropped the boot. Smoke filled the air and the smell of cordite lingered with the smoke. He noticed a mist of red blood in the air, all that remained of a 115 pound Russian woman, except her boot.

As the group moved forward to check on her, Private Lisenka stepped on a toe popper, which the Russians called 'ball poppers.' Most of their troops were injured in the groin area if they stepped on a shotgun shell with the primer resting on a nail, so they disliked them immensely. They had a mine detector, but using one in the field slowed any unit down a great deal.

Lisenka screamed and blood flooded down the front lower part of his trousers, near the zipper. The Medic, cutting the material away, saw his left ball and half his penis were gone. He was bleeding hard, clawing at the snow and screaming. The medic quickly gave him a shot of morphine to kill his pain and to quiet him down.

"Uh, Base this is Polar Bear four, over." the radioman said calmly.

"Go, Polar Bear."

"We have one dead and one severely injured due to mines, over."

"Copy."

"Request immediate evacuation of my wounded and dead, over."

"Negative, the winds are gusting to around 96 Kilometers an hour. It is too dangerous for helicopter flights right now. The wind is expected to die down in about four hours and that is the time I can send you a ride home for your wounded. Can you keep them alive that long?"

Looking at the medic, he asked, "Can you keep him alive for four hours?"

"Yes, Master Sergeant, but he will be useless to us and will slow us down."

"Helicopters cannot fly in this wind, so we will bring him with us."

"Affirmative Base, we can keep him alive. Let me know when the taxi is ready to pick up my injured."

"Roger, Base out."

"Polar Bear, out." Akulov pulled out his compass and said, "Move a few more degrees to our left, Point. You are drifting slightly to the left and I know it is difficult to see right now."

An hour later, the weather worse and the winds even higher, they moved into the safety of trees to block the wind. They were done moving for the day. It was too hard to see and the weather had not improved in the least. The snow was piling up and the winds were fierce, and the Master Sergeant knew they had to stop. In camp now, with most of the winds blocked they got shelters up, insulated the bottom of each shelter using pine boughs, and gathered enough wood for the night. They each had a long pull from a vodka bottle and then settled in to eat their green frog rations. The Sergeant wasn't a hard drinker and none of his troops had alcohol problems, so he didn't mind if they all carried flasks in the field, but if he caught one drunk, he would file charges against them. He knew on cold evenings and even when hurt at times, booze could improve things.

They didn't speak much on missions but they wondered how far they'd cover in weather like this. His team had been issued snowshoes, while others were given skis. Surely the resistance would be holed up as well.

"Do we need night guards with the weather like this?"

"Yes."

"Do you not think the resistance is in a shelter too?"

"Yes."

"If the resistance is under a shelter, why do we need guards?"

"I always have guards when in the field, *always*, and no matter the weather. It is when you do not expect the enemy that you die."

"It is cold. I have not felt cold like this since my training in Siberia. It was cold there too."

"Yes, it is cold in Siberia and if you survived there, you will survive here. If the snow slows or lets up tomorrow, we need to be moving. We will never find any partisans in snowy weather and the helicopters cannot fly in this either. There is too much wind and it is too high in speed. They couldn't even come for Lisenka."

"I may need to take blood from some of us to care for him. I have used most of the blood I had with me, so we are growing short. If other units have had injuries, then men will start to die on us in another day or two."

Master Sergeant Akulov said, "It is the way of the army. Someone did not think this storm would be so strong and we are out living in it as they remain on base sipping vodka and eating well."

One of the men laughed and said, "It is always the enlisted men who pay for the mistakes of senior officers."

"No, not always, but usually. We will have to wear snowshoes tomorrow, because it is coming down hard."

"I do not think we will move an inch for days." the medic said, "And if that happens, we will end up with a dead man on our hands."

"It cannot be helped as it is, so let it go. Lisenka knew the risks when he joined the army, then when he volunteered for airborne school, and when he jumped yesterday. We all know the risks. I hope the man lives, too, but if he dies, then he dies. This war is serious business and combat is no game; no, not a game at all."

The medic lowered his head and gave thought to the Master Sergeant's words. Like many of them, Lisenka had volunteered for combat duty in America, mainly motivated by the **591,803 rubles offered by the government.** At about $10,000 it was considered a great deal of money by all Russians and it was offered to all who volunteered to serve in America for one year.

"He volunteered for this tour." the medic said.

"By God, I did not!" one of the Junior Sergeants said.

"But your pay goes up here and we pay no taxes."

"And, as Lisenka shows, I can lose my balls and pecker here too. No, this is my third combat tour in four years, and I am getting out once home again. I have had enough. Hell, we are no closer to winning this war now than we were on my first tour, and do you know why?"

"Tell me, why?" the medic answered and his tone was full of sarcasm.

"Because it is impossible to win a partisan war. The resistance owns the people and the countryside. Look at all the wars where the country fought the resistance, and there has never been a victory by any outside nation. The partisans win in the end, just like they will win this one."

"Stop talking like that. That kind of speaking will get you sent to a gulag."

"At least I would be alive. I grow tired of this war."

The Master Sergeant said, "We all do, but it is our jobs to fight the enemies of Mother Russia."

"Did someone call in our night position? I do not want to be blown to hell because someone sees the light of our fires."

"I did, about fifteen minutes ago." the Master Sergeant said.

"We are going to need two fires all night, I suspect."

"That is all whoever is on guard will do, tend to the fires. If they go out, we might all die by morning."

"No, it is not that cold, but it is cold enough we need these fires." Akulov said. He pulled his flask out and took a long drink of his vodka.

"I dread tomorrow and walking in snowshoes."

"They are not bad, once you start walking bow-legged naturally." the Junior Sergeant said and began laughing. "And the fact your legs ache from the pain of using them all day."

"I do not get much pain, but I trip a lot, at first anyway. Well, I am going to bed. Since tomorrow will be a rough day, I need to get to bed early. Wake me when it is my time to guard."

In ones and twos, the men headed to their sleeping bags.

The night was quiet, and when Master Sergeant Akulov got up to check camp at close to 0300, he found the guards alert and the fires burning. It was lung hurting cold then, a good -34, and he expected -40 before the sun dawned again. He crawled back into his cold sleeping bag to rest for another hour. He catnapped until 0430 and then climbed out of his sleeping bag for the day.

As the troops ate another green frog, the Sergeant said, "Still snowing, with 24 inches on the ground, and currently it is minus 40. We leave here in thirty minutes."

"Tonight we will have to make a fire on a platform of green logs, or that is what we did in Siberia in deep snows." the Junior Sergeant said.

"I have to get through the day, then I will think about this evening. This will be a rough one."

"Once walking, take it minute by minute and make the best of it. It is hard enough to walk in snowshoes as it is, but add a 27 kilogram backpack and it is awkward at best. Just be sure to avoid sweating or we will have some serious problems."

"We have all been trained." Master Sergeant Akulov said, and then began packing his gear for the day.

"Quiet! I hear something." the medic said as he worked on Lisenka.

"Someone is coming." the Junior Sergeant said, and slipped the safety off his weapon.

CHAPTER 11

We had radio calls by the hundreds it seemed from folks reporting they'd seen Russian paratroopers first in the air and then on the ground. Of course, I ordered them to attack when the times were right and we'd lose the least people. Most chose to do nothing with the weather as bad as it was. The reports I was getting indicated the Russians landed and when the bad weather hit, moved for cover. I expected them out and moving during the second day and for sure by the third. I ordered ambushes set up and then gathered up a squad to go Russian bear hunting. There is no limit on Russian bears either, and no hunting license needed.

When we left base this morning, it was -40 and with a light wind out of the north. The high was expected to reach -15, which is almost tee-shirt weather, right? We wore stolen Russian snowshoes and parkas. Around each left arm went a red or orange piece of cloth to help keep us from shooting each other. Our parkas were white snow pattern camouflage, and we had enough white parachute material to cover our heavy backpacks. I went so far as to wrap a little white material around my Bison. Then off we went. I kept the pace slow to avoid overheating in the cold. It's hard not to sweat when we're often carrying half our body weight, or more, on our backs.

First Sergeant Andrew "Andy" King was along to stay current in our operations. I required everyone to go on a mission at least once a month. Andy was an average sized man, 150 pounds, five feet and ten inches tall, and with short brown hair. His green eyes were intelligent and his mind quick. His teeth were even and white and usually seen often due to his sense of humor.

We'd covered about five miles when he said in a low whisper, "I smell smoke."

We stopped and I smelled it as well. Someone was camped nearby and it was wood smoke. Snow was coming down at a regular rate, fast, and it was minus 20. Finally, after glassing the area, I spotted a thin finger moving for the sky upwind and maybe a half a mile away. I knew we had no units this close to our base camp, so we prepared to attack.

Base was informed and we then made ready. I'd keep my folks all together and try to overrun the camp. Hopefully I'd catch them off guard and we'd be successful. If not, maybe I could reduce the numbers enough the survivors would call for a ride home and I'd bag a chopper. I sent Andy and Sergeant Stone to Injun up on the place and see what we had. They would then return to me with the information. At that time I'd decide if we attacked or not. How they were armed and their numbers would influence my decision, but they might have armor too. I'd know more when they returned.

My wait was short.

"Squad sized with a variety of different weapons, including a machine gun. I saw one man badly injured, and they were getting ready to leave."

"I want an L shaped ambush site, and I want it now. No moving or talking as we wait in ambush. Let's move, and hope the wind and snow covers our tracks." Blowing snow along with falling snow was filling our tracks in quickly. Ten minutes later, we had two Claymore mines planted and were in position.

Now we waited.

I felt the small animal called fear nibbling on my gut, but knew we'd do fine. I hoped we killed enough of them to remove them from the field. I felt with each Russian death, we got closer to gaining our freedom.

"Here they come." Andy whispered.

I could barely see them in their camouflage clothing and the falling snow. I grew nervous as I watched their point man walk by us and then I waited for the main group to enter the kill zone of my mines. I picked up the clackers and waited.

The leader stopped and looked around. I knew he felt something out of place or perhaps danger. I lowered my head to avoid looking at him. People have a way of feeling when they are being watched. If you don't believe me, stare at someone for a few minutes and they'll eventually meet your eyes. I have no idea how it works but some feel your eyes on them quicker than others. Finally, after not seeing anything out of place, he moved slowly forward.

Once the whole group was in front of my mine, I squeezed the clackers and a loud explosion, followed by screams, filled the air. Most fell with the explosion, but the two or three still standing fell right behind the others from rifle and machine gun rounds. A red cloud hung in the air over the fallen forms.

"Give 'em time to bleed!" I called out.

I heard a burst of automatic fire and then someone yelled, "The point man is dead."

I counted the downed forms and I was two short of the known tally.

"We have two missing. We'll look for them in a minute." I said. My tone was hard and harsh, but I was shaking inside from the adrenaline rush. I knew from experience, I'd be fine in about ten minutes.

When we moved forward, the bodies were torn to hell and back by the steel ball bearings and most had limbs missing. We found none alive.

"Andy, I want you and another trooper look for the two missing. I suspect they stopped to use the bathroom, or fell behind for some other reason and were to catch up later, but I don't know."

"How is their injured man? Thomas, you come with me."

"Dead, they're all dead from the ambush."

"Are you going to wait for me?"

"No, it's too cold to wait long. Return to base after you find them or when you get too cold looking for them. The call is yours."

"Later then. We'll find 'em."

Andy had no idea he was soon on the trail of Master Sergeant Akulov and a Junior Sergeant named Aleskeevich. The two Russians heard the firefight and suspected they were the only survivors of the squad. The sound of the two Claymores exploding caught their attention.

"Move east and into the trees." They had remained behind as the Junior Sergeant finished his morning toilet. He'd come down with the squirts and was suffering from stomach pain too. His belly was all that saved both men up to this point, but the Master Sergeant suspected they'd be followed. They'd be easy to track in the snow too.

"We are lucky because neither of us is wounded and we have all our gear."

"Uh-huh, but we are leaving tracks a baby could follow."

"The wind is picking up, so maybe we will get lucky and the blowing snow will help fill our tracks in. It is not falling hard enough now to fill them."

"I just heard an engine. There it is again. Do you hear it?"

"Helicopter." Akulov stopped and opened his backpack.

He pulled out a survival radio and extended the antenna before he said, "Any Russian aircraft that can hear me, please respond. This is Eagle Five, over."

Instantly he heard, "Uh, read you five by five, Eagle. Do you need help? This is Raven Two."

"Need a ride home. We are the only survivors of a squad, over."

"Turn your beeper on and leave it on until you hear me fly over you. I will home in on the beeper."

"Copy and here goes."

"Someone comes!" Aleskeevich said, his tone filled with fear.

Gunshots were heard and the Junior Sergeant fell, but he'd only taken a bullet to the fleshy part of his left arm.

The helicopter flew over and the Master Sergeant, said, "You were just over me, Raven Two. Be advised I am being shot at, but only by a couple of men, or so it looks."

"Move to the clearing, oh, maybe 30 meters in front of you. I will land in the field. Approach the aircraft toward the nose and only the nose."

"Copy and will do. Eagle Five, out." Then turning to Aleskeevich the Master Sergeant said, "Move forward, maybe 30 meters to a field. We will approach the helicopter running and both enter by the aircraft's right door."

"I understand, right door."

Akulov nodded and then pulled a pin from a grenade. He tossed it behind them and then turned and started running. By the time they were at the field, a helicopter was just setting down, so they took out running and right for the nose.

Suddenly the Gatling guns on the right side opened up on the trees they'd just left. As they neared the helicopter, they could both hear the occasional bullet strike the metal skin on the bird; *plunk-zing*, was the sound of each round hitting the metal. The Sergeant tried to push Aleskeevich into the door faster when suddenly he felt a hot poker strike him in the back and heard the Private scream as the round went through him, too. The gunner reached down and pulled the injured Private into the helicopter. Sergeant Akulov had his feet on the helicopter skids when the bird began to go up, the Gatling guns both making noise now. The medic pulled him the rest of the way into the helicopter.

The Sergeant was sleepy and looking up, he saw a medic giving him a shot of some kind. Bullets from the two Americans were still hitting the helicopter, and then the pitch in the aircraft's engine changed.

A headset was placed on Akulov's head and the medic said, "Your Private is dead and you would not have lasted another hour in the field. One of the two bullets that struck the both of you hit his spine."

"Uh, I have no idea, Base, but I'm in serious trouble." the pilot was heard saying.

Smoke, starting light and then turning darker, was coming from the crew section and the pilots were seen fighting for control.

"My console is lit up, mostly in red lights, and the bird is becoming hard to control. I will keep us in the air as long as I can. I am at about a thousand feet and can get no higher with the weight

I have on the aircraft. I will have everything not needed tossed out the doors. Copy and out."

"Want to keep the body or throw it out, sir?" a gunner asked.

"We will try to keep it, but get rid of all Gatling guns and all ammunition. I want everything not nailed down tossed out the door. Hurry, because every second counts." the pilot said.

The aircraft began to shudder and shake as the smoke grew dense and dark. The engine was making a high pitched whine along with its normal sounds. And glancing around, the Master Sergeant saw the gunners were worried too, because their eyes were showing their concern. The Master Sergeant was helped to an olive drab nylon seat and then a seat belt was placed around him. The gunner pulled the strap tight as the medic wrapped the Sergeant's back injury. Once done, he attached the shoulder straps and tightened the works. He then gave the Sergeant a thumbs up.

The medic gave Master Sergeant Akulov a shot of morphine and as he was falling asleep, he heard the pilot saying, "Mayday, mayday, mayday, this is —" and his world turned black.

The Master Sergeant woke hearing people talk and then a piece of metal struck a metal bowl or pan.

"How do you feel, Master Sergeant?" a voice asked.

"I . . . have no . . . pain. Where . . . am I?" The lights were too bright and it hurt him to try to open his eyes.

"You and the whole helicopter crew are in a hospital in Seattle."

"We . . . had one . . . dead."

He burned badly after the crash, but the medics said he was already dead. I am afraid your army days are finished. The bullet that struck your back caused enough damage that you are no longer fit for active duty. I do not think after you heal you will be able to pick up a suitcase, much less a heavy backpack."

The Sergeant nodded and then drifted off to sleep again.

Colonel Yakovich walked into the room and the interrogator stopped talking and went to a position of attention.

The Colonel asked, "As you were, Sergeant. Is she telling you anything?"

"A little, sir, but not much. I may have to turn rough in a few minutes."

"Do what is needed and when it is needed. Mother Russia needs the information she has."

Turning to the woman, the interrogator said, "If you do not answer my questions, my Colonel wants to turn you over to the men and let them use you. That would be a fate worse than death for most women."

"No, please. I have nothing to do with the resistance. I had a child with me and you sons of bitches killed my baby."

"You know about the resistance because a gun was found in your home."

"For our protection, that's all. All American homes have guns in them or they used to have them."

"It is illegal to own a gun now. Only criminals and the resistance have guns now."

"Not true. Many have guns but they're hidden."

"If they are discovered with a gun they will be killed, just like you will, if you do not answer my questions honestly."

"I have, and I know nothing of the resistance."

"How many prisoners are here?" Yakovich asked.

"I have twenty rounded up last night, sir. Why?"

"Bring in another prisoner, then kill this one in some horrible fashion and see if the other will talk. Not all of them know of the workings of the resistance."

Walking to the door, the Sergeant ordered another woman brought to him. In the meantime, he moved his prisoner outside, tied her to a fence post and then placed a chair about 20 feet from her. When the other prisoner was brought out, he had her tied to the chair.

"What is your name?" the Sergeant asked the new woman.

"Sandra Hinds."

"Sandra, what do you know of the resistance?"

"Nothing, nothing at all."

"I am going to ask you one more time and if you lie to me again I am going to hurt the woman tied to the post. What I do to her is your responsibility and you are the only one to blame. Now, what do you know of the resistance?"

"Nothing. I have seen shadows moving around at night, but I'm not in the resistance, none of my family is in or helps them, and I have never met a member of the partisans."

"You are a liar. See the woman tied to the post? She is a liar too. Do you know what I do to liars? I kill them."

Colonel Yakovich stood in the doorway of the building watching his Sergeant. He suspected he'd kill one of the women to get the other to talk. He casually removed a cigarette and lit it, wondering what his Sergeant had in mind.

The man walked to the corner of the building, picked up a can of gasoline and said, "Now, let us see how you take watching someone burn to death, all because you are a liar." He moved to the woman tied to the post and drenched her in the flammable liquid.

"Sandra, what do you know of the resistance?" he pulled out a pack of matches.

"N . . . nothing. Nothing at all."

The Sergeant ran the match head over the striker strip and when it ignited he asked, "Are you sure?"

"Yes, I'm sure. I know nothing."

He tossed the match at the fence post and with a loud *woosh*, it ignited.

The woman jerked at her bonds as she screamed and tried to use all her strength to break loose. As the flames grew hotter, she jerked to get away and a smell, not unlike burnt pork, filled the air. Dark black smoke moved for the low overhead clouds. Her screams were hideous now, as she danced against the flickering flames. Her hair was gone and just a few tatters remained of her blouse and skirt when she suddenly collapsed in the dirt and jerked. A few seconds later she was dead.

The Sergeant yelled, "Guard, bring me two children, under the age of 6. Get me a boy and a girl. Maybe after I burn them, Sandra will talk."

"Please burn no more. I will tell all I know."

Ten minutes later, she stopped talking and refused to answer more questions. The Sergeant picked up a steel pipe and striking her right arm hard and her left leg, broke both bones. She screamed and then passed out.

"Take the bitch back to her cell. We will talk again tomorrow. And, when you return, Private, get rid of this burnt body."

"Yes, Sergeant."

Stepping from the doorway, Colonel Yakovich asked, "Do you always have to go to such extremes to get them to talk?"

"Not usually, sir, but she has more information and she stopped talking."

"So, what is next for her?"

"Personal punishment with a great deal of pain. Ripping off fingernails, twisting broken bones, or removing an eye with my knife tip. Then again, electrical shock or water boarding usually work too. Of course, I will give her to the men to use later."

"Those are more traditional methods, and I am more aware of them."

"The fire method is unusual for me, but it works, and quickly too."

The Commander thought as he moved for the door, fighting the urge to puke, *I need to return to my office and see how Operation Fish Market is working.*

CHAPTER 12

Back at camp, I was eating Chinese rations with Cynthia when I was called to answer the radio. I was rather surprised since it was almost 1800 and never spoke with Base this late in the day, unless something bad had happened. Cynthia went to the tent with me, but waited outdoors.

"Base, Cobra One, go." I said.

"Cobra, Base. We have LAPES deliveries for you everyday next week, which starts tomorrow. Your first pallets will be motorcycles, 350cc dirt bikes, and they'll be ready to ride. You will receive 20 motorcycles in tomorrow's delivery."

I smiled and replied, "Thanks much, Base."

"Base One asks if you caught any fish? He has a strong desire for a huge fish."

"No, not yet, and not sure if we will. If we do, I'll let you know, because I have no place to keep 'em."

"Roger, any questions? Over."

"Negative on questions, Base, and thanks."

"Base, out."

Wow, I thought, *motorcycles, and twenty of them too.*

Over the course of the next week, we received the motorcycles, shoulder-fired missiles, a dozen flamethrowers, and well over a thousand pounds of munitions. We felt like our birthdays and Christmas were in the same week. Then things began to settle down.

The following week, right at dawn, we were beside a major highway waiting for a large convoy. It was still mostly dark, but the air was filled with the grayish fog. I expected the fog to be gone by 0900 hours, but right now I couldn't see 50 yards.

By the time I heard the truck engines, I had them almost on top of me. I let the first half of the convoy pass and when I thought half had gone by, I squeezed the clackers and the blast of the Claymore mine was loud, but so were the screams of those hit by the steel balls. Small arms fire followed and the tat-tat-tat of the two machine guns raking the trucks was comforting.

One of the tracers from the guns must have struck some explosives because two cars exploded, along with a truck, into huge fireballs. Russian bodies and pieces of bodies were thrown high into the air, landing on the other side of the freeway. Grenades wiped out groups of resistance in the convoy and then it grew quiet except for an occasional moan from someone injured or dying. The trucks could be heard burning, the cracking and popping of the flames loud against the stillness.

"Move forward, but keep your eyes open for survivors. Treat any wounded and put down those too seriously injured to survive. They might lay here in pain for days. Any taken alive should be brought to me." I yelled as my troops stormed the vehicles.

A few pistols popped and then all I heard was the excited voices of my people as they took all they wanted from our enemy. Food, ammunition, medical supplies, whiskey, Russian uniforms, sleeping bags, missiles and even some rubber arctic boots. There was much more, only I didn't hang around the trucks looking. The ATVs were loaded, bicycles, and even a couple of horses and they started for home. They'd go about halfway home, hide the gear, and come back for one more load. We tried hard to pick a convoy apart.

One of my men went down the row of trucks, pushing grenades into the fuel tanks—the pins pulled but the levers being held down by a rubber band. Weeks from now, after the diesel ate through the rubber band and the lever popped off, the truck would explode, no matter where it was located. Hopefully we'd kill more Russians.

Some Russian grenades were picked up, the timers moved to zero and then they were thrown around the battlefield. We even forced the tips from bullets, poured the powder out, and replaced it with as much C-4 as we could get in the empty shell. Our final act as we left was to mine the area, and heavily too. Soon the pines and hills hid us from view as we moved toward home.

About halfway back, I heard the whop-whop-whop of helicopters and moved my people into the thick brush. The choppers were moving slowly, obviously looking for us, but I didn't think they'd be lucky this day. We had a little sprinkling of rain falling and the temperature was going down. The area we were in was so dense with brush, if we left the trail we had to use machetes to clear enough underbrush to move.

After about ten minutes, the aircraft flew away from us, and I lost them.

I waited a few minutes for my drag man to near and then I said, "Be sure to plant mines and toe poppers when you can."

"I will, sir." said an unknown Private. She was thin, like the rest of us, short blonde hair, full lips, nice shape and deep blue eyes. She looked all professional to me and that made me happy. I liked those who knew their jobs and did what was needed without being ordered all the time.

I had never seen her before and that told me I needed to be spending more time with the cell than with Cynthia. I wanted to personally know my troops, but especially their names and where they were from. We'd been spending most of our free time together and looking back, some of that was a mistake. I moved forward and got back into my position.

It would take up to two days to walk home because it was about forty miles one way. That evening I poured anyone that wanted a drink a cup full of whiskey as a small celebration of our successful kill. The Russians would be mad, but they'd know the resistance was alive here and doing well now. As I sat beside Cynthia sipping my cup of strong amber drink, she was on the radio.

"Headquarters said the Russians were seen loading dogs and handlers on choppers at the main base. The handlers were all wearing parachutes, so they may be coming our way."

"That's possible." I replied and took a sip from my tin cup.

"You ever worked against dogs before?"

"Many times, and the best thing we can do is try to kill the dog. There are two types of dogs that track. One that smells the tracks of the target on the ground or those that smell the target's scent in the air. Both can do the job, but I've had better luck getting away or avoiding those dogs that smell tracks on the ground. It's good to know about them, but they don't concern me a great deal."

"John, what would you say if I told you I love you?" She looked right into my eyes.

I know I smiled, because while I felt something for her it wasn't love yet and I told her as much. She nodded, but was grinning as well. It's a wonderful feeling in a war torn nation to feel loved and I think it gives us a sense of real honest hope. As long as we can love we have hope for the future, and we can recover from anything.

As we waited, it began to rain paper, sheets of paper.

I had one float almost into my lap and when I grabbed it still in the air, I was overwhelmed with shock. It had a younger photo of my face, almost an 8 inch by 10 inch, and at the top read, "Wanted Dead or Alive. Reward of $1,000,000.00 by Russian Government. John Williamson, Colonel, US Partisan. Paid in Gold or currency of choice."

"Oh, John, this is terrible." Cynthia said, and then burst into tears.

I gathered up a goodly amount, because toilet paper was hard to find.

Later, I had a hard time sleeping because I knew the reward might tempt someone to try to kill or capture me. A million dollars is a hell of a lot of money. The problem is, there is no place in America to spend the money, but it's enough to tempt many people, even good people.

I slept poorly and tossed and turned all night. I had to get the posters removed, destroy the building where they were printed, and kill those behind the reward. The poster was nice enough to give me a Colonel Yakovich as the Wing Commander, Colonel Slava as the Base Commander, Colonel Chupakhin Vitomir Chief of Intelligence, and a General Yurkov Georgiy as the man with the. government money behind the printing. All three names were on the poster. I might be able to track and kill the three Colonels in the United States, but the fat General was out of the picture. It was very likely the General was in Moscow.

Over morning coffee with Cynthia, who hadn't slept well either, we discussed my plan. I had spies on the base who worked for our Headquarters and I'd try to get images and information about all three men. The General was safe and there was absolutely nothing I could do about him, but I could always arrange the Colonels to be killed by a sniper or killed in a bomb blast.

She didn't think it'd work because it would take balls to enter the base and try to steal personal information and images of the two highest ranking men on the facility. I knew we had spies that stole what we needed and often at great risk. In the meantime, I had to worry about one of my people putting a bullet in my back. If it got too rough, I'd have my Headquarters transfer me to another region of the United States. I didn't really want to do that. I dislike running from anything or anyone, and wouldn't this time, unless I took some near misses or attempts on my life.

"Top?" I said as he neared.

"Sir? How can I help you today."

I handed him a wanted poster, he grinned and said, "You're worth a million dollars to the Russians, and that's enough money to bring out the greedy. How can I help you?"

"See all posters that can be found are gathered up and burned. Then, tell our folks the Russians might offer that money, but we don't think it would be paid. First, to kill me, it would take a partisan and I don't see the Russians allowing them to live, reward or not. They want all partisans dead. They'd probably kill the person when they went to collect."

"Your words are more truthful than you realize. I think they'd kill them too."

"Make sure the threat to my life is reported to Headquarters and see what they think. They might have some ideas. I don't want to be reassigned, but I'll do what they order. If I have to go, see that Major Cynthia Morgan goes with me."

The Sergeant Major hadn't said a word, but I could tell he was thinking. Finally, he said, "We might be able to get a janitor or someone who works for us to smuggle out photos of the three Colonels and then we give clean copies to our snipers with orders to take them and no one else out. They need to do their normal routine for the day and then keep an eye out for either man. Make killing them a priority."

"Think that will work?" Cynthia asked.

"I think so, and members of the resistance know even if they killed John, they'd never be able to live and not worry about being assassinated. We'd track the killers down no matter where they relocated, not that it'd matter to you or John."

"Uh-huh, because I'd be dead."

"Yep, I'll get some spies to working on this, sir. In the meantime, I'm assigning five men to you for security and safety. I want five so some can rest at times and not always have to work. I want two outside and around your tent at night when you sleep, one with you during the day. I want them seven days a week and twenty-four hours a day."

"What of Cynthia? You know she lives with me now, right?"

"What you do is none of their business, and who you do it with even less so. They are there for one and *only* one reason, to keep you alive." Top said.

"See what we've talked about happens and within the hour. I want the information sent by code to Headquarters. From this moment on, I can trust no one and must be prepared to take action any second. The only people I can really trust is you Top, and Cynthia."

"I'll see this is done." he said and then left us heading to his office.

"Oh, and what makes you think I wouldn't kill you for this kind of money?"

"Come on, be serious. You said you love me and that you want to be my mate."

"I do want that. So, you should see security beefed up a great deal. All briefcases or boxes should be checked before they are allowed to enter a building with you. All they have to do is set a timer and make an excuse to leave the room. Once the blast is over, then they'd contact the Russians. Make it hard for anyone to kill you. I love you, John, and if you get killed, I'll not want to live, so I hope they kill me when they do you."

"Noble, but not needed. There is no need for you to die as well. I'll do all within my power to keep you and I alive."

"You mean me and your baby, don't you?"

I was shocked, and hoped this time my lover and baby would survive. The last time Spetsnaz killed both of them. I pulled her into my arms, kissed her deeply and felt her desire kick in and that alone triggered a change in me. Passion suddenly ignited, but it was 1700 and I had meetings to attend until around 1800.

"Did the medical folks tell you about the baby?" I asked, trying to get my mind on something other than loving her.

"No, it's not been confirmed yet, but I've missed two periods, so I'm sure I'm with child."

I glanced at my Russian watch and said, "I have meetings until 1800 but wait for me and we can eat in the mess hall together. After that, we can cuddle up on my bed and listen to Free Partisan Radio as we talk. I hope you are pregnant, because I want a baby to love."

"Uh, I had more than talking on my mind, sir."

"It'll happen. I will love you before we sleep." I pulled her to me, gave her a hard hug and a deep kiss. This would be an easy woman to learn to love, and deeply too. She loved pleasing her man.

Headquarters agreed with me trying to take the three Colonels out, except with a time limit. If I couldn't take them out within 30 days, they'd reassign me to the Southeast portion of the US. I agreed, because what else could I do? I'm not a coward, but I don't have a death wish either. As everyone stated, "A million dollars is a lot of money."

Less than three days later, I had information on the top three Colonels on the base. I even had color images, which meant I was able to provide my snipers nice clear photos. The images were from their personnel records. Of the three snipers, I considered Staff Sergeant Roper to be the best shot of all of them. I wanted the base watched 24/7 with no shots taken except on one of the three Colonels.

Roper went to a different location each day and lay prone for eight hours, waiting for one of the Colonels to exit a building, but so far he'd seen nothing. He grew hot as the day progressed, but he didn't move, not even for a canteen of water. It was the third day and late afternoon when he spotted Colonel Chupakhin Vitomir, Chief of Base Intelligence, exit what Sergeant Roper thought was the Headquarters building.

It was just starting to turn dusk when his spotter elbowed him. He'd already seen the man, so he just nodded. The Sergeant moved the cross-hairs on his scope to make up for any drop in the bullet in about a thousand yards, then lined his sights up on the Colonel's chest. Sergeant Roper took a long deep breath and as he released it, he squeezed the trigger. He was rewarded by a slight thud as the supressor kept the noise of the 30.06 rifle firing to a minimum.

In the scope he saw his intended target fall as the bullet passed through his chest and exited as it threw blood and gore out his back. He suspected his target screamed when hit, but Roper heard nothing. When bystanders neared the man, Roper waited, not wanting them today. He wanted to make sure his target was fatally injured, so he waited for them to lift him. Then he would shoot him again.

Two men with rifles neared and were ordered to guard them as others lifted him. When Colonel Chupakhin Vitomir's body was picked up and fully extended, Roper sent two more bullets into his chest and the Colonel's chin dropped; he was dead.

Sirens sounded and their high pitch wail seemed to just add to the overall confusion. A couple of men pointed off in the distance and not one finger was near the sniper. An airstrike hit minutes later, only it wasn't even close.

As Roper and his spotter ran, the shooter radioed Base.

"Uh, Base Three, Quick Draw One, over."

"Go Quick Draw."

"Cobbler three." He said, the code indicating Colonel Vitomir, the number three man, was dead.

"Repeat, Quick Draw One. Over."

"Cobbler Three is no longer a player in the game."

"Copy, Quick Draw One."

"Starting our escape and evasion. Out."

"Good luck, Quick Draw."

Roper moved quickly through the trees and brush. In a matter of minutes the Russians had choppers in the air, but the witnesses were confused because he'd been no place near where they were searching. He smiled and kept running.

On the base, Colonel Slava knew after talking with witnesses the death of the Chief of Intelligence was no isolated case of luck. The Colonel had been murdered. Of all the people walking around the grounds, the senior man was killed, which meant the sniper knew Russian uniforms and ranks. He'd been selectively killed.

The Colonel suddenly felt a chill go down his spine and moved out of the open. Once in his office he poured himself a double shot of vodka and found he spilled much of the liquid due to his hands shaking. He didn't like knowing the sniper killed by rank, because he was the next ranking man on base.

Over the next four days it was quiet and Colonel Slava found himself drinking more vodka than usual. He was drinking each morning, early, just to walk two blocks to his Headquarters building. The sniper had not returned, so maybe it was safe for him to relax a little.

The weather was perfect as the Colonel walked to a Black Shark two seat attack helicopter and was to go on a flight to keep his status current and to still receive flight pay. Everyone was in a good mood, with all of them joking. He'd just moved up the external steps to climb into a seat when the canopy glass took a glancing bullet and the chunk of lead zinged off into space. There followed three more shots and each one was close, very close. While the bullets didn't pierce the aircraft armor plating it did send each bullet off as a dangerous ricochet. The launch crew was going nuts with bullets bouncing all over. One man fell screaming, with a bullet to the shin, and the broken bone clearly seen sticking from the mangled flesh.

One portly Sergeant screamed and fell, his left arm bleeding hard, and the crew chief fell with a bullet to the back. As they lay screaming the sniper was cursing with each miss. Colonel Slava ran into a nearby hanger and went out the back door. He then called his driver and had his car, minus the flags, brought to him.

Just as he stepped from the hanger, he felt a red hot poker enter his back and watched the bullet, along with part of himself, strike the car door. Off in the distance someone was screaming. The concrete of the sidewalk felt cool to his face as he hit hard. Less than a minute after being shot, he was pulled into the back seat of his car and was moving for a hospital.

"He hit you high and in the shoulder, sir." Sergeant Victorovich said, "So you are lucky. Here, let me push some material against the wound to stop the bleeding. We will be at the hospital in a few minutes."

He was very confused as he slowly lost consciousness.

CHAPTER 13

Three days after the wanted posters were dropped to the ground, someone shot into the outhouse with four rounds, which normally wouldn't be a big deal, but I was in the small smelly place at the time. How they missed, I have no idea. I'd dropped a pocket knife in a sheath from from my belt and bent over to pick it up from the floor. Four holes appeared right above my head and then continuing on, the bullets made four holes behind me. It's very unnerving to experience something like that. While the bullets hit no one, the attempt on my life made everyone a little nervous, especially me.

No one had seen anyone with a rifle and there was not much I could do except to warn folks at all meetings, "If you try to kill me and miss, and I catch you, I will kill you right then and there. You will get no trial, no hearing, not even a chance to explain your action. You will either be shot or stabbed to death."

I turned security over to Top and lived my life as normally as I could. All boxes and briefcases brought into any tents I was in, or would be in at some point that day, were checked closely by my military police. Dog teams moved around us at all hours.

Cynthia was a loving woman, and I was slowly falling love with her gentle and soft ways. When not out on a mission, she was all woman, and dressed the part too. She had the ability to go from deadly partisan killer to sweet Southern Belle in less than five minutes in dress and behavior. I respected her for that, because it showed she cared about our nation. She also cared about herself, it showed plainly, and she wanted me to be happy too. She was all lady, a woman, my friend, and my lover. She knew when to be a professional partisan and when to turn intimate with me.

One morning, right at dawn, Cynthia was standing beside my cot as I slept. She'd just returned from the showers and was wearing a robe, with her hair wrapped in a towel. She removed the day's uniform from my locker, when she noticed movement out of the corner of her eye. She looked and spotted a grenade rolling into my tent.

"John, grenade!" She screamed and then kicked the explosive out of my tent. I heard screams and yells, but had no idea what was going on. I sat up, but heard no explosion. I did hear two gun shots.

"I got 'em! Here, help him stand. Hard to stand after a .45 strikes a man in the leg." I heard Top say.

I pulled my Russian pistol and made my way outside.

"Move closer to me, sir." Top said. "The grenade didn't go off, which means we're lucky. It's Chinese made and they have about a 70% failure rate. If it had been Russian or American made, we'd not be having this talk out here."

A tall skinny kid of about 18 stood, supported by Top and another man I didn't know.

"Who is this boy?" I asked.

"He's the man I saw roll a grenade into your tent. I actually stood over by the ATV and watched him pull the pin and saw the handle fly into the air. He was alone."

"Did you do this for the money?" I asked him, only before he could answer me, I fired two shots from my pistol. Both bullets struck him in the head and he was dead instantly. Blood and gore splattered on the ground behind him. I could see my actions shocked Top.

"Hang him by his ankles in the center of camp so others may see him. Place a sign on him that reads, "I wanted to be the assassin of our Commander. I failed. Will you be next?" Let the body hang for 48 hours. Then pull him out into the brush a couple of miles from here, but no burial."

"Yes, sir." Top replied. "Oh, Sanders, I can tell you have nothing to do. I have a job for you, son."

Shaking his head, the young man said, "You usually do have a job for me or you find me one pretty damn fast. What is it now, Top, dig a new latrine?"

"No, we are going to hang a man."

"Hang a man? Who?"

"Never mind who, just know he's already dead."

"Then why hang a dead man? It looks to me like hanging wouldn't be needed."

"To make an example of his ass. Now, come here and you take his feet."

A minute later the body was gone.

Once in the tent I told Cynthia what happened and warned her to go no place, not even my tent, without being armed. They could try to kidnap her to get at me.

I grabbed all of my field gear and said, "I'll be back in the morning. I have an overnight mission with Andy King and his troopers."

"You be careful and take no risks." she said with that sexy smile of hers.

"I won't take any risks. You be careful here, too, because the Russians want me badly. I know they'll hit this place when they discover my location. They'd take you in a minute to get back at me."

She pulled me into her arms, kissed me deeply, and said, "Plenty more where that one came from, so be safe and return for more."

"I'll return as soon as I can."

Andy ran a professional group of men and women, with absolutely no talking in the field and very little moving around when stopped. He was well prepared and organized for this and any other mission he ran.

When I asked him about it, he replied, "Either keep them professional or watch 'em die out here. Most partisans are professionals in action now, but as recent as two years ago that was not true."

As we started down the trail, my camouflage face paint was already itching and bothering me, and I had another 12 hours or so to go. My pack was heavy, close to 70 pounds, but most of what was in the thing was there to help keep me alive. I could think of nothing in the pack I didn't, or might not, need on the mission. It would be a long night with little sleep and poor food, and I was sure I'd end up with indigestion from the rations.

It was mid afternoon before Andy took a break for a 'noon' meal. He stopped later than usual because everyone, including me, had eaten breakfast in the dining facility. While not much, powdered eggs, bread, bacon and hot coffee beat a ration to hell and back.

As we sat eating our meals I noticed some had Chinese rations, and I hated those things. What American eats a pickled turnip root or rice and squid? The closest I'd found to a real American meal were the Meals Ready to Eat and they were very good. We were eating some now that were over 20 years old.

"Sir, if you have a second, I'd like to show you our objective, so if I'm killed or wounded you can take over." He had a map opened in the dirt as he squatted.

He then continued, "You okay'd the mission some time back and I got it late last night. Now, I want to do this job with no losses if possible, but we're to blow the Diablo Dam." He pointed the location out to me on the map. I nodded but knew nothing of most of the dams in the state.

"Located in the North Cascade range along the upper Skagit River, the Diablo Dam is absolutely beautiful, or so I think." I said, having been there about ten years ago. It was one of two I could remember ever seeing before.

"We'll visit there to take out the power generators, not take images, but the area is stunning. You must have seen it during the summer." Andy said.

"Actually, during the fall."

Glancing at his watch, Andy said, "Saddle up and let's move. I want to be able to see our objective before we stop for the night."

The trail soon turned rough and every mile or so we planted mines on our back trail. Close to dusk we looked out over a beautiful lake and to our left was the Diablo Dam. While it was larger than some it was smaller than many, but was gorgeous. I can still see that dam in my minds eye.

We unloaded our packs, pulled out everything except for explosives and ammunition. We also took grenades, just in case we had to fight our way home. Leaving one woman with our gear, we moved closer to the dam, where we waited for full darkness. Near 2000 we'd hit the 129-megawatt facility and see if we could blow all the transformers. As we waited, I watched Russian soldiers, men and women, moving around the damn, with most at the top. I estimated maybe two squads of military stationed there. I envied them, because the view was beautiful.

I had Andy give his pack to one of his troops and I did the same. We pulled our knives as I said, "Andy and I will silence the guards, then I want everyone on the stairs going down to the transformers. One way down is inside the building at the other end of the dam, but the exterior steps will be used by most of you. I need about half of you to follow me. Once we start, remember we do not want to be a prisoner of the Russians, because they are vicious and will mistreat us. On this raid, no quarter given or expected in return."

Silence.

"Okay, check each others face paint and then let's go." Andy said.

A few minutes later I spotted the first guard near the road. I moved toward him, knife in hand, only I stayed in the shadows. He seemed to be about half asleep and kept shaking his head at times as if trying to stay awake. I paused when he pulled out a pack of cigarettes and lit a smoke. I gave him a few minutes to get comfortable with his cigarette.

I was able to walk to the man, throw my arm around his neck, and then stab him four times near his kidneys with my 12 inch long knife blade. He attempted to scream a warning, so I cut his throat. I tossed his dying body aside, heard him choking, and moved forward, as his blood ran down my hands. I wiped my hands off on my trousers.

I saw no other guards and waved my people to me. Once together, I led them down the exterior stairs toward the generators. The closer we got, the louder the noise became. Finally, I slipped ear plugs in as I entered the generator room alone. I saw a group of ten men sitting and working with computer monitors. All were dressed in sparkling white lab coats or Russian uniforms. I had no idea what their jobs were or even their nationalities, because just being here made them my enemies.

I pulled the pin on a grenade, let the spoon fly, and held it two seconds. I then tossed it over the heads of the workers. A second later, I sent another grenade flying toward them. I heard a scream in English and heard what I assumed was a warning in Russian.

With a loud *blam*! the first grenade exploded, throwing shrapnel in all directions, then the second grenade went off. Screams were heard, and I saw one worker stumbling around with a cast iron fragment sticking out of his forehead. Blood streamed down his face as he kept promising his mother he'd be a good boy if she'd stop punishing him. It was then I realized I fully understood him and I'd just killed some Americans. By working for the Russians, I felt they'd deserved their deaths.

One man was on the floor, his back against a wall, and his fingers were trying to stop the flow of blood from his neck. His lab coat had blood all over it, because it was spurting from his throat. He calmly met my eyes.

Not a word was said by either of us as I shot him in the chest. Seconds later the light behind his eyes went out forever and he was dead.

"Quickly, set the explosives!" I said to those who had entered after the blasts. I heard gunfire outside. "I want four men guarding the entrance to this place, because I don't want to be trapped inside here." I said, as the men positioned two outside and the other two on the inside.

My people were fast and I watched as the explosives were placed against the generators to cause the most damage, especially the huge turbine blades and engines. Within ten minutes the explosive were placed and timers were set for 30 minutes, I gathered up my troops and as we were leaving, the door at the top of the stairs flew open and Russians poured in. I fired and watched my bullets stitch the Russian troops at waist level. Some fool from my group tossed a grenade that exploded at the top of the stairs, sprinkling all of us with some shrapnel. We killed that batch of troops, with the loss of two men to serious injuries. Two of my larger troops threw the wounded over their shoulders and out of the building we went.

I expected to be met by thousands of Russian soldiers, but no one was there, but I could hear fighting from where Andy was. I sent the men carrying our wounded to the trees and the rest of us moved for the building.

Our attack on the Russians caught them by surprise. We struck their backs, and hard too, killing over half with the first pull of our triggers. Of course, like most experienced combat troops, they quickly recovered and began an organized withdrawal. They didn't enjoy being sandwiched between us. I'd estimate they lost over half their men within twenty seconds or so. Andy and his folks came out of the building like a flood, pouring out and looking for blood.

"Link up on me!" I yelled. I moved to a dead Major and placed an ace of spades card in his mouth, then pushed his chin closed. My folks were already taking what gear they needed from the dead Russians.

"Let's move, people!" I yelled to be heard over the shouts of victory and the turbine engines. "We don't have much time!" I took off at a jogging pace toward the trees.

We no sooner got there and stopped to catch our breath when I heard a loud explosion and then heard a high pitched whining noise coming from the turbine blades. Dark black smoke mixed with diesel fuel rose for the sky from the shattered windows in the generator room.

"Let's get back to our gear and make tracks. This will be a long night as we attempt to get far enough away so I feel safe." I said and then thought, *Usually, following an attack we would guess the mileage a group with, and without, injured would cover in ideal situations. In this type of terrain, twenty miles would be tops, most likely. I want to cover twenty-five miles, but that might not be possible.*

We moved at a steady pace and my wounded were able to move with the help of crutches or another person. They were weak, but I could not endanger all of us for the sake of two fighters. They continued to move knowing if they quit, I'd overdose them on morphine and leave them. I had little choice except to save as many of my troops as I could. I'm not a coldblooded killer either; I ate, lived with, and knew these people, most by their first names now.

The first four hours were brutal on all of us, but I needed the initial distance to feel safe. I was giving this thought when our woman on point went up in an exploding sheet of flames, rocks, and soil. I watched her come apart in the air. I felt it was a fast, clean, and better way to die than most. Here one second and gone the next.

When it grew quiet again, Andy said, "We're in a minefield. We need to walk back the way we entered, and step in your footprints if you can see them."

"Colonel, I'm standing on a mine."

"How do you know?'"

"I felt something snap under my foot and then heard a loud click. Jesus help me, I don't want to die." a young Private said.

"Just relax and let me get everyone out of this minefield and then I'll return to help you. Don't move at all, if you can help it, because if your weight shifts or becomes less, I won't find much when I get back. Do you understand?" I said.

"Y . . . yes, sir."

I moved all of my people to a safe distance and then, as they ate a meal, I returned to help the Private on the mine.

He was new, and this was not the way to start a move to a new unit.

"I'm going to dig around the metal and see what kind of mine you are standing on. Some, like a Chinese mine don't even explode half the time, while the Russian or Americans have about a 95% successful detonation rate."

"Okay. I'm not going anyplace, so do what needs done. I'm about to fill my pants right now."

"Son, I think, in your place, most folks would be scared." I squatted, pulled my sheath knife, and began poking and stabbing at the ground looking for metal.

After I checked all around his foot, I said, "I want you to step off the mine, but then fall to the ground."

"Won't the mine explode?"

"I don't think so, and you can't keep standing here for days. Now, I'm going no place, so I'll be right here beside you. If I thought it might explode, I'd not stay with you."

"Oh, Jesus, I don't know if I can do this."

I need to do something if he won't move, I thought, so I punched him dead on his chin and down he went. He fell a good 4 feet from the mine and landed flat on his back.

"You're about a crazy bastard, do you know that?" he asked as he sat up.

"I've been called worse." I intentionally smiled at the man. He had every reason to feel as he did, because I'm sure my actions terrified the man.

"How were you so sure it'd not explode?"

"This mine is an anti-tank mine and requires more weight than you have to arm it. The click you heard was a triggering device moving down a little, but not down far enough to trigger an explosion. If it had exploded, about half of us would have disappeared. Now, lets get back to the group, they're expecting us."

When we returned everyone was glad to see the new man, who I learned was called Duck for some reason. Many members of the resistance use fictitious names or nick names to protect their families in the event one of us was taken prisoner. We couldn't get a man's family murdered if we didn't have his real name. Take me, very few people knew my last name, but I knew the Russians had it from the wanted posters. All of my family was dead, so as the family of a partisan, they would not be gathered up and placed in a gulag.

"Smyth, you're my point and Madison, you bring up the rear. Let's move, folks." King said and picked up his heavy pack.

I heard choppers overhead as we moved through the trees, but some sections in Washington have large dense forests and you can fly over them and not see a thing. I knew we were safe from eyes in the sky unless we ran into someone who could radio for fire support, and then we were in trouble. So far, with the exception of the mine, we had no indicators anyone was around.

It was just before we stopped at noon, when I ran into "Chief" sitting beside the trail. He was our point man.

"We all just walked through an ambush. They were good but I spotted it about halfway past the Russian troops lining the trail. There was no way to warn you and it appears now, they didn't want us. It makes me wonder why they are out here, if not to kill us." he said.

"Maybe to follow us back to our main camp and then schedule it to be hit."

"Damn, I never gave that any thought." he said.

"Why settle for a few of us when they can kill hundreds?"

"What now, because we can't lead them to our main camp?"

"We ambush them, or overrun them first thing in the morning, just as they wake up."

"Now, that makes sense."

"Continue on now, but slowly take us in a wide circle."

"I can do that easily enough."

As we stood and he started walking, I realized I'd been breathing pretty hard and he wasn't even winded. Of course he was twenty-something and I was in my early fifties. Before the fall, not many men my age could hump all day in the woods with a sixty pound pack, and be able to get up in the morning and repeat the day. I could and did, often.

I fell back to tell Andy what was going on.

Andy understood, and liked the idea of ambushing the ambushers. It was about fifteen minutes before dusk when I had everyone line the trail for the ambush. Time to put an end to being followed, if we were. My drag woman said she'd seen no one behind us. Mines were placed and everyone was ready.

Just as I stepped off the trail, the woods erupted into a battlefield and I mean in a split second. I heard screams for help, cries of pain, and yells of victory. I was shooting at shadows and quick movements but some shots brought a scream. Then it grew quiet. I could smell blood and human waste. I heard moans and groans, so some of my people were hurt. I crawled forward and moved behind a log.

I saw movement, but it was too dark to see which side it was, so I remained still. I didn't want to be a guest of the Russians. I heard someone praying in English and another talking to her mother, then a choking sound from both.

A pistol fired and a body fell with a thud.

I heard a command in Russian and watched as black shadows moved against the dark gray sky. Minutes later, they were gone. I thought it might be a trick, so I waited a good hour before I stood.

CHAPTER 14

Colonel Slava woke in his car as medics and doctors were screaming orders, and all it did was add to his confusion. He hurt and knew he'd been shot, but was unaware it was by a sniper. His mind was dulled and confused. The Americans had a sniper near the hospital too, to kill those Colonels the other snipers missed or only wounded. It was a long gamble, but today it paid off.

The Colonel was pulled from his car and placed on a gurney. Just as a doctor came over to check his patient, his head exploded, throwing gore on Slava and splattering those nearby with blood. The doctor fell, his body jerking and shuddering as it shut down.

"Sniper!" someone yelled.

He must be using a silencer, Slava thought, *because I hear nothing.*

As everyone went to ground, leaving the injured Colonel exposed and on the gurney, Slava's driver pushed the injured man away at a run, toward the emergency doors. The driver suddenly dropped, a bullet to his left arm, but he stood again and finished pushing his boss inside the building.

Once inside the driver yelled, "I have the Base Commander here; someone assist me in seeing he's treated, and do it *now*!"

Folks were returning from outside and three of them were packing the dead doctor. The dead man's body was taken to another room. He'd be home in Russia within 48 hours, and then he'd become just another number, a statistic if you will, in the Russian American War.

The Colonel was wheeled into surgery instantly, once they saw who he was. As the ranking officer on the base he had a lot of power. It took them over four hours to fix his shoulder and all prayed he would mend and recover quickly.

Across the base, Senior Sergeant Victorovich was dispatched into the field to find and kill both snipers. Knowing the snipers could kill at great distances made the members of the cell with the Sergeant nervous. But, each knew to disobey an order in the Russian army would lead to being hanged or shot, so off they went. Each member of the squad was apprehensive of leaving the relative safety of the base. Having hunted down and killed his share of snipers in his twenty-two year career, the old Sergeant didn't give this mission much thought.

"You people in the middle, spread out more. One bullet would kill two or three of you."

Some mumbling was heard, which was normal for any army.

They moved slowly, checking for mines. If nothing else, the war had given each soldier a healthy respect for mines and their destructive power. All of them had seen legs and arms blown off, or seen a careless victim die as they attempted to hold their guts in.

While the weather was mild, everyone but the old Sergeant was soon sweating. There is something about looking for a killer who happens to be an excellent shot that bothers a man. These soldiers were veterans, all serving honorably, but snipers worried them all. Each soldier wondered, *Which of us will die next?*

A shot rang out and a woman dropped, struck hard in the thigh. The medic grimaced and ran forward, fully expecting to die, only he didn't. As he bent over the wounded woman, he felt a bullet strike him in the shoulder, so he dragged her behind some brush and rocks. He was bleeding like a stuck pig, but her bleeding was even worse. Her femoral artery had been hit and if he didn't get it to slow or stop, she'd be dead in a few minutes. As he worked, Sergeant Victorovich spotted the sniper.

"He's in the huge pine, straight ahead of us, maybe 200 meters, half way up the tree and on the right side. I want everyone to fire at that location now, especially the machine gunner, because your rounds will go completely through the tree. Now, fire!"

The blasts of the various guns were loud and even a grenade launcher was fired. Bark and wood splinters flew in all directions as the tree was shot to hell and back. Removing his binoculars, the Sergeant viewed the tree. He could see a chunk of bloody meat in the tree, but nothing else. The meat did not move.

"Uh, Base, Hunter One, over."

"Go, Hunter."

"Looks like one sniper taken out. I will check for a body and let you know."

"Roger. The Colonel wants you to bring the body in with you."

"Copy and will do, over and out." He said on the radio and then turning to his people he said, "Let us go and get the body. I guess Headquarters wants proof we killed the man."

They approached the tree cautiously and were happy to see blood running down its trunk. When they were directly under the tree, the Sergeant said, "Private Demian Savelievich, climb this tree and push the body to the ground. When we get back to the base, I have a bottle of vodka you and some friends can share this evening."

"I can get the body down, Sergeant." the Private said. It was hard to believe less than six months ago he was a simple farmer in Siberia. He climbed the tree like a squirrel and when near the body, yelled out, "Watch out below." Not thinking to check a dead body, he gave the sniper a hard push and down he went.

The second the body fell the Private saw a lever from a grenade fly into the air and he knew he had five seconds to get out of the tree or he'd die. He closed his eyes and jumped, as he screamed, "Grenade!"

Most of the Russian soldiers were standing under the tree when the grenade exploded and all screamed. For two it was their last sound made on this earth and for six more, they screamed in pain. The hot cast iron blew completely through arms, legs, torsos and heads.

Private Demian Savelievich lay on the ground unable to move, yet more or less uninjured. He had no wounds, but medics would soon discover his back was broken. He would be sent home where he'd spend the rest of his life unable to move from the neck down. The Senior Sergeant had a number of injuries to his face, including a mouth injury that was bleeding profusely. The medic ran to the men and women, shook his head at the carnage, and picked up the radio.

"Headquarters, this is the medic, all the team members are down and injured. I need medical assistance and a helicopter to pick up my dead and wounded."

"How many dead do you have?"

"I have no idea. The entire unit, except for me, is down. I need help here, because I have more wounded than I can treat alone, over."

"Roger, copy, and I have a helicopter on the way."

He moved toward the Senior Sergeant who waved him away and said, "Treat my troops first."

Two were already dead, one fatally wounded, and five wounded that would live, but all would take months to recover. The Senior Sergeant had some fragments of cast iron in his lungs and stomach. He'd need surgery, and quickly too. The medic stuck him with a syringe filled with morphine after the man asked for a local to kill his pain. He knew the kind of man the Sergeant was, he'd bleed to death as his lesser wounded troops were treated.

The fatal injury was a Private who took shrapnel to his heart and head. The victim was unconscious and barely alive, which was good. This way, he felt no pain.

Ten minutes after talking on the radio three helicopters arrived; one was a medical chopper while two were gun ships and provided cover. The medical chopper landed and two medics ran to the injured and began loading them. Within five minutes of landing, they were all airborne.

Roper received a return to base call and was soon teamed up with the other snipers and heading home. There were a total of six men returning and due to them being so few in numbers, they'd avoid all trails and cut cross country. Usually that was a safer method to travel in small groups.

It began to snow the first day, but the wind was light, so they kept moving. They saw no one all day and quit an hour earlier than they wanted to gather wood, collect water, and get an early supper. Shelter was a lean-to back in the pines and the fire, not much bigger than the crown of a cowboy hat, kept the place warm. It was still above freezing, but not by much. The snowfall was light, but lazy and constant. It was slowly adding to the two inches on the ground.

Roper didn't really want a fire, but it was cold enough to warrant one, and tonight would get much colder. He pressed the mic button on his radio twice every hour, so Base knew all was well. They ate American MREs for supper, with the meals being older than some of them. They'd learned after a couple of years of no government to make do with what they had or do without. While the rations were old, they were edible and that's all that mattered these days. What they ate seemed less important when going hungry was the only other option.

The wind was picking up and the temperature was dropping near bedtime. Finally, all but the radio monitor, who was also the guard, went to their sleeping bags. The bags were quality Russian winter sleeping bags, guaranteed comfortable to -20 degrees, and they were good. Soon all but the guard was asleep.

Near 0400 choppers were heard flying overhead, and all knew they were searching for the resistance and their fires. As cold as it was, most would have a fire overnight. Glancing at their fire, Roper saw it was small and under a huge pine tree. He relaxed a little. He suspected these Russians didn't have thermal imaging yet, because it changed the game a great deal. But it would come. Just a year ago they had few helicopters too, but it wasn't the case now. Things changed and with the new resistance commander came an increase in Russian efforts.

Soon the chopper was heard flying away.

The next morning, as they drank coffee, Roper asked, "Should we move when our footprints will be clearly seen in the snow? Be easy to find us with tracks like that."

"I think if we stay off the trails, the easier it will be for us. Stay as deep in the woods as we can and hope for the best."

"After our coffee, let's saddle up and cover some miles. The sky looks like more snow coming, so let's be ready for that too. Jones, you're on point and Smyth on drag." Roper said.

The day was slow and uneventful, but miles were covered. Near dusk, Jones discovered an old barn. It was cold and snowing again, so they moved inside and set up a home. Roper looked the place over and said, "Plenty of openings and exits in this place. I like that, so I don't feel trapped. Damn me, but it's cold out and well below zero."

"I don't think anyone will be out much in this weather. The Russians could be, especially any Siberian troops. Hell, this is tee shirt weather to them."

"I'm originally from Mississippi," Jones said, "and this is cold enough for me. I'd not be here now, but a bunch of us were transferred here with Colonel Williamson. I'll survive, but I do better in warm weather."

Roper had just changed one damp sock and was reaching for another when Smyth asked, "Do any of you hear that engine running?"

"I hear something with an engine, but don't know if it's in the air or on the ground." Someone agreed.

"Running too rough to be in the air. It sounds like a truck or armored personnel carrier." Roper said.

"Or a big-ass tank." Jones said "And if it is, we'll soon hear the treads jingling and clanking too."

"Fellers, their newest tanks have IR systems on them."

"I heard they don't work worth a shit in bad weather."

"They don't in rain, but I have no idea about snow. If it comes here, scatter and stay that way until daylight. I've fought them before and they're no fun. Don't worry about the cannon as much as the machine guns and IR capability. Hard to hide if they can see us glowing in the dark." Roper said, and then added, "but this old barn may hide our images. If not, we'll know in about ten minutes from what I hear."

"Do we run now or stay here?"

"We stay. I think they're hoping to flush out some partisans and kill them as they panic." Roper said.

"It's working on my ass. I'm still here, but my gut impulse is to run, and fast too."

"We have missiles and some RPGs, so we're not defenseless." Roper said as he pulled a Russian missile and prepared it for firing.

Jones went outside and stood in the cold, listening. It was moving closer, and somehow they must know the old barn is here and occupied. How they would know, he had no idea.

Sticking his head in the door he said, "The tank is moving toward us, but how could they know we're here?"

"Easy. They have satellites that see through cloud cover and IR, but I'm not sure. The wood and tin roof of the barn might obscure our heat signature. Then again, someone may have seen our tracks in the snow today and, knowing the barn was here, suspected we'd spend the night here. So, we fight the big ass beast, huh?" Jones said.

Roper grinned and said, "I think we need to make a token resistance and then flee. Who knows, we might get lucky and destroy it, but I doubt that will happen. When it gets near, all of you will leave the barn and fight from outside. I'll climb into the loft and fire a missile at the thing. Once the missile is gone, I'll leave the structure too, and at that point we scatter. Then tomorrow we all meet up again five miles down the trail and five miles exactly. Good luck to each of you."

"What if it has infantry along for protection?" Smyth asked.

"Kill all you can. I just want to let them know we are here and then melt into the night. By scattering, they can only follow one of us. If they follow you, move to the roughest and most difficult terrain you can find. I would not be taken prisoner either, because I hear it's a rough life in a Russian cell."

"I'll save the last shot for me." Smyth said.

Jones stuck his head inside and said, "Y'all need to move, because I hear the tinkling of the treads moving. It sounds like a T90 to me. I'm moving now."

Each sniper and spotter lowered their NVGs and slipped into the darkness, except for Roper, who moved to the hay loft. When the big beast was seen for the first time, the sniper's heart skipped a beat. It was much bigger than he remembered a T-90 to be. He was tempted to turn and run, very tempted, but the missile gave him courage, as well as hope. The T-90 was loud too.

The heavy 12.7 mm machine gun opened fire, but Roper had no idea what it was shooting at. He aimed his missile to strike where the turret met the body of the tank. The target locked-on light blinked and he squeezed the trigger. He watched as the missile struck. There was a loud explosion and the tank stopped moving for a few minutes. A little smoke appeared out of an open hatch on top of the tank and it then began moving forward once more. A man started climbing out of the open hatch when a single shot rang out and the man fell with half of his body out of the tank and his upper torso laying on the turret. Blood ran down the cold steel and the man was unmoving.

Jones moved and the machine gun fired, knocking the sniper to the ground where he screamed in pain. The big T-90 moved toward him. His legs or spine must have been injured, because he couldn't move. The closer the tank got to Jones, the more apprehensive Roper became. He tossed hand grenades at the tank, but unless one went down the open hatch, they'd do little damage to the big beast of a machine.

Roper kept screaming for Jones to move, but he seemed unable. The closer the tank got to the wounded man, the louder Jones yelled for help. Russian infantry now moved out from behind the tank and it's protective armor. They all fired their weapons, but most of the snipers were gone now. Roper thought the infantry firing their weapons and the tank continuing to fire both machine guns was done to spook anyone in the barn so they'd run out into the open. The tank was less that twenty feet from Jones now and Roper watched, mesmerized, knowing the tank intended to run over the downed man.

When the tank was about a dozen feet from Jones the driver's hatch opened and a man's head popped up. The tank rolled forward slightly, the rear of the tank fishtailed a little to line it up, and then it moved forward. Roper watched in captivation as the tanks treads struck Jones' feet and then slowly moved up his body. The wounded man's head was back and he was screaming as the heavy tank began to crush him alive. By the time the tank tread was at his waist, Jones was either unconscious or dead, because he was no longer screaming or jerking. Roper knew every bone in Jones' body would soon be crushed.

Roper pulled his sniper rifle, sighted in on the driver's head and squeezed the trigger. The kick was hard and the bullet true as it struck the man in the forehead. The area above the hatch was now coated in brain tissue, blood and bone. The dead driver's foot must have pushed on the fuel control harder because it lurched forward, flattening Jones' head. It then struck the side of the barn, causing one side to collapse. From where Roper was, still in the barn, the open turret was clearly seen below him.

He was still in the loft, so he moved to the open hatch, tossed two grenades inside the tank and then moved out of the barn. The infantry tried to shoot him and while some came close, no one struck home. Before he reached the trees, there was an explosion, followed a second later by another explosion, and finally a much greater explosion. The last explosion lit up the night and a member of the tank crew crawled out of the vehicle, fully engulfed in flames.

Then there was a huge explosion and, looking over his shoulders as he ran, he saw the turret thrown high into the air. The infantry were firing in all directions now and Roper knew they saw no one. His men were gone and had been from the moment the tank got near the barn. He knew most would look at the explosion and lose their night vision.

After he'd covered over four miles, Roper moved for a grove of tall pine trees to spend the rest of the night. It was too cold to keep moving. He moved to a tree with low branches and trimmed off a few of the lower limbs. He then crawled under and up the lower limbs, knowing he'd not be seen. But he needed a source of heat or he'd be dead in an hour or so.

He opened his pack and pulled out a portable Russian ration stove and a bunch of fuel cubes. He opened the stove, place a cube on the aluminum stove and lit it with his cigarette lighter. The fuel cube burned clear flames and hot. While not a huge fire, he felt the heat and held his cold hands near the invisible flames. He knew his tracks were seen in the snow, but the wind was getting stronger and the snow falling harder, so he had to stop for the night. To continue was to risk hypothermia, which could

easily kill a man alone.

Besides he was sure the Russians had stopped too. They had dead and wounded to care for. Roper knew he'd not sleep well tonight, not after seeing Jones run over by the tank. All the man's inner organs and brain had popped from his body to stain the treads of the tank. Never before had he seen such a horrible way to die. He knew he'd have nightmares for years after what he'd seen.

The night was long and slow, but no one came near him. It was not until dawn, when he heard the crunching of the snow as someone moved that, he came wide awake. When he'd gone out earlier to pee, he noticed his old tracks were already filled with snow. No one could track him now no matter how hard they tried. Only, if the noise was made by his enemies, would he fight the Russians or allow them to pass by him?

Would the tracks from his earlier trip to pee give him away? If they'd not filled in by now they'd lead a child to his shelter.

He heard Russian voices and his fear became alive. He was tempted to run, which was exactly what they wanted him to do. It was like hunting rabbits; you moved around until you scared one into running and then you could shoot it

He had two Russians walk right by him. They knew the general area he was in, but not his exact location.

CHAPTER 15

I was in pain, but had no idea I'd taken an injury until a good hour after the battle. I had a deep cut on my left arm and I was missing the tip of my little finger on my left hand. I'd felt absolutely nothing until the adrenaline from the fight wore off. The finger was bleeding the most, but the cut was what hurt me. The cut was about six inches long and to the bone, but how I got either injury I had no idea. I had morphine for pain, but didn't want to use it because I'd get sleepy and the weather was too rough to sleep right now. If I fell asleep once in a shelter, the fire would eventually go out, and I'd freeze to death. I was lucky, I still had gear and weapons.

I heard noise on my back trail, so I flipped the safety off my Bison. I waited and a minute later was met by the bloody face of Andy. He looked like hell, and had moved under some brush once he took a bullet to his shoulder. Another bullet had creased his head.

He gave me a forced smile, nodded and then whispered, "We're the only survivors. I watched them shoot all injured. Ain't we in a fine mess right now? Here we are, both injured and no help, without a radio, and a good 20 miles from camp."

"You forgot we're still alive, determined, and know where we are. We'll make it back as long as we take it slow and easy. For right now we need a shelter, small fire, and some rest."

"I'm still in shock from the suddenness of the attack."

"Let's move for the trees and try to find a shelter. We need to dress our wounds, drink something hot, and get some rest. But, we can't take any morphine or we'll fall to sleep." I stood and struggled through the snow, which was a good 12 inches deep and still falling.

"I can deal with the pain, at least for 24 hours. I make no promises after that, and we have to be wounded during a bad snow storm. We need to hole up until this front moves on. Right now a child could track us in the snow. If we get under shelter now, maybe by dawn our prints will be covered with snow."

"I agree, so let's find a place." Less than a mile later I found a nice sized tree blown over on its side. It was a huge pine. I went to the middle of the tree and removed about half of the limbs on the bottom side and we crawled in and pulled some boughs up to cover the opening. I used the extra pine boughs and others I cut from the underside to insulate part of the floor, where we'd lay and sleep. Someone would need a dog or smell our wood smoke to find us now. I knew we could not be seen by the naked eye, no matter how hard they looked.

I got a small fire started, about the size of a tea cup, and warned Andy, "No bigger than this or we'll catch this place on fire. This will keep us alive for now. In a few minutes, I'm going to check our wounds and doctor them."

"How are we going to stop your bleeding?"

"We'll have to cauterize my wound, and maybe yours too. I'll try sewing yours up, but I know I don't have enough cat gut to sew both injuries closed."

"I don't have much, except a standard first aid kit with bandages, gauze and things you'd use to treat small injuries, not anything for major wounds like gunshots or deep knife cuts. Damn, sir, burning your arm shut will knock you out."

"That's why we'll burn me last. I'll take some morphine which will kill my pain for six hours or so. Do you think you can stay awake that long?"

He gave me a forced smile and said, "Airborne, sir! I'll do my best, Colonel."

"If we can just survive the next twelve hours, we have a good chance of getting back home alive."

He nodded, but by the dim light I could see the doubt on his face. Like me, he thought our odds of surviving were slim to none. I carried a metal flask full of whiskey on me during every mission. I only opened it when I had someone injured that needed a pain killer when we didn't want to use morphine. My usual medic, now dead, had all sorts of painkillers, but they were out of reach at the moment. I carried some meds for pain, but they were what we once called over-the-counter medications and they were almost useless with the injuries we had.

I pulled a curved needle and thread from my pack and placed both in about a ½ inch of whiskey to clean them before use. Then I cleaned Andy's shoulder with alcohol and started sewing the entrance and exit hole. I know it had to hurt him, but other than a grunt when the needle first pierced his skin, I heard nothing out of him. Once done with the sewing, I placed two large bandages on his wounds and wrapped him. I then placed two knife blades in the fire so he could cauterize my wounds. I took a long pull from the whiskey bottle, because burning would hurt me.

"Take the morphine now." he said.

"I might not need it. Burn me first and we'll see how badly the task hurts me."

I pulled my shirt off, and it was cold. I moved closer to the fire and waited, dreading the red-hot knife touching my flesh. A few short minutes later, Andy picked up the first blade and touched my skin. I gave a short scream and then passed out.

I awoke to the smell of burnt flesh and an aching arm. He handed me the whiskey bottle and said, "Sleep a bit more. I have been and it helps me feel stronger. I see no need for a guard, but we do need to keep the fire burning."

"Why no guard?" I asked, with my mind confused.

"It must be 40 below zero out there and anything that walks or flies is holed up waiting for warmer weather."

I nodded, not wanting to speak. I was suddenly tired and achy. I saw it was dark, and nighttime would be much colder.

"Well? Do you think we need a guard?"

"I . . . I'll leave that decision and any others up to you. I can't think straight right now, so I'm going to take morphine and get some sleep."

"I'll give it to you, because I can reach your arm easier than you can." he said as he reached for the syringe.

Within seconds of getting the shot, my pain lessened and I began to get sleepy. I had my sleeping bag tied to the top of my backpack, so I untied it and crawled inside. I was asleep within a few short minutes.

Early the next morning two snipers, along with Porter, showed. The three of them were made welcome in our shelter and we discovered the Russians were not out in force looking for us. The snipers had seen no one since they left the base. They found my dead squad and they'd been stripped of anything useful by the Russians. One had been bandaged, so they remembered how I treat their wounded, but he was dead, likely from the cold.

Porter must have seen me open my eyes, because he said, "Mornin', Colonel."

"Mornin', Sergeant."

Just the body heat of three more people warmed our shelter a great deal. Now, both Andy and I could sleep and rest. Over the next four days we did a lot of both, and by the fifth day we were ready to move. We still had some pain, but not as much as before. When we returned, I needed to speak with my supply and medical folks and see about putting some pain pills of some sort into the first aid kits. Not being able to kill our pain made our stay rough and morphine would have been like killing an ant with a hand grenade, just too much. I wanted something less than morphine but more than an over the counter pain killer.

We saddled up, and for the first time I noticed the bullet holes in our gear. Both our packs were blood stained too, with bullet holes in each. I soon discovered to my dismay they were still heavy and uncomfortable. Every pack I ever wore dug into my shoulders and eventually I grew sore there, and this one was no exception. Mile after mile we covered, and at a pretty good speed. Then, aircraft were heard and we went into hiding for about an hour. I heard helicopters and jet aircraft looking for us or inserting troops.

We walked until darkness found us in a dense forest surrounded by blackberry bushes, and yep, with thorns too. We bedded down there with two small fires. After eating a ration, everyone except the guards hit their sleeping bags. We were all bone aching tired and were asleep in seconds.

Shortly after midnight, someone touched my heel and I opened my eyes and listened. I heard no night sounds and a few minutes later I heard Russian being spoken. It sounded like they'd selected almost the same spot as we had to rest overnight. I removed a grenade, pulled the pin and then tossed it toward the conversation. When it exploded, screams were heard, and some of the Russians started firing in all directions. I took cover and returned fire.

My snipers were all using day/night capability scopes, so one by one the Russians were seen and then killed. Technology was making it harder and harder for an infantryman to stay alive. We all wore NVGs and they worked well, but most of us had fallen asleep without putting them on. I realized then we needed them around our necks or readily available while we slept. I'd see to that from now on.

It grew quiet and the gunfire stopped.

I could smell the blood, cordite, and human waste, so I knew someone was dead, and near me too.

"Porter, take another man with NVGs and check them out. Take anything we can use and that means military weapons, ammunition, gear, and clothing, along with personal jewelry or money."

"Will do, sir."

"Cook, you cover me as I look them over."

"Got you, so move."

A few minutes later I heard automatic fire and Porter said, "He was playing 'possum on me."

I was surprised we had no one killed or injured, so we'd gotten off easy this time. We quickly donned our packs and moved into the trees, moving overland.

Near dawn, when we took a break to eat, Roper asked, "Do you think they were searching for us?"

"I don't think they were specifically looking for us or they knew about us all joining together, but they were looking for partisans. If they'd been a little bit quieter, it's hard to say how that battle might have ended. I just tossed the grenade where I guessed the voices were."

We were less than a mile from camp when I noticed aircraft overhead and the sound of gunfire. I watched a jet line up his approach to camp and then he came down low and fast, dropping napalm as he pulled the nose up, so he sort of flipped the two containers on my friends.

I heard screams and cries for assistance, but we were too far away to be of much help. We moved away from camp and waited for the fight to stop. I thought once the Russians broke off the attack, people would return to salvage what they could before they moved to a new location. I prayed Cynthia was a survivor. If not, I'd have lost another woman I loved, and it was growing old. It seemed like every old friend and new lover I had was gone these days. I'd learned over the years that a man cannot survive easily without a mate he can pull to him late at night and just talk. I think God made women to keep men from being lonely.

"There go the last of the choppers." Porter said.

Andy shook his head and said, "Be a high casualty rate from this attack. I'd suggest sir, we gather our troops and move closer to the Russians. The closer we are the more we can hurt them."

"While we gather our troops and see to our wounded, I'll give that some thought."

Over the last few days, the weather had turned warm again and most of the snow was gone, except for some that remained in shadowed areas. That meant there was also mud in some spots too. I worried about how many people I'd lost in this Russian attack. They were getting smarter here now, and I'd have to do the same.

I neared the camp and all I could see was fire, smoke, and people running around madly. We needed to get organized and out of here before the Russians sent in ground troops to finish the job. I soon had senior men trying to gather people up. We needed to break into small cells and disappear for a week or so.

Finally after three hours I sent the troops out, all of those left alive, into cells of ten people each. Out of maybe 200 folks, 140 were still alive and uninjured. I ordered the hospital staff and injured to stay with me. My injured numbered 23, with 4 fatally so, so I had them put down. Soon, we were deep in the forest and I prayed the Russians would allow us some time to rest.

But, that was not to be.

Russian aircraft were constantly looking for us, day and night. I knew they were hounding us to keep us off guard and deny us any rest and all the sleep they could. It was working, but only to a point, and I'd requested additional missiles to deal with the aircraft overhead. Once I had arms, we'd turn the momentum back into our favor. We'd encountered more ground troops, too, but I could deal with them. I finally decided we'd attack the main Russian base in Seattle and do just enough damage that it would shock them. That meant I needed information. I needed to know all I could about the base and the buildings there.

I went out with Andy's cell, and his mission was to look at the Russian side of the big airport because at one time it'd been a large commercial airport. We had no information on the place and I mean nothing, really. We'd take photos, mark aircraft parking on our crude map, and check out security. Since Roper had been a sniper there, he went along, too, to help us locate various hot spots, meaning those areas of importance to any air post.

When we left, I'd leave Roper and his spotter to kill a few of the air traffic controllers in the tower, as well as any high ranking officers. He thought he might get lucky and get a couple of landing jet or chopper pilots. I'd leave the targets up to him, but to take no risks on poor or low priority targets.

The night before we left, Cynthia and I were together and I enjoyed myself.

She suddenly asked, "How much longer do you have to go into harms way in this damned war?" Her tone hinted of anger.

"I imagine until the Russians leave, but I'm not the only person risking their lives here, baby." I glanced at her and could see she was angry.

"You are the Commander here and you go because you want to be on these damned missions, not because you have to go. One day you'll be killed. I know you don't have to go, but yet you do, why?"

I'd opened a bottle of bourbon earlier in the evening, so I poured us both a drink and replied, "I have to go because I want my troops to respect me as their leader. A big part of leadership is showing your people you can and will do what they do, and share in the dangers of it all. I'm sorry if you dislike that trait in me, but I lead by example."

"But, as a Commander, you could stay back here where it's safer, only you never will."

I knocked my drink back, wiped my mouth off with the back of my hand, and replied, "No, I never will, unless I one day make General Officer, and that's not likely."

"I don't understand why you take the unnecessary risks, is all." I could see the tears in her eyes and really understood for the first time she loved me. Oh, she'd told me before, but this was different.

"Sweetheart, when the Russians invaded this country, they came into my very home, wanting to turn me into a slave and rape my nation. Like most Americans I am damned proud to be an American and I'll fight until death to deny them ownership of this land I love. I didn't even realize how much I loved the United States until she was seriously threatened." I filled my shot-glass once more with the strong amber drink. Dolly moved to my side and placed her head in my lap, wanting her ears scratched.

"I love this country too, but the risks you take and to think of the chances for you to be killed when you could be safely running the show from here."

"I'm sorry you dislike the risks I take, but I will do what my people do or resign. I must see, hear, feel, and smell what they do, or I'll soon lose the knowledge of the cold harsh acts needed in combat to win against a cruel and determined enemy. I cannot allow that to happen, or I'm useless as a commander." I threw that drink back too, but it would be my last of the evening.

"I don't know if I want a man with a wish to die. I love you, John, but I don't want to end up loving a dead man."

"So be it then. You knew the kind of man I am when you and I started this relationship. I'm truly sorry you feel this way. Only, my country comes before myself and even you. I love you, Cynthia, but I'll not change what I am for you or anyone else in the world. I am a Colonel in the Partisans that leads from the front and I will always lead by example."

"I think it would be best if I left then." She picked up her hat and walked to the door. She stopped with her back to me for a few long seconds, then turned and met my eyes as she said, "Goodnight and goodbye, Colonel."

"Goodnight, Major."

I knew she was crying when she left and I knew I'd just lost a good woman, who would or could not accept me for what I was, a warrior. I could no more change than a duck could become a goose. I am what I am, and always will be. The long cut on my left arm began to ache.

Having second thoughts about the drink, I picked up the whiskey and took a long pull straight from the bottle. I sat on my bunk holding the bottle in my hand, my injured arm throbbing, wondering why my behavior was that hard to understand. Near midnight I fell asleep sitting on my bed, the bourbon bottle half gone and Dolly laying beside me, her big brown eyes concerned, but not overly so.

Morning arrived earlier than usual and I had a hangover. I rarely have more than two drinks, and last night I'd had a good pint of bourbon. Now I faced a long day of walking in some rough country as I fought the urge to throw up. I gagged a few times brushing my teeth so when I returned to my quarters, I picked up the whiskey bottle and took me a long pull of the hair of the dog. Within a few minutes, I felt normal again.

"Feeling better, sir?" I heard Sergeant Major Birdie ask from his side of the tent.

"I'm fine."

"And the lass will come around, sir, because she loves you."

"Uh, enough about my personal affairs." I wasn't comfortable discussing my 'woman' problems with someone else.

"Yes, sir. I was just offering my experience with women, is all. I'll not mention another word about it." His apology sounded genuine to me.

"I appreciate the offer, but I'll deal with her and on my own." I said, and slipped my pack on my back. I glanced at my watch and added, "You and the Major take good care of this place while I'm gone. I suspect we'll be in radio contact."

"Yes, sir. The Russians are mad and looking for blood, so be careful."

I grunted in reply and left my tent.

CHAPTER 16

Colonel Slava's temporary replacement, Major Ruslan 'Rusya' Gennadiyevich, stood at the head of his table and shook his head as he said, "When our troops entered the camp, they found no one living and there was no resistance. Bodies were scattered all around and we counted right at one hundred and forty-two dead. We lost four men in the main camp from booby traps and land mines. Of their wounded left behind, we took eight prisoners and put three mortally wounded down. The prisoners are being interrogated as I speak."

"Moscow must be very pleased with us right now." the chief of supply said, a man who'd never been in combat or seen a shot fired in anger.

"Gentlemen, we now have more pressing news and it is not good. This is doctor and surgeon Colonel Boris Danovich, the hospital Commander, and he wants to discuss two problems we have, and they're both serious too."

The surgeon stood and said, "Gentlemen if you look at the slide I have on the wall, you will see two in every ten soldiers we have is infected with a sexually transmitted disease. It is our belief the resistance is encouraging infected women to have sex with our troops as a way to damage our morale. We think they are intentionally sending infected women here to help the spread of Gonorrhea and Syphilis, but we have no proof. The best protection would be for our troops to keep their trousers zipped up, only that will not happen."

"How are you handling it, then?"

"Through base wide lectures and placing free condoms all around the base. The first time a soldier get an STD he is warned and made to attend a briefing on the illnesses. The second time he gets it, he is fined and loses money based on his/her rank. Current percentage of Russian female soldiers with the problem is around twelve percent, which is much less than our men and they, we think, are contracting the sickness through our men."

"I think this STD problem is common in most combat zones. The enemy has used STDs as a way to fight an enemy for years. But, you can treat it with a handful of antibiotics." the Base Operations Lieutenant Colonel said.

"I realize that, colonel, but they have also sent another disease to us and it is harder to control and cure— smallpox, or as it is known in the medical field, Variola major or Variola minor. As you know, in Russia the disease was eradicated but it is alive and well here, and many of our troops are infected with the illness. We never thought to give inoculations for the illness prior to deployment here. I currently have 60 men and women in the hospital ill with the disease and we have started an American theater effort to give the preventative shot to every Russian stationed here. Since the shots take time to give, plus we do not have any serum in the country, we will soon have many more than 60 in the hospital with the pox."

"What is the fatality rate if untreated?" the Acting Wing Commander asked.

"Left untreated, oh, we would probably lose around 62%, if we are speaking of the malignant-type of smallpox, or with other types of pox it depends on the physical health of the individual. With Hemorrhagic smallpox, it is usually fatal. However, the folks in the hospital now have the ordinary type and the fatality rate for it is around 62% as well, if left untreated. We can prevent and treat the illness, but not cure it. Most doctors suggest using the drug cidofovir, but it has to be given with an IV. Then the patient has to be closely watched because the medication can cause liver failure. Our best bet is to use the shot to prevent it to start with."

"If I have the disease and get the shot early enough, let us say within the first week, will it help me any?" the Chief of Base Security asked.

"If given within three days of the illness starting, an inoculation can lessen the impact of the disease a great deal. If the shot is at the seven day mark from the beginning of the sickness or less, it will lessen the disease a little. I have 10,000 vials of the medication due in any day now."

"I wonder how many of our men or women have both illnesses in their systems right now and have no idea?" the Chief Fire Marshal said.

"I would guess at around 70% or so." the surgeon replied. "Since smallpox is highly contagious and transmitted by inhaling the variola major virus, and since our troops live and work very close together, this issue will become epidemic to us within 30 days. I suspect within 30 days, our army will grind to a stop. They can fight with an STD, but not with smallpox."

"In the meantime, I will talk with Moscow and have additional troops that have been vaccinated sent over to provide security." the base commander said. "Then, once we are back on our feet as a unit, they can return home. Now, Intelligence?"

"Yes, sir?"

"Find out if you can, if the partisans are responsible for either of these illness in some way. Now, let us finish this meeting and get back to work."

The day was quiet, or it had been so far, so this evening the Russians expected the same thing. The partisans with me were ordered to attack the base to check their reaction times and how they responded. I figured it would be an excellent time to destroy some aircraft and kill a few of my enemies. I planned the attack for a few minutes after midnight.

We spent the day counting aircraft, vehicles, anything the Russians had to bring to the states. I hoped over time to destroy a lot of their trucks, tanks, and aircraft. Tonight was an attack to really just get a feel for their readiness. I had no idea half the base was down with smallpox, or I would have hit them with every person I had.

The base was a normal airfield, except it had two fences around the place, and in the middle of the wire walked a dog handler and his dog. I saw two dogs and both were German Shepherds, and they're a noble animal in my eyes. I knew killing them tonight would be the hardest part of the attack, so I gave the job to Andy. We would then cut the wire, enter, and then divide into three groups. One group would be sent to raise hell in the Russian living area, another group toward all oil and fuel tanks, and then the group I led, toward the airfield.

Until midnight, we'd all kept to the trees, ate cold rations and tried to sleep. Our biggest issue was not to be seen, so everyone was ordered to stay in the trees all day. At 2315, I had my sappers move forward and cut the wire to the fences. We were to enter 10 people at a time.

I was soon on the other side of the fence when I heard the dog team coming. Andy waited until the dog was close to the hole in the fence and the soldier was reaching for his radio before he fired his silencer equipped sniper rifle. My man shot twice and I watched both the soldier and the dog fall. The next group through the fence brought both the dog and dead man with them. As we moved toward our targets, Andy waited near the fence for the next dog team. He rolled the body of the man and dog into a ditch beside him.

I expected the loud sirens that indicated the base was under attack to sound any second, but long minutes passed without a sound. We were less than fifty feet from the runway before the high pitch warbling sound of the sirens was heard.

Each of my troops carried an explosive charge filled with nuts, bolts, rocks and broken glass mixed in a canvas bag of C-4. All they had to do was pull the fuse to ignite and toss the charge. It would explode about 3 seconds later. I began to hear explosions and the sound was music to my ears. Then across the base I heard an earth shattering boom and watched a huge fireball moving for the sky. The main POL facility had just gone up. With their Petroleum, Oil and other Liquids going up in flames, I knew they'd be hard pressed to resume a regular flying schedule any time soon. I unknowingly smiled.

Tracers of all colors began to zigzag in front of me and when one hit the concrete of the flight line, it made a loud "*pee-zing,*" and the colorful round would suddenly change its visual direction. A Russian worker dressed in blue overalls suddenly rounded the tail of a chopper with a gun in his hand. I pointed my Bison at him and squeezed the trigger. The bullets struck him in the left knee and went all the way up to his right shoulder. He was dead and almost cut in half before he realized he'd been shot.

Fires were all around me now and explosions were starting to go off as fuel tanks and munitions on aircraft exploded. I saw one of my men toss his explosives charge into a hanger where a fuel truck was refueling an aircraft and the resulting explosion knocked me off my feet. My soldier disappeared and the resulting fireball was huge. Giant balls of black oily smoke rose to the sky as maintenance men engulfed in flames staggered from the fire. The Russians aflame would have looked comical if not for the fact they were burning to death. We reached about the halfway mark on the flight-line when a dozen big deuce and a half trucks arrived and began to unload Russian soldiers. I blew my whistle to withdraw.

As we pulled back to the fence, I saw the Russian infantry moving toward us, but they seemed to lack the desire to catch us, or perhaps they were fatigued. We broke into a jog and quickly outdistanced them. I knew something was wrong with them but had no idea what it could be. I started thinking maybe we'd be hit from the air as the Russian infantry didn't want to get to close, but I heard nothing flying overhead, which was strange too.

While we pulled back to the fence, so were those attacking the barracks and POL. The base was in flames from one side to the other.

Andy yelled, "Tank!"

A T-90 rolled to a stop and the cannon fired, striking the fence, and blowing a much bigger hole for us to exit through. The machine gun on the tank began to rat-tat-tat and people began to fall. Suddenly a flamethrower lit up the night and screams were heard coming from the tank. I figured the tank crew was safe from the fire, but it must have scared the hell out of them. I watched two of my people near the tank and jam their explosives between the treads and fenders. They pulled the fuses and ran like the Devil was on their asses. Just as they cleared the tank, a shoulder launched missile struck it in the ass and it was a killer. Smoke and flames came from the destroyed motor.

The hatch on the turret opened and a man exited, only to be chopped to pieces by small arms fire. The driver was half out when the fuel tank went up with a huge blast. I actually saw the force of the blast tear him in half. All around me we could see as clearly as daytime.

"Move it! Get through the fence and now!" I yelled to be heard over the noises.

I stayed beside Andy as we hurried folks through the fence. As my people moved through the opening, I stuck an Ace of Spades card in the dead dog handler's mouth. Other cards had been left on the base too. I wanted them to know who'd attacked them.

As the last man left the airfield, I wonder about the slow zombie-like movements of the Russian soldiers. Something was wrong with them, and they didn't follow us to the fence either. They fought us until they saw we were leaving and then stopped, which was unlike them.

About a week to ten days after we left the bombed out Russian base camp, Carter, a Sergeant Medic I had caring for the injured came to see me. I had a mission going on this night and it was to be a big one. We were to hit the Russian base in Seattle again. It was a probe and feel attack to check their readiness again. He only stayed long enough to remind me not to rip the stitches open on my arm, or he'd staple it closed the next time and with no local. For me, it was a great chance to hurt the Russians once more and to blow some of their property to hell and back. Cynthia hadn't come to see me since she said goodbye and stormed out of my life, so I had nothing else to do.

About an hour later, there was a knock on my door.

"Enter."

"Sir, I need to speak with you again." He said as soon as our salutes were done. I wasn't one to force salutes, not like some officers, because I felt as partisans we were pretty much equal. However, if saluted, I returned it with the best of my ability.

"Have a seat, Sergeant; tell me what's on your mind." I said after he reported. I could tell this was more important than my stitches.

"Thank you, sir."

He sat in my chair as I sat on my cot.

"Now, what brings you to see me today?"

"Sir, I have a number of ill soldiers and they appear to have Variola major."

"I've never heard of it, so should I be concerned?" I asked, not sure what in the hell it was. I smiled at him.

"Uh, you may know it as smallpox."

"Jesus. It killed hundreds of thousands in the dark ages."

"It may do the same here and now. I have no way to treat this, and our only doctor was killed when the Russians attacked our base camp a while back."

"Birdie!" I yelled, seeing him working at his desk.

"Yo, sir?"

"Contact base and let them know we have smallpox here and I need the vaccine and three doctors. I need both in place ASAP."

"Will do, sir."

"We already have men dying and there will be more. At first, I thought they had the measles or I would have reported it earlier."

"It's okay, after all, you're no doctor. I'll speak with base and we'll see what we can do. In the meantime, you are in charge of them and I want you to prepare me a list of what you'll need to treat them."

Soon most Russian activities on and off the base ceased due to the illness. Troops could no longer be placed in the hospital because it was filled. Then schools, recreation centers, meeting halls and any large buildings were used to house the ill. Men and women with high fevers were providing guard duty and cooking soups for the sick. While it would have been an excellent time for the partisans to attack, we had sick folks now as well, but the Russians didn't know this.

Some of the older Russians had taken an inoculation as kids, so they were not affected by the disease. Each day the numbers of dead were given at stand up and they were growing more and more as troops died in their own blood from a disease that killed ruthlessly.

They'd taken to burning the bodies of those who died and all they owned except weapons, and they were sealed in metal boxes and labeled as dangerous/hazardous material. They were then sent back to Russia where they were cleaned in a laboratory established to do nothing but clean contaminated guns from America. Some of the weapons were brought in with radioactive particles on them from the state of Mississippi and others were brought in from Washington, contaminated with smallpox. Very few people worked in the large airtight building.

In the Commander's office his phone rang and he answered it, since his receptionist had died three days before.

"Base Commander's Office, Major Gennadiyevich speaking; how may I help you?"

"Rusya, General Josef Svyatoslavovich here. What is this I hear of smallpox at your place?"

He'd been feeling sick this morning and now he was uncomfortable speaking with the General known as "Gulag" Svyatoslavovich. The Major said, "It is true, sir. I have about 60% of my base down with the disease and more die each day."

"Can you not do anything to combat the spreading of the illness?"

"I have my medical teams doing all they can, sir. My head of the hospital, a young Captain, told me this morning they expect to lose almost 70% of my personnel to the illness before this is over."

"I thought the hospital Commander was a Colonel."

"The Captain is my senior medical man still alive, sir. My Colonel died well over a week back."

"I see. I will check around and have anything you have requested rushed to your base."

"Make sure any troops that show here have been inoculated against the illness or they do me no good, sir. Out of the last fifty troops I got, only six are still alive. The others contracted smallpox and are dead."

"Yes, yes, I understand. I will see what I can do for you. Goodbye."

Placing the handset back in the cradle, the Major stood, poured himself a drink and noticed it was 0523, and he was drinking already. He took a gulp and enjoyed the way the strong vodka burned all the way to his stomach.

He sat in his chair and thought, *What will they do to me when I return home? Will I be treated as a hero or placed in front of a concrete wall and shot? I have done all I can here and with the best of my ability, too. Those lard-ass Generals we have, most have never seen a combat zone, yet they send us orders each day on how to fight a war in the country they have never visited. They have no more of an idea how to fight this war than my wife does. Maybe I should take my pistol out and blow my head off. No, that would just please my enemies. When I return, I will be forced to retire, so let us hope it is done with full military honors. It is hard to believe 30 years have passed so quickly, but they have.*

Knocking back the remainder of his drink, he poured another one. He'd drink until he passed out and would be discovered by a security policeman making his rounds, near noon.

CHAPTER 17

I was sore from falling asleep at my desk as I did paperwork. The last three nights I'd stayed late, catching up on paperwork, and fallen asleep at my desk. I'd close my eyes for a few seconds to rest them and before I could pronounce my name, I'd be sleeping. I glanced at my watch and saw it was 0100. I stood, took a drink of water from my canteen, and moved for my bed.

Suddenly, Dolly growled and looked toward the wooden door of my tent.

Don't let it be some crazy fool after the one million dollars. If so, I'll have to kill them and I dislike doing that with my own people. People are so greedy, I thought as I slipped the safety off my pistol.

The door opened and in stepped Cynthia. She smiled and said, "It's cold in my tent; I saw your light on, so I came over here to warm up."

"Come in; we need to talk. I've missed you." I said, and pulled my sleeping bag open.

Over the next month things were rough and we burned a lot of bodies. I found many of my cells almost wiped out by smallpox. While the Chinese dropped vials of serum and we inoculated all our people, for some it was too little too late. When it was all said and done, I'd lost about 30% of my fighting force, and they were mainly young men and women.

One morning I was dressing for a mission and learned of a roadblock on the way to where we were to take out a supply warehouse. The military often has supplies stored off base in secured buildings or bunkers and some are guarded and some not. All are locked, and in different ways too. Some may have padlocks and others will look like a bank vault, with tumblers and all. Every storage area will be surrounded with a tall seven foot fence with razor wire on top and security cameras.

It was misting now, like the Northwest often does in the winter. It seemed to me all it did here was rain, snow, or mist. I hate a cold rain, because nothing keeps me warm but wool, and I'm allergic to the blamed stuff. I break out in a rash that itches. I had to place a layer of cotton under the wool to wear it, which I did, because even when wet wool insulates well.

Soon, twelve of us were walking near a trail that would take us to the storage area. We never walked on a trail if we could avoid it, because of mines and booby traps. The Russians had learned that fact too, but at times I'd caught them on a trail. So far we'd only had to avoid two mines, which was few. I planted some behind us as as we moved.

The storage area I wanted to hit was isolated but had cameras, hardened bunkers, and steel doors. I had no idea what was stored there, but usually I'd find rations, ammunition, guns, and everything except chemicals or fuels. At times, according to Andy, who'd been here a good ten years, the Russians would post a guard or two. Guards were no problem.

My biggest concern was did they have a security system installed and where was it located. I wasn't worried too much about that either, because this place was remote and it'd take a helicopter a good twenty minutes to get here. By that time we'd be long gone, if things went right. I hoped it had foods in big cans, because rations were getting old. I wanted a thick juicy steak, only my last one was over three years ago and it was venison.

We walked the whole day without any problems, except I was tired at about dusk. I was fine for about eight hours, then the pack became very heavy. Most partisans my age were not out actively fighting anyway, but in camp helping in a variety of ways. I figured I had five more years, then I'd remain behind. Running with a cell was rough on anyone over 40 years old.

The evening was quiet too, and by looking at my map I could see we'd be there in about an hour, just as the sun came up. Normally, I'd hit a place like that at night, but this one was so remote I didn't think it mattered. There were no other structures closer than five miles.

The next morning we were there early, and I circled the place twice. I saw nothing out of place and no guards. We had two ATVs with trailers hooked up, a horse, and two bicycles. I hoped to use them to carry the valuable loot we'd find once among the supplies. It was really hard to say what we'd find here.

One quick snap with the bolt cutters and the padlock to the main entrance was gone. I warned each person to check any locked doors for booby traps. We then entered and started our rampage though the place. We found shoes, overcoats, rations, goggles, uniforms and all kinds of things. The last three were filled with ammunition, grenades, mines and explosives of all kinds. I even found some shoulder fired missiles and RPGs. The munitions I had loaded on the ATVs and wish I could have taken all of it. As it was, I barely made a dent in the bunker.

I sent all but Andy and I ahead as we mined the place. I mined each open and closed door to the storage bunkers. Some of the bunkers we didn't enter, because I wanted to be in and out in less than an hour. Andy had discovered the security cameras were not connected and the only security they had was a 60 watt light over the main gate. From a log book we found it looked like someone visited once a month and logged in and out. I moved back about five miles and hid the supplies I had. While dangerous, tomorrow we'd return and see what the unopened bunkers held. This place was there for the taking, and who knows what we'd find tomorrow. According to the log book, it'd just been visited three days ago.

The evening was quiet and I left Andy and another partisan at the supply dump to keep an eye on the place. They'd know if any troops or vehicles visited the place. I didn't think the Russians would know we were there for almost another three weeks. The log book showed a monthly visit, all of them made during the last week of the month. Over-night the supplies we already had were taken to camp by the ATVs and the horse. I'd use them to transport again in the morning.

By dawn we were in the supply depot with the mines removed from the doors. The first bunker was filled with winter camouflage uniforms and other cold weather gear. The snow patterns weren't much good to us right this minute, but they soon would be. I found mittens, gloves, boots, snow boots, skis, and all kinds of cold weather stuff. I took it all. The last bunker held rations, canned water, and some medical supplies. I took all the medical gear and left the big machines, along with the water. It started snowing just as I locked the gate and booby trapped it. I'm like a kid around snow and it fascinates me and always has, plus in the country it's so beautiful.

I was one happy man when we got home and avoided walking in the blizzard I suspected was approaching. Just a few hours later the wind picked up and snow began to fall hard and fast. I knew by morning we might have 12 inches or more on the ground. We could have survived on the trail, easily, but we'd have been colder. One of the items I took from the supply bunkers were heaters the Russians had for tents. We already had some, but eventually I wanted one for each shelter.

As I ate breakfast, my weather man briefed me on conditions, and I felt neither side was going far for the next week as storm after storm would hit us. It looked like there would be 40 inches of snow on the ground by the end of the week. I relaxed and made myself comfortable. Intelligence briefed me that the reward for me was still valid, but as far as they could tell, no one was interested in the money. I felt they were wrong and I told them so. A million dollars would buy a very comfortable life in another country, especially Mexico, because of it's poor economy. I kept the guard posted just outside my door.

Since the weather was bad, I had the doctors who'd flown in to help us with the smallpox administer physical exams for all members, check their dental health, and if needed evaluate them psychologically. Any unfit would be returned to Texas or released to work here, but only in headquarters. I didn't want unfit folks on the line and maybe causing the death of others.

It was during the blood and urine tests that Cynthia was definitely confirmed to be pregnant. Her doctor broke it to me, thinking I'd already been told by her. He apologized when he realized I knew nothing at all about the pregnancy being official. I was filled with joy, but scared for her and my baby. That night she told me she was pregnant and I acted surprised and happy, which I was. Before I slept that night, I had a long talk with God pleading for the safety of my child and Cynthia. I'd loved my other two wives, I really had, but I know in my heart, I loved neither of them like Cynthia. Ours is a special love, and to just be with her makes me happy. I worried about raising a child in the middle of a war, but we don't always get to pick when things happen in our lives. I knew in a war whole families could be here one minute, then gone in the blink of an eye.

I was deep in thought when Andy neared, stuck his head in my door, and said, "We've got a problem. We have two people who were riding ATVs gathering wood and water. Neither are from this area and both have some bad frostbite."

"What did the doctors say? Coffee's on the fire out there if you want a cup."

He had a tin cup clipped to his belt. He left the tent, filled his cup, returned, and said, "They left yesterday, ahead of this front, so they just barely got out in time. We have two medics and neither knows much about cold weather injuries. I know some about treatment, so maybe I can help. We need to gradually thaw the frozen tissue out using warm water. Then, in a couple of days, any part that turns black has to be removed with a knife."

"That's about all I know too."

"Both have frozen toes, fingers and ears. I have the ears covered with bandages, and they almost had hypothermia too. I've got them warming up now."

I stood and said, "Let's go look at them, and I'll help to warm up their feet and hands but they'll not like it much. I've seen grown men cry when their cold hands touch the warm water. I won't use painkillers or whiskey until we see if body parts have to be removed or not." I stood and we made our way toward the hospital tent. Unlike in the movies, this one did not have a huge red symbol on top. The Russians would bomb the medical logo just for fun.

"Be rough to lose a body part without a painkiller of some sort, don't ya know?" He asked as we entered the tent.

"I have morphine, but I won't use it unless the part being removed is major. For fingers and toes I think we can use a local and some codeine pills. A major body part to me would be a whole hand or foot."

"I agree, because we need to save it for more serious wounds. They're in the back left corner of the tent." he said as he moved toward them.

Both were in cots, wrapped up well with heavy wool blankets and sedated. I grabbed a passing medic and asked about their condition.

"Sir, all we really know right now is their hands and feet were frozen. We thawed them out using warm water and they took that poorly, too. We'll keep them warm and with us for about three days and see if the frostbitten areas turn colors on us. If they do, we'll use surgery to remove the dead flesh from them."

"If you need anything, let me know." I said in closing, and meant it too. There were many ways to die or become maimed in this war.

"I'll remember that, sir. Now I have to make my rounds, so please excuse me."

"Take care of these people, they are this nation's true heroes." I said, and then walked to Andy by the first cot.

"They're both asleep. I think the medics are keeping them that way so they get stronger."

"I have no idea. Let's let them rest." They both looked pale and peaceful, but I imagine just the warm bed felt good to them.

Off in the distance I could smell someone burning human waste, and it was a weekly task for some random Private assigned the detail. Our outhouses had 55 gal. steel drums cut in quarters and placed under the seats of our outhouses. Each week they were removed, a fresh drum placed under the seat, and the old one pulled into a clearing. Gas, diesel, or even aircraft fuel was added to the human feces and then ignited. As it burned, a man using a long steel rod worked the waste and fire. Over time, the drum was burned clean. The problem was, the man doing the burning smelled like crap for a day or two and taking a shower didn't help much at all. It was affectionately called the shit detail.

As we walked back to my tent, a man right beside me suddenly fell with a bullet wound to his lower back and there'd been no sound of a gunshot. He screamed, fell and then thrashed around like a fish out of water.

"Sniper!" someone yelled.

"I'll flush him out!" Andy yelled as he took off running to get his cell.

It could have been an attempt to kill me, but I wore no rank and I didn't think anyone who knew me would attempt to kill me, but a million dollars was a lot of money. That the Russians knew where we were I had no doubts, but would they make another costly effort to attack our base camp? Questionable. Just a few weeks back they'd done just that and our intelligence suspected they'd lost over 200 dead, wounded or missing. No unit could afford that many losses at one time. I did expect them to start hitting us with aircraft. I expected bombings and strafing to become common.

The sniper fired again and I heard a woman scream and from listening to her, she'd taken a round in the left leg as she lay behind a huge wooden box. Twice more the sniper shot and while all I could hear was a low thud, which meant he or she was close, two more times men screamed. So far, the sniper was batting a thousand.

Ten minutes later, I heard the explosion of a hand grenade, a good dozen weapons on automatic firing, and screams. I suspected Andy had just put an end to our sniper problem. A few minutes later he returned to camp holding a Russian sniper rifle.

"She was up in a pine not 100 yards from here. It was one of the few women snipers I've encountered." he said with a dry smile. I saw the rifle was covered with blood and it had a day/night scope. He continued, "Eighty-three notches on the stock, so we put down a good woman."

I nodded and then said, "Have the body pulled away a good mile and left. She deserves a military funeral with that many kills, but I just can't do that here. While I may respect her ability, she was an enemy."

"It's being done now, sir."

"If you need me, I'll be in my quarters." I said and made my way back to the tent. As I walked, I thought, *Eighty-three victims of her shooting ability and eighty-three dead Americans. It's a good thing we've done here today, killing this sniper. As soon as this nasty weather clears, I need to move this camp too, especially now that the Russians know where we are. All it would take is one fully loaded jet aircraft to put us out of business.*

A month later, in a new camp, I sat in my office planning another attack against the Russians when Birdie walked in and said, "Grab your gear and catch a Chinese chopper in an hour, sir. Headquarters wants you back in Texas for a bit. A new Colonel is coming to take your place, but only for as long as you are needed."

"Can I take the two out with me that lost their feet and hands to frostbite? They're not much help here with us and I think they'll do better where they can be assigned admin duties."

"Let me ask them on the radio, sir."

"Find out quickly so we'll know when they come for me."

"Any idea what is going on?" I asked, suddenly feeling butterflies in my stomach. The last time they 'needed' me, I detonated a suitcase sized nuke bomb. That I would refuse to do again, even though I knew we had a second bomb. I was part of the group that stole the two bombs from a Russian train shipment.

"They said no, because another chopper will come for the frostbite victims in a few days. This chopper inbound is for you only."

"Why just me? It's unusual as hell." I said.

"I have no idea, none at all, sir." Andy replied, because I know I gave him questioning look.

"Well, I'll let you know if I can later. If it's classified, you'll be out of luck." I extended my hand and as we shook, I said, "Good luck, Birdie, and tell Andy the same thing."

"I hear you just fine, boss, and you stay safe." Andy said from his side of the tent. He then laughed hard and long.

CHAPTER 18

S o, grabbing my gear, I ran to the pickup point, where a Chinese chopper picked me an hour later.

We flew low, mainly to avoid Russian radar, and I didn't like it at all. I'm no coward when it comes to flying, having been a military passenger in three wars and a number of state side training missions, but these Chinese pilots were fools. At some points we flew lower than the trees. Small arms fire from Russians guns reached out for us and some even struck the aircraft. I was worried; if we flew over just one person with a shoulder-fired missile we were toast.

I guess we were at 500 feet when I heard a loud beeping sound and one of the Chinese said in English, "Shit, dey hab lada lock on us." I noticed he could not pronounce r's well and they came out sounding like l's, thus lada for radar, with a long first a.

I cringed and waited for the explosion. My wait was a short one, less than 15 seconds I suspect, when a loud noise caught my attention, along with a fireball in the sky just slightly overhead. Pieces of aluminum began to fall, smoke filled the cabin, and the co-pilot was laying limp in his seat, with the top half of his body covered in blood. I noticed part of the windshield was gone, likely blown out. The crimson blood of the co-pilot was now caught in the slip stream and spattered on the walls of the cargo area where I was sitting.

The door gunners were sending out short spurts of fire and obviously only at targets they could see clearly. Then the one on the left fell back into the helicopter with top of his head missing. He jerked and twisted madly on the floor.

"Mayday, mayday, mayday . . ." the pilot said in English and then in Chinese.

He tried to gain altitude, but it was not to be. The bird began to shudder and shake as the engine seemed to experience it's death throes mid-flight. Fluids were leaking now and I figured most were flammable, so I tightened my seat belt.

"Captain to passenger, I must sit helicopter on ground. No can fly now." the Captain said casually and when I looked at the door gunners, one was dead and unmoving and the other moved to where I was and sat beside me. When he met my eye and smiled, I figure him insane.

"We hit ground soon. After we hit, go into trees fast." the Pilot informed me as I said a silent prayer. I then closed my eyes and waited to hit.

The aircraft struck hard, rolled on it's side and then rolled back upright again. The door gunner and I jumped from the helicopter, his hands had something in each, and made our way into the woods. I'd jerked the first aid kit from the now burning aircraft when I left along with my backpack, because I figured I'd need them. When I turned and looked behind me, I saw maybe fifty Russians making for our crash site. The pilot jumped from his seat and, using a semi-automatic rifle, began shooting. Russians dropped left and right. Then the Russians returned fire with dev- astating results. I saw the pilot struck at least five times in the torso, so I wrote him off as brave, but dead. I increased my running speed.

The aircraft was on fire and small explosions were heard. Then a larger boom was heard and an oily black fireball rose high in the sky, and rolled into itself as it tried to meet the clouds. The large explosion was followed by more lesser booms. I figured the smaller explosions were the ammunition and oxygen bottles blowing up.

The Russians were pleased to have downed the Chinese chopper. Unknown to us, they stopped by the wreckage to take photographs instead of chasing the two men who'd ran from the aircraft. Then they propped the dead pilot up and took photos sitting beside him with their individual guns. Finally they called headquarters about an hour later and reported the aircraft was down and while blown up, the Chinese star was clearly seen on some of the metal. If they'd not stopped, things might have been different for us. I noticed the little man had his door gun, a Chinese machine gun, and a can of ammunition.

About an hour later, we stopped in a thick grove of pines, because I knew the gun must be hard for him to carry.

I was out of breath as I told him, "My . . . name is John, John . . . Williamson." I pointed at myself. I then put both hands on my knees and bent over slightly trying to breathe.

"Wan . . . Tu" he said looking at me. He was gasping for breath too.

I noticed he also had a pistol and a rifle of some sort, a container of canvas, and a canteen. He was short, maybe five feet tall, black hair, brown eyes, white even teeth and about 105 pounds. He was smiling and I didn't see why, only some folks react differently to life and death situations. He handed the pistol to me, and two more full 9 MM magazines.

"Do you speak English?" I asked.

"I speak some English." he replied. I noticed, he pronounced it as Engrish.

"We must move quickly because they will look for us. I will carry the machine gun for a while."

He handed the gun to me and then opened the canvas bag, pulled out some camouflage face paint in what looked like a water colors set with a brush. He used his fingers to smear it on the high points of his face. He used a blotched pattern and I just smeared it on my face, neck and hands. I also removed my stainless steel watch, so the sun would not flash on it as we moved. He tossed me two Chinese rations, but I had others in my pack. I figured we were lucky to have gotten out of there alive.

"Are you injured?" I asked.

"Hu't back, and you?"

"I'm fine. Can you still run?"

"I can lun."

I took off at a slow jog, because you can't run too fast with a 60 pound pack on your back. I couldn't figure out what our next step was, so I continued trying to cover some distance from the crash site.

We ran for a good two hours but it was really just a fast jog.

"Stop, no can lun no mo'. Mines here, see line?" He pointed in front of me.

Not six feet away a thin clear plastic fishing line extended across the trail. I guessed it to be about two pound tensile strength. I moved forward to look it over, spotted another mine, near where the line was tied to a small sapling. I checked the other end and it was tied to a Chinese grenade. The use of a Chinese grenade meant it was a booby trap of our making. The grenade was armed and in a can, with the can holding the lever against the body of the explosive. If the line had not been pointed out to me, I might have pulled the line, the grenade would have been pulled from the can and then exploded. The delay could have been set from 0 to 5 seconds. The problem was, Chinese grenades were undependable at best. I know it would have come out of the can, but would it have exploded? Even in the best of times they only worked about 70% of the time. I stepped over it and now scanned the ground for mines much better than before.

After noon we heard choppers flying near, only they didn't seem to be searching for anyone. But, each time they got close, we had to hide in the underbrush. By dark, I figured we'd covered almost fifteen miles. While I know that doesn't sound like much, it was on foot. My gunner's back was hurting him and I was just plain tired.

I selected a bushy area that looked like it was nice spot for a den of snakes and one at a time we crawled into the brush. We saw no snakes, but a stick did poke the gunner on the arm and he said some things I didn't understand. I suspect he was talking bad about the stick, maybe thinking it was a snake. Once in the brush, he pulled out the survival kit and we looked it over. We'd been moving fairly steady and we were both more tired than we realized.

The kit had basic survival gear; signaling mirror, whistle, flares, compass, matches, radio, spare radio battery, first aid kit, survival sheath knife, survival pocket knife, morphine, small tins of food, vitamins, and a survival book written in Chinese, which I handed to him. I also discovered a sleeping bag and casualty blanket. We divided the gear up, so we shared the weight of the items and each had something to signal with.

"Here, you use the sleeping bag. I've used a blanket many times. Now, we need to gather wood because it will be a cold night."

"Yes, cold." he said, and began to gather wood for a fire.

An hour after dark and before we had a fire, I heard movement down the trail. I prayed there was no dog team along if it was a cell looking for us. Usually I have a fire when the sun goes down, but didn't because we were late eating supper, which we ate cold. We sat perfectly still as the troops neared and I could hear the Russians talking to each other. I wondered if they could hear my heart beating.

The little Chinese warrior was ready to fight, I'll give him that much credit, but 40 people walked past us, so as soon as they were gone, I moved us further back into the trees and started a small fire. By now it was below zero and a fire was needed, especially if they were done for the day and in a night camp. I honestly didn't think the Russians went far either, not as cold as it was. A person can actually stay pretty warm walking in cold weather but the moment they stop, they start losing body heat and a fire is needed. If the sweat on them freezes, they'll die, usually.

I wore my NVGs, but the Chinese had nothing. Hopefully we'd not need them. Speaking in a low tones, I said, "You are a Sergeant?"

"Sergeant, yes. Me Army ten years."

"I am a Colonel."

He shrugged and said, "Okay. I no know what that be."

"Officer."

"I see. Okay, *sir.*"

I laughed as quietly as I could and thought, *I'm not telling you that for any reason other than to let you know. It means little to me. When they pick us up, it will help, I think.*

"Call me John in the woods.""I understand. Some Chinese officer the same you. First name alone, but all name and lank when alound others."

"Yes. We will take turns using the goggles at night. We do not want to fight, not anyone, because there are just two of us. If it looks like a fight, wake me."

"I see, and understand."

I hope he really does and isn't just saying that because it's all the English he knows, I thought but said, "Now, I sleep then you wake me later."

"Okay."

I slept, but it was a restless sleep with me seeing both my first two wives and trying to explain to them how my life had turned out like it had. I tried to explain that I didn't want to lose either of them and how much it hurt me when they died —and it had. My first one accused me of leaving her all the time and not protecting her, which was partly true. Only, I had no idea at the time how lawless we'd become as a society and I was always working, trying to make a living. Then, after the fall, trading and stealing was the only ways to get what a family needed to survive. I had four 500 gallon gas tanks I used to refuel my security trucks each week. I kept big dogs chained to each tank. I had a Rottweiler, two German Shepherds, and a Doberman I kept near the tanks and all lived in dog houses better than some of the places people live in in town. I treated those dogs like my babies. During the day they ran free and had free access to my house. I'm getting off track, but gas had greater value than gold, so when I needed something, I'd fill up four five gallon gas cans and head to town, five miles away.

The day she was murdered, I remembered trading for what we needed and then going straight home. I felt a sudden urge to get there quickly because something bad had happened. Something horrible had happened; I entered my house to find my wife raped and murdered along with my kids. I almost lost my mind seeing them butchered and used. I can still see the blood splattered walls and the horror on the faces of my loved ones. I stayed drunk the first week, then slowly tried to put my life back together and while I came close with my second wife, it didn't happen. I lost her in combat, as well as my soon to be wife just last year. Last year I lost both the woman I loved and my unborn child. Three good women and God took them all away from me. That's why I'm leery of a relationship with Cynthia, because every woman that gets close to me dies a violent death. It's a bit late with her now, because I love her, and do want my baby. I want to be happy, but the past always raises its ugly head and reminds me of bygones.

I felt someone shaking me and when I opened my eyes, Wan was looking at me. He held his finger to his lips and then cupped his hands behind his ears. He was right, why no night sounds? I got up, pulled the pistol he'd given me and slipped the safety off. We saw or heard nothing and after a bit the night sounds returned.

Sergeant Wan Tu said, "You no sleep good. Talk in sleep and jump all over the place."

"Nightmare."

When he looked puzzled, I said, "Bad dream."

He nodded in understanding then.

"I t'ink I sleep now and you watch us."

I agreed and wondered what had been near us earlier. If not a man that left grizzly bears or cougars, and either one was bad news for just two men. Just the thought of either kept me awake my shift. When I went to bed again later, I slept better, but it was raining when I woke. It wasn't a hard rain, but a steady one that folks who lived here knew could last a week or more.

A quick look on the trail at dawn indicated a large number of troops had moved down the trail last night and they had to be miserable in this weather. I know it was well below zero when the movement took place and that's a terrible temperature to be moving. I woke Sergeant Tu and after a cold ration, we saddled up and started walking.

Near mid-morning a chopper flew over, but it was too high to see which side it was on, so we didn't signal it at all. We stopped for lunch at near noon and despite the rain and mud, we were making good time. Surprisingly, I was so hungry even a green frog tasted good. We moved slowly, but at a steady rate, so the miles soon disappeared behind us.

Escape and evasion is always a very slow process. Most folks don't realize the first thing most folks see when looking for someone is movement, and when trying to avoid capture you want to blend in and not be seen, yet still be able to move. The most you can hope for is to see them first and in some cases that is hard to do, especially if they're sitting still looking for you and you're trying to move. It was lung hurting cold at night, so moving during periods of darkness was out.

We stopped near dusk and moved away from the trail to rest overnight. I'd just placed some water on to boil, using the aluminum canteen cup that fit over the bottom of my canteen, when I heard English being spoken. I glanced at Sergeant Wan Tu, and he was smiling.

I knew it was risky, but so was just two men moving north, so I called out, "Hello, we're Americans and need help. There are only two of us."

I heard a bunch of safety switches on weapons snap to the off position.

"Both of you move forward, and keep your weapons in your left hand and over your head. Do not lower the weapons until told to do so. Any quick movements will get you killed. Come forward, now."

I moved forward until a man appeared out of the brush to take the pistol from my left hand and Tu's rifle from him. We were moved to what looked like two squads of people on the trail. A tall middle aged man moved to me and asked, "Who are you?"

"Colonel John Williamson."

"And him?"

"Sergeant Wan Tu, Chinese Army. Our chopper was shot down."

"What's your dog's name?"

"Dolly."

"What is your current girlfriend's first name?" the man asked.

"Cynthia, why?"

He smiled and said, "We've been looking for you. While we've seen plenty Russians, you're the first Americans we've seen. Any others from your chopper survive?"

"No, all the others were KIA."

"I'll report we've found you to Headquarters later. Right now, we need to cover some distance because we're being followed."

We were pulled into the line, handed our guns back and I was also given a Bison sub-machine gun, since all I had was a pistol. My weapon of choice is a Bison. I noticed Tu moved in close to me and I suspect it was because he knew me. I'm sure being around all the big, tall American strangers intimidated him a little. We walked another thirty minutes or so and then moved back into a grove of pine trees. I counted 24 people, not counting me or Tu. Claymores were placed near the trail and anti-personnel mines circled us. One small fire was soon burning, as we all ate our meals cold.

The leader, who I discovered was named Steve Pitts, was a Major with the Partisans. His sole mission was to find me or my body and return.

Over cups of hot tea he said, "You're a valuable man to the resistance, sir. They must have 20 groups of folks out beating the bushes for you. When I called Headquarters a few minute ago they were happy you'd been found alive. You are to stay with us until they decide what they want done with you."

Before I could answer, a guard neared and said, "Russians will be here in less than ten minutes so I suggest we put the fire out." I noticed he was wearing his NVGs so I lowered mine too. Later today I'd either be home again or on my way to the Base in Texas, unless I was dead.

CHAPTER 19

The Colonel in charge of prisoners, civilian and military, was standing tall this morning as he explained how his prisoners were kept on a 900 calories a day diet, or less. This was done on purpose to keep them too weak to escape his gulag.

"We mainly feed them scraps from our military dining facilities. They get the trimmed fat from all meats, fruit and vegetable peelings, served in a watery soup twice a day. Their bread is 50% bread and 50% sawdust, which adds fiber."

"Surely you jest. I mean, that is not enough to keep a person alive." Lieutenant Colonel Ruslan Gennavich, the temporary acting Base Commander, said.

"I am speaking the truth, sir. The average prisoner will die at slightly longer than six months."

The Colonel slammed the table hard with his right fist and replied, "By God, that will change today. Do you not realize the Americans will feed our captured men exactly what we feed theirs?"

"It is to be expected by our men, because this is war, sir."

"I will not have our men half starved because you wish to demonstrate your power over our prisoners. Starting today, they will eat what we eat. I want all officers fed from our officers mess and the enlisted or civilians from the enlisted mess. Their serving sizes will be the same too."

"I . . . I do not understand, sir." The Colonel's face was crimson and he was obviously confused.

"The Americans have a few Russians as prisoners and they have promised to treat them as we treat our prisoners. Three of the men they have are Russian Generals and they are not used to starving, sir. So, from now on, treat them firmly, but fairly. I also want all torture to stop effective immediately because of repercussions. Not long ago one of our interrogators burned a captive to death, using petrol, attempting to make another prisoner talk only it did not work. Somehow the word got out and ten Russian captives were found burned to death beside a main highway earlier this week. They all smelled of petrol and there was a note warning us. They promised to kill ten of ours for every prisoner of theirs to die, and by the same manner. So, your gulags will need to be cleaned up a little, comrade."

"The Americans will do nothing. They are weak and like children." the Chief of the gulags said. "How do we know our men were alive when burned?"

"The eleventh man was not burned, but shot in both knees. He told us what happened and even explained why he was left alive. He was to speak for the resistance and to warn us to change some of of our standard procedures, like the menu at your gulags. Moscow has issued the orders for you to change, not me, but I do agree with them. I trust that is sufficient authority for you, sir."

"What makes Moscow so sure the Americans will really continue to do this?"

"Mainly because they have done it for years in Mississippi and Alabama. This retaliation was started years ago by a now deceased partisan named Williams, and his partner Williamson, both members of the famous partisan group 'The Aces.' As a matter of fact, Colonel Williamson is now the commander of this three state area, so we are sure the message was no idle threat. By God, this is no joke, Colonel, and besides, you have your orders. Make them happen."

"Sir, I must —"

"Sit down, sir, damn you! You are making a fool of yourself." When the Colonel didn't move quickly enough, he added, "Or I will have your ass shot!"

The Colonel took his chair and lowered his head to his hands.

"The next sonofabitch that questions me, I will shoot." He pulled his pistol from the holster and chambered a round. While junior in rank to the Full Colonel, his position as the Base Commander gave him full responsibility and authority to do as needed.

"Now, let us proceed with my morning briefings. I am sick of having Moscow on my ass, and need your support in making things happen. If you cannot make things happen, I will replace you or start shooting."

The rest of the meeting was uneventful, but he had their attention.

The next morning at breakfast time, Colonel Gennavich showed at the gulag and when met by the camp commander, he asked to be shown the food being fed to the prisoners. He was taken to a cell, the door opened, and the food given to the prisoner was evaluated.

"Is this what we had this morning at the open mess?"

"Uh, no, sir. I can explain."

Without a word spoken, Colonel Gennavich pulled his pistol and fired one round, which narrowly missed the gulag Commander's head.

He said, "There will be no second warning. Now, find these people some decent food! There will be no more of this watery soup with a few pieces of gristle for food. Improve on it by lunch or you will be eating it for your supper, sir!"

Colonel Gennavich was under a tremendous amount of pressure since the partisan activities were up in his area. Moscow had just notified him this morning they'd made him the permanent Commander, so he had to make things happen and quickly, too. His name was on the Full Colonels promotion list coming out next month. His states, long since thought pacified, were finally active and the resistance activities were costing the Russians lives. Moscow was on the phone day and night now, wanting answers, answers to questions the Colonel didn't have. He was honestly close to shooting people.

He'd been raised in a modest home in the country, but a far cry from a farm because his father had money and was in politics. He'd had a private tutor, went to the best universities for his degrees, and had moved up the promotions ladder ahead of his classmates. His father had connections, which meant Senkin had connections as well, and as a young man he'd used his fathers power and influence rarely, but when he did, things happened.

His wife is the daughter of a powerful manufacturer of Russian tanks and arms, and the American equivalent of a CEO. Her father is a rich and omnipotent man, who knows few equals in Russia and is owed many favors by those he's helped. She is pretty, but not beautiful, and was raised to behave like a sophisticated lady. She usually dresses simply, but neatly. Her education and bearing shines through all she does, and more than once she'd used her connections to advance Rusya's career. While he was unaware, there were times when she'd used more than simple connections to see him promoted or selected for a career advancing position. She considered nothing more important than his military advancement, so she did what was needed. Theirs was an arranged marriage, with the power of both fathers behind them and between the two, they could move mountains. If he was able to do a fair job in America, he'd been promised General when he left. Once in the General ranks, he'd advance rapidly, due to his connections.

Now, with all the partisan activity in the northwest for the first time, he was being watched very closely by Moscow. There were those Generals who wondered what he was doing wrong all of a sudden, and then others were pleased to see the Russians finally weeding the partisans out of that region. No one, not even Yakovich, had a clear picture of what was really taking place, which was nothing more than the birth of the resistance in the three state area. I'd just assisted in organizing it and now allowed it to run on it's own momentum. Once up and running, I didn't think anything could stop it from doing what it was designed to do, kill Russians.

He walked to his desk, sat in his leather chair, and took a sip of his cold tea. As he placed it back on the saucer he thought of having it replaced, and then changed his mind. It didn't matter if his hot tea was cold or if the world was round or flat. All that mattered was Moscow had to be convinced he was a great success, but how could he do that?

He picked up some older reports and read about Sergeant Wan Tu's chopper being brought down. He picked up the phone and called the base Information and Media Affairs Office.

"Hello, Captain, this is the Wing Commander and in the morning, I want a photographer and two writers to go with me into the field. We are going to visit the crash site of a Chinese helicopter we shot down. I want big news made out of the fact the Chinese are here and illegally, too. I want the Chinese bodies and the whole mess photographed. Do you see any problems doing this?"

"I didn't think you would. Do this properly and you will see your name on the next promotions list to Lieutenant Colonel. No, there is no mistake. If you do this right, you will never wear the rank of Major. Then, you know Colonel will be assured for a man who never put on Major. Have them ready two hours before sunrise."

He hung up the phone, opened his desk drawer and removed a bottle of vodka. He pulled the cork, poured a generous amount into his cold tea, and then sat the bottle on the edge of his desk. He took a slight sip, closed his eyes and wished his wife was with him to give him a massage, or at least to discuss his problems with. She saw things in situations he never did and usually had brilliant ideas. Only she was home and could offer him no assistance.

I must make General when I leave here or my whole life has been for nothing. I was born to be a General and now I will fulfill my destiny or die an old man and a failure. I must be promoted, he thought as he picked up his tea and downed the drink.

He wiped his mouth off, stood and thought, *"Tomorrow I will send Moscow proof of Chinese involvement and my interrogation of the Chinese pilot before he died of his wounds. He confessed much to me and I must send that information to Mother Russia. I will be shown dressing his wounds, and speaking with him. I am sure we have some people who can make a dead man in a photo look very much alive. Perhaps I can first be shown dressing his eye injures, which will be severe."*

Early the next morning the crews and media folks were all standing around the Russian helicopter before they departed. The media folks were all excited and the aircrew members were bored with the mission. The Colonel arrived and then boarded the aircraft. Minutes later, they moved slowly into the air.

The Chinese had been dead a few days, but the cold weather had preserved the bodies well, only the co-pilot and other door gunner could not be used because they were torn to pieces. Photos were taken of the dead pilot and the Commander went through the motions of doctoring him up and caring for him and once he had the eyes wrapped, it looked good, but even with all the effort made by the Colonel, the man died anyway. They were gone about four hours. The smell was enough to gag all of them and the military reporters had a hard time keeping their breakfast down. Then, once they boarded the aircraft for the trip home they took some small arms ground fire, but only a couple of rounds hit the helicopter and none that caused much damage. It was mostly to the aluminum skin on the aircraft.

Once back at the base, a brilliant story, along with images, about how Full Colonel select Ruslan 'Rusya' Gennadiyevich had tried his best to save the life of the Chinese flier, was soon airborne for Moscow. He also stated that the pilot had recently died due to his injuries. Since he had experience in other wars, his images were most convincing.

Weeks passed and he finally got a phone call from his father stating his photos and story were the talk of Moscow. The Russian media made a huge push at showing how humane the Russians were, along side images of WWII of the Chinese decapitating prisoners. It clearly spoke, no, it shouted of the Russians being the good guys in this war.

The phone calls to him were suddenly less harsh and rough, indicating he was now a favorite of the Generals. To make things look even better, he launched a huge attack on partisan areas, led by his airborne troops.

The first sign of something being wrong was when a machine gun in a chopper door coughed and my troops on the ground began to fall. Our point man was chewed to pieces by the gun and when the firing stopped, little was left except for a red puddle on the trail. He was dead in a heartbeat. I'm sure he felt little, and what he felt was not for long.

Then Russian missiles struck, killing even more, especially when combined with the devastating gunfire on the ground. It felt like we'd run into a couple of companies of troops, but I knew better. The Russians were just getting better at ambushes was all. Casualties grew as we withdrew to fight another day. I never fought them if I could avoid it, on even terms. I'd lose every single time. It's hard to beat ground troops with experienced air support. It was a sad group that moved toward base camp.

I discovered I'd lost over 150 killed, maimed or missing. Of my maimed, forty folks, four were not expected to live. Some had horrible wounds, so I had the ones dying for sure put down with morphine. Otherwise, some would take days to die and I had to leave them. I knew the Russians would just kill them or hurt them to gain information. I never intentionally left a wounded person behind to become a POW.

When we left, we took all the guns and ammunition, along with other gear, as we booby trapped all the bodies. Russians, like most troops, are souvenir hunters, so the traps would kill some of them. We'd leave most watches, rings and necklaces on our dead to entice them.

The next few days I had cells moving in all directions. I had a feeling the Russians had some forward operating bases I knew nothing about. I intended to find the bases and take them out, one at a time, destroying all the property and gear I could, as well as killing the troops. Only we had to find the bases first. I soon discovered two that were large enough they were hiring civilians to do the jobs they didn't like. Our people now washed dishes and manned the dining facilities, as well as the clubs where they could drink. I intentionally sent women to and around the bases that had sexually transmitted diseases or other illnesses that would spread quickly. My goal then was not to kill, but take a man or woman out of action for a day or two and affect their morale. To me, nothing is more degrading than a person catching an STD.

I also wanted to bomb them, but how? I knew I had no support aircraft and couldn't get any right now. I could get some small drones that were more like toys than weapons and I had bicycles. I could drop explosives from the drones and use them over and over. I could also fill the hollow bicycle frames with C-4 and set them off during peak hours at busy locations. Mix a few nails, rocks and broken glass with the clay-like explosive, and I had a horrible bomb. I decided to try them both, since I was the boss, to show my folks I could and would do what I asked them to do. My first attempt was using the small drones. I soon discovered a perfect place to try my drone attack.

Between myself and Seattle there was a Forward Operating Base (FOB) with a portable fuel bladder uphill of the two clubs, officer and enlisted. I selected that base for my first attack. Of the two attacks, using a drone was the safest. I had my Explosives Ordinance Disposal folks make me one explosive the drone could carry weight-wise and I had a quick release button on the drone.

Sergeant Andy was coming with me, along with Captain Simmons' cell. We left early in the morning, while it was still dark and misting rain. It was cold too, which made it perfect hypothermia weather. We were all dressed in Russian rain gear, with red or yellow material tied around our left arms. I carried the drone and explosive to maybe 100 yards from the fuel bladder. My drone was small, almost the size of the child's toy, and maybe 14 inches from tip to tip. Not big, but large enough to carry a pound of C-4.

"Is this too far away?" Andy asked from the brush beside me.

"No, we have mile range, so this is ideal. I want to drop the explosives with a timer and then get in a good position to ambush the survivors. If it works well, we'll start hitting various targets on bases."

"What kind of targets, sir?" Andy asked, his tone almost at a whisper.

"Commanders quarters, Headquarters, and supply. There are others, but you get the idea."

I connected the explosives to the quick disconnect and tested the engines, no problems. I had the drone fly up near the fence around the base and then back. I could see my target and the Russians were nice enough to keep the fuel bladder area well lighted at night.

I met the Sergeant's eyes and smiled as I said, "Here we go."

The drone lifted nicely and in seconds was airborne. I noticed I heard nothing and I was sure those in the clubs heard nothing either. When it moved over the fuel bladders, I lowered to the point the explosive was almost touching and then released my package in the middle of the fuel. I then brought my drone home to use once again. Now, we waited to ambush those who survived the blast and burning fuel. Hopefully we'd bag a good number this evening. I had set the timer for five minutes and now sat watching my watch.

Exactly five minutes later the C-4 exploded and the fuel erupted into a ball of flames that moved toward the sky. It mushroomed out, resembling a nuke blast, and burning fuel ran down the gentle slopes right to the two clubs. Since both were nothing more than canvas tents, the canvas quickly caught fire. I could hear men and women scream as they tried to exit packed doorways and felt nothing when I realized they were burning to death. Others walked from the tents completely covered in flames. We opened fire with small arms and two machine guns.

My troops then began shooting into the two tents and before long I heard aircraft nearing. I had my people move deeper into the woods and return home. I then flew the drone over the damage and dropped the Ace of Spades cards as I took color photos and videos of the place.

Later, Chinese Sergeant Wan Tu walked with me a great distance, smiling.

Finally, he said."We hab good fight." I could hear the pride in his tone.

"Yes, tomorrow we'll try the bicycle bomb."

"Dat one will work good." he said, and continued smiling.

Early the next morning I moved to a base we'd not attacked yet and had one of my lady troops approach the main entrance and ask about a job on base. The Russians, being like most troops, liked having others do the jobs they hated. He gave her directions to base personnel. She rode her bicycle filled with C-4 to the building knowing the busiest time of the day was near lunch and set the timer for noon. The small timer was connected from its position under her seat to the detonator, which was inserted into the C-4 in the hollow frame. We'd even filled the handlebars. At various places around the base, she cautiously slipped the Ace of Spades card where it would be found following the bombing.

She then mixed into the crowd and made her way toward the main gate.

At the main gate the same guard stopped her and asked, "Did you not ask about a job?"

"I do not have all of my papers with me. I only have my identification card and I need my social security card and drivers license."

"Come." he demanded, which frightened her.

"I will call the office and speak to my friend, Igor, and see if they have job for you."

He called, spoke to someone in Russian and said, "You will need a birth certificate and then you can have a job. They have many on the list." He put the phone back in the cradle, shrugged and added, "When you return, go there and ask for Igor, tell him you have a friend that works the main gate. He will know it is me. If you hurry, you can do this today."

"I will rush."

"Where is your bicycle? Did you not have a bicycle?"

"Yes, I have one, but the tires have gone flat. I ran over some nails. I will have my father pick it up on his way home from work. He works on the base and can bring it home for me later."

Smiling, the soldier said, "Go, and best of luck with the job search."

After she exited, we sat waiting patiently with our small arms loaded and ready for the explosion. We could see the front of the personnel building and were aware it was also the base Headquarters building. Minutes move slowly when you wait in a war.

CHAPTER 20

Colonel Yakovich was growing nervous as he was briefed by the Base Commander of the new forward operating base. They were in the Lieutenant Colonel's office having lunch with most of the Colonel's staff from Seattle there. The base was doing well, with 101 confirmed partisan bodies as of 0600 this morning. It had been operational for two months, but it was the first time he'd been able to visit. The first 45 days were spent adding security, mines, barbed wire, and towers along the fence line. There were shouts heard outside and then the loud sounds of engines running.

The Base Commander, Lieutenant Colonel Select Ruslan 'Rusya' Gennavich, stood, walked to the window and said, "The fuel trucks to fill the propane tanks have finally arrived and here it is, almost noon. They were to have been here yesterday. Master Sergeant Yurievich, see they hold off on refueling until our meal is completed and we leave the area. The smell of the propane can make some ill, especially after we have just eaten. Tell them to wait fifteen more minutes."

The face of the watch under the bicycle seat showed three minutes until noon.

Soon after the Sergeant disappeared the noise stopped and the Colonel moved back to his seat. He picked up his water glass and said, "As I was saying, I look forward next month to the arrival of the thermal systems for our helicopters. I am sure my Black Sharks will be much more effective with the updates."

Master Sergeant Yurievich entered, closed the doors and waited patiently in his chair for the meal to finish so he could call the room to attention when all the brass left. The face on the watch now showed one minute until noon.

Colonel Yakovich stood, moved to the window and smiled. Since he'd provided proof of the Chinese being in the three state area, his name could do no wrong in Moscow. He had a half a glass of vodka in his right hand and an unlighted cigar in his mouth when the world as he knew it turned white and a loud explosion filled the air. Glass from the double windows no more than fifty feet from the blast shattered sending sharp glass shards into the room with the force of a shotgun. The room instantly filled with flying debris, flames, and dust. Blood floated in the air, mixed with dust.

The steps in front of the personnel building were full of folks coming and going to lunch when the bicycle exploded into thousands of small pieces of metal. The metal, rocks and broken glass mixed with the C-4 only added to the body count, as it killed fifty straightaway and wounded a good hundred others. Then, the fuel truck went up. The propane tank left a fifteen foot crater under the explosions and the workers with the truck simply disappeared. Three quarters of the personnel building was blown out onto the quarter acre of grass behind the facility toward the base gymnasium. Bodies, broken, burned, and ripped, littered the grounds in all directions.

The fuel tank on the truck exploded last, killing many who'd only been injured by the propane tank explosion. Smoke from all the fires now raging was turning the overhead sky dark gray and the flames continued to roll inside of themselves. Oily black smoke mixed with the smell of burnt bodies filled the air. The crackling and popping of the flames could be heard, along with the screams of the injured and low moans and groans of the dying.

Forward Operating Base Oscar had just become a living hell for all assigned there. People screamed for help as others screamed for their mothers. Master Sergeant Yurievich removed his belt and placed it on the stub where his left arm used to be. He tightened it as tight as it would go. He then crawled out from under the heavy solid oak table and saw nothing but rubbish and bodies. Blood, still wet, dripped from the walls, and those not burned were torn to pieces. He moved among the injured, the few there were, looking, and finally found Commander Yakaovich, who lay in the remains of the hall with a six inch wide shard of glass in his stomach. His hair was smoking, his eyes were both gone, and a grimace was on his face as he lived his last few minutes.

"Sir, are you in pain?"

"Inga . . . my . . . love, I . . . hur . . . hurt." the Colonel said, his words slow and drawn out. His pain was obvious now.

Yurievich squatted beside him, took his filthy hand in his and said, "It was . . . the . . . partisans, sir."

The Colonel moaned and said, "Kill . . . them. Kill them . . . all." He gave a loud sigh, a rattling was heard in his chest, and his bowels relaxed. The Sergeant read the Colonel's lips, because he could hear nothing. A second later, as a foul smell joined others in the room, the Colonel gave a long moan and was dead. His hand was still grasping the Sergeant's hand against pain when his head fell back limply.

Suddenly the room was filled with medical personnel and military police. It was then Master Sergeant Yurievich remembered the base medical clinic was across the street and the police headquarters not a half a block away. He was sure both of those buildings were damaged from the explosions too, but nothing like this.

A woman dressed in all white neared him, said something his shattered eardrums did not hear, and then gave him a shot of morphine in his left arm. As she wrote morphine, 1210, on his forehead with her lipstick, the medicine began to work. Seconds later, his world faded into black and he was asleep.

The nurse stood and screamed, "Orderly! I have a live one here! Stretcher needed here!"

The rescue crews worked night and day pulling bodies from the rubble and I pulled my main force back, leaving four snipers to select targets of opportunity. We'd done what I wanted to do and that was to leave the building smoking. The propane tank truck was just an added bonus. Now, my snipers would kill anyone of any importance that come to see the damage done. Over the next four days, nine more lives were lost and each was a Major or higher in rank. Lucas, my newest sniper, killed a brigadier General who came to see the damage with his own eyes, and that was on the fourth day. He seriously injured six more men who tried to rescue the General. According to my snipers, they were still pulling bodies from the rubble on the fourth day.

I withdrew and moved to the west to an old saw mill I knew of, to rest and then break into cells once more. I needed a few days to brief my cell leaders on targets, places to leave alone and some spots just to watch.

Once the cells left, I decided to use the saw mill as a temporary base camp because it was located in almost the center of the state, the building was still sound and well insulated for cold winters. After a few weeks, we settled down and made the place a home. Folks were coming and going regularly, but usually at night to avoid being seen by the Russians. Then, overnight that changed.

"Base, understand you want me to turn command over to Colonel Rivers, code name Bird. Will do, as soon as he arrives. Roger, I realize that was planned when the Chinese chopper went down. When I come, I will bring Sergeant Wan Tu with me. I think it's time he returns home, over."

"Roger, Cobra One, the Chinese have asked about him. Be advised the Russians have or will soon be getting thermal systems in their choppers, armor, and perhaps even binoculars for officers and squad leaders. We discovered that in an intercepted message we got from them to all units."

"Copy on the thermal and it's a pain in the ass, over."

"Additionally, they suspect you are at the at the old saw mill, but will not attack until all their systems are updated with thermal.

That means a night attack to us. You can expect your package in the form of a bird to arrive this week, over."

"Understand my bird will arrive this week and we are in danger of a night attack. We will relocate once the bird is in his cage, over and out."

"Roger that, and Base out."

I handed the handset back to my radioman and yelled, "Andy!"

"Yes, sir?"

"Get everything and everyone ready to move one day this week. The new man, Colonel John Rivers, will be parachuted into our area in a day or two. Once he is on hand we are to relocate, and I'll then turn command over to him. They'll send a Chinese C-130 or chopper in to pick me up. Sergeant Tu will be going back to Base with me."

"I've known Rivers a long time, since he was Sergeant Rivers and worked for me. Now, he ain't worked for me in twenty years, back when he was on active duty, and I was an E-6. He's a good man who I've kept in touch with over the years, and you'll be leaving us in good hands. Any word on your next assignment, sir?"

"They mentioned the South East or North East. I imagine they'll use me to get them organized and then pull me out and have a new person come in. More or less what I have done here."

"I see a sparkling star over you." Top said, and then laughed.

"I'm afraid being a General in a partisan unit is not something that is all that rewarding; well, not like peace time anyway."

"Perhaps not, sir, but it would still be a great honor and you deserve it too."

"Enough loose talk. Get this place ready to move." I ordered with a grin. I liked Andy, because he had great attitude about life and that was hard to maintain in a partisan unit. I was thinking more about seeing Cynthia and loving her again.

"Yes, sir." Andy said with a big smile.

Swearing revenge, the new base commander in Seattle was briefed on what intelligence had learned about the partisan attack that seriously crippled the base. Colonel Yuliy Bykov, fresh from Moscow, sat stone-faced at the head of an oak table as charts and slides explained the details. He saw no way it could have been prevented, except for a dog team that sniffed out explosives, and he only had one of them. He wrote on the pad in front of him, *'Get six dog teams for explosives detection.'* He had four dog teams for hunting men, three more for illegal drugs, but only one for explosives.

"Sir, Intelligence thinks we can expect more attacks like the one that killed Colonel Yakovich in the future, unless we increase our searches before civilians are allowed on base and get more dogs capable of detecting explosives."

"Do those dogs even work?" A Major from personnel asked.

"Three days ago a man was entering the base when the one dog we have went crazy trying to get at the man. He carried nothing in his hands, his clothing and shoes were clean, and it appeared the dog had made a mistake. The man was taken into custody and checked out further. It was in the hospital that we discovered gun powder residue under his finger nails. So, to answer your question, yes, they work."

"Where is this man now?" asked Commander Bykov.

"He is in a gulag, sir." the chief of security police said.

"I also understand that gun powder is visible under ultraviolet lights." the Commander said and then added, "If that is so, have them installed at the main gate for all civilians to use before they are granted access to the base. I suspect with the dogs, lights, and the T-90 tank that will be positioned at the main gate at some point today, we will have less problems with terrorist attacks."

"Maybe, sir. This base has miles and miles of fence line, so if they want in badly enough they will find a way. It takes guts, you know, to set explosives up in the middle of your enemies."

"Cowards, is what they are! By God, call them what they are!" Colonel Yuliy yelled as he slammed the flat of his right hand on the table hard. Then after a minute or two he sobered and asked, "And, what of the cowardly woman who placed the bicycle there to kill our brave comrades?"

The Chief of Security Police said, "She would not talk at first, but she did not deal well with pain. After the interrogator broke her left arm in three places, and poked out her left eye, she told us all. She was still living with her parents, who she got to see hanged before she admitted working for the resistance. Nothing worked on her except pain. She is scheduled to be executed for murder this Friday morning at dawn."

"Good, have it done at morning roll call so the assembled men can see how we treat murderers."

"Yes, sir, I will see to it."

The intelligence chief said, "We were told the man behind blowing up some temporary fuel bladders, which killed a large number of our troops a few months back on another FOB, and the man who planned our attack was the same man, John Williamson. In both cases, we found the Ace of Spades card scattered around."

"Aces, huh?" the Colonel said. "I fought those bastards on my first and second tours here as a Captain and then as a Major. They are ruthless. Are they still killing ten of our men for every one of theirs we execute?"

"We no longer execute prisoners except for murder, rape or terrorism against our troops."

"Good, I never thought that would work as Moscow thought it would. Hell, how can you scare a country into liking you? I do not care if they like me, as long as they obey the laws."

"This execution Friday will be the first one in over two years." the Chief of Security Police said.

The Colonel nodded and then asked, "Weather, any idea when we will have a week of dry weather?"

"Later this week will start about eight days of dry weather, sir."

"Ops, I was told by your Major that all the thermal detection systems will be installed tomorrow, is that correct?"

"I was told that by the Chief of Maintenance, sir."

Looking at his Chief of Maintenance, the man said, "We are testing the last installations today, sir, and they should be installed and ready to use tomorrow."

"Good, because in the morning, we are going to hit the Base Camp of the partisans, at the saw mill, and I want every man we can afford from here to be involved in the fight and I mean, admin, cooks, bakers, and even vehicle mechanics. We will keep about 20% of all manpower here and I want the rest in the field."

Base Ops smiled and said, "The aircraft will be ready, sir."

"Uh, what about us, sir?" An unknown Lieutenant asked.

"If you have enlisted in the field, then your Commander should be in the field. Now, notice I said Commander and not his representative, Lieutenant. When you return to your office, be sure to tell your boss what I said. He had better be there and not some man he sent in his place."

"For how long, sir?"

"Hard to say, but I would bring enough food for between ten days to two weeks."

"Yes, sir."

"Uh, this meeting is adjourned, but Master Sergeant Kovarov, I need you to remain behind for a few minutes. The rest of you need to return to your units."

After everyone was gone, the Lieutenant Colonel said, "Roberta, I will need your help with this assignment and the backing of the enlisted men. I intend to let the army, navy and air forces do a lot of the work we used to do by hand. However, I need you to keep me up to date on the morale and mood of my people at all times."

"Yes, sir, that is part of my job."

"I also want you in the field often and along with some of the patrols, so we keep them honest. On my first tour here, some men would pretend to go out, but they would only go outside the base and then radio in later that they were miles away. I want them eager to go into the field, which means I want to win more fights than I lose. I know you have been in the army longer than I have been alive, so help me fight a good war and warn me before I do something stupid. Deal?"

"Deal, sir."

"Dismissed, but my door is always open to you, always."

The next morning was a real goat roping as well over a thousand Russian troops were airlifted to near the saw mill. The helicopters from all three states were used to begin the largest Russian operation of the war. Of course, all of that, along with our resistance and ground fire, brought about some confusion. My troops would fire on the Russians and then move in close to them to avoid any return fire by choppers. We partisans had no air power, so we used a lot of mines and booby traps to slow them down, and when that failed, we fired shoulder launched missiles. I had no serious desire to stop them, why should I? Besides, I couldn't with the number of people I had on hand, but I could slow them almost to a stop.

As the resistance, we could have run and waited for them to leave, but I wanted this attack to cost them in material and lives. In war, taking an objective doesn't always mean you are the winner and in many wars the loser wasn't obvious at first glance. I wanted every inch of ground they took to cost them in blood. My replacement, Colonel John Rivers, was there and I explained all of this to him as we battled the Russians.

I fired a shoulder launched missile that struck a Russian Black Shark in the engine. The pilot was attempting to auto-rotate to the ground but as visible as he was, he was a bullet magnet. His engine mounting was covered in flames and smoke, a dark gray, was spewing out behind him from his engine exhaust. One gunner was hanging from the door, dead as hell, only retained by a thin nylon strap connected to the helicopter floor.

Even from a distance, I saw bullet holes walking up the sides of the aircraft and while the pilot was a brave man, his efforts were wasted. He wanted to gain altitude and fly home, but that was not to be. On this day, God had decided this man would crash land his helicopter. He made a rather rough landing in an open field about 100 meters from me. I was in a wood line. Instead of a landing it was more of a semi-controlled crash. He landed hard and the windshield flew apart as my machine guns concentrated their efforts on his aircraft. I watched as the big guns struck him and his co-pilot, killing both instantly. I sent a squad of men to try and steal any parts or all of the thermal cameras from the aircraft. Maybe by having a system, we could come up with a way to protect our folks from it's detection.

I took Rivers and we moved close to the saw mill.

"The structure will blow in a minute. My troops have a good 500 pounds of explosives under the place and it will be command detonated." I said. Russians were all around the building.

Zing, zing, two bullets sounded as they struck rocks beside us and then flew off into space.

A minute later, there was a loud explosion and the building went up in flames, killing all the Russians inside and wounding a good handful on the outside. Now my snipers began their bloody work. They'd severely wound a person and then pick off those trying to save them from death. Often they'd get a good half dozen before the first one shot would bleed to death.

I watched one brave squad charge the woods only to encounter mines, and walls of flames went up when each one was triggered. Those not killed by mines were shot to death.

Colonel Rivers blew a whistle three times and we began to withdraw. I was struck once, hard in the left side, just as the Colonel took a bullet to his head. I was spun around, fell, and crawled to him. I found him alive, just grazed by the slug. Very few partisans passed us and in the noise of battle, my cries of help were not heard. Then it grew quiet, except for the occasional *pop* of a pistol or loud *bang* from a rifle.

I pulled us both under some brush and then bandaged our wounds. I was starting to hurt, but couldn't take any morphine or I'd go to sleep. I did take two codeine tablets, but they didn't help me much. I knew I had to wait and we'd escape and evade back to our unit, maybe. A great deal depended on the extent of Rivers' injury and if he ever woke up. I decided, come dark, I was leaving and I'd try to take him with me, but he had to be conscious before I could do that. There was no way I could carry him for miles as I attempted to avoid the enemy.

I heard Russian voices, and while I only speak a word or two, I knew by the tone they were angry about their losses, which had been high. I heard the loud pop of a pistol at times and said a silent prayer for my troops as the injured were being executed. I knew they were like me, in that the fatally injured were being put out of their misery and the other wounded would be taken prisoner. It reminded me of Mississippi, where I had no cages for prisoners, and I had to kill or permanently disable any Russian troops found alive. I'd usually shoot them in the knee and move on.

They were gathering weapons, counting the dead and injured and looking for intelligence. I'd left some Ace of Spades laying around the blown up building, so they knew who had attacked. While we'd hurt them today, we didn't cripple them. Injured troops and media troops were flying in and out the rest of the afternoon.

Colonel Bykov and Master Sergeant Kovarov were in the command helicopter overhead when my troops were pulled out of the battle. The Russians had quickly moved forward, only to encounter mines, snipers and booby traps. After it had grown quiet, the chopper landed and the two men exited the aircraft. It then flew off to fly 360 degree circles until the Colonel was done looking the battlefield over. He would then call the helicopter and it would return for him.

The Colonel immediately had photos taken with him beside the dead partisans and picking up their weapons. His was all publicity images, but the old Master Sergeant walked around looking at his dead troops who just 24 hours earlier may have laughed or had breakfast with him. He shook his head at the cost in supplies, gear, and Russian lives. He then moved to the First Aid Station and held the hands of some of his seriously wounded. He prayed with or for the fatally wounded. He was used to seeing this and had seen the same thing in a dozen other countries and ten years later, Russia was no longer interested in the places all the blood had been spilled and pain suffered for. Why pay the high price if they were not going to stay?

He approached the Colonel and said, "Sir, I think it would be good for you to be seen with our dead and wounded. The folks back home need to see and know you care about your men and women."

"Excellent idea, Sergeant." he said, and then moved to the First Aid Station, with the Master Sergeant with him. A handful of photographers and TV news reporters followed them around like dogs, now that the shooting had stopped.

As they walked, the Sergeant said, "I will have all the squad leaders fill out paperwork and submit it to us for medals and awards. It is amazing how just a piece of tin and cloth can mean so much to some folks back home. I suggest we be generous with the medals, too, sir. Especially for our dead."

"Yes, of course. Uh, radioman, have the helicopter come back for us." the Colonel said, and the Master Sergeant knew the scent of the dead and dying disagreed with him.

As they climbed on the helicopter, the Sergeant looked over the battlefield and said a silent prayer for those who died on both sides to be able to find peace through death. He then shook his head at the cost.

CHAPTER 21

R ivers and I spent the entire day in the brush trying to prevent discovery. Rivers was still sleeping and I found that was best, because I couldn't leave until after dark anyway, just to be safe. At one point, late afternoon, I saw a trooper approaching and he must have seen something in our brush. I knew if he pulled the brush apart I had to kill him, so I pulled my sheath knife and made ready. He was humming when he neared, but stopped not two feet from me.

Suddenly, he pulled the brush apart and in an instant I buried the 10 inch blade in his belly and took a wild swipe at his throat. I felt warm blood run down my arm and then felt it splash on my face as it spurted from his severed neck as he choked. He fell and his eyes met mine as he jerked and twitched as he bled dry. He seemed to be asking me why, but we both knew the why of his death, because he was in my country uninvited. I would continue to kill them until the last Russian left.

When he stopped moving, I grabbed him and pulled him into the bushes with us. An hour after dusk Rivers woke and we began to walk north toward our base camp. I suggested to him he move it once more, just to be safe. If my luck held, I'd be back at our base camp in Texas a week from now, only first I had to get home and I had to see if John's head would keep him from serving as Commander. Head wounds were tricky.

I heard the Russian radio before I saw a soul. I motioned for Rivers to stop, which he did. He froze in place. I had no idea what was being said, but it'd kept us from walking in the middle of their camp. It was early morning, still dark, so we backed up and went around them. The whole time I expected to hear them open up on us, but our NVGs were life savers as well. We stayed in the darkest shadows, moved little unless walking, and never spoke unless necessary. In two days, I only said one word I could remember, "mines."

When we sat, we blended into the background and rarely moved. We rolled across roads or one would sweep our tracks as another allowed dirt to fall from our hands, dusting out our tracks. There is no way to completely hide tracks, but we tried our best. We avoided roads and trails, but we did encounter some that had to be crossed. There is no way to move cross country and not find a trail or roadway. We stepped on large rocks to avoid boot prints and made sure we didn't scuff the rock or leave mud on them.

We were close to home when Rivers, who was in front said, "Awww, shit."

For some reason his tone and choice of words made me think we were dead. He glanced back at me and said, "We're in the middle of a minefield."

"Are you sure?" I asked because it was dawn and not full light yet.

He didn't say another word, but he did point out about ten mines buried in the soil around us. I froze, felt my heart beat increase and then felt sweat on the palms of my hands. I met his eyes, gave a weak-ass smile and replied, "Move, but slowly."

He pointed to every mine he spotted and it seemed to take us five hours to cross forty feet of mine field, but it indicated we were close to home. Once on the other side, he fell to his knees and I could see he was praying. I felt so weak from the stress I almost passed out.

"I need a shot of a stiff drink after that, and I don't care what it is either."

"We'll have that, if we get home in one piece." I promised, knowing I had some whiskey in my footlocker. We continued to move.

At one point at night a chopper flew over, stopped and then backed up. I think the pilot didn't believe his thermal gear showed two people on the ground. I saw his Gatling gun start to pivot and pulled my poncho over me as I fell to the ground. I then had Rivers do the same thing. We pulled it over us, then pulled it off and then covered ourselves a few times. Then bright lights came on and flooded the area. After about twenty minutes the aircraft flew away and I'm sure the pilot thought his system was really jacked up. I don't think what we did would have confused an experienced pilot, but he must not have had much faith in the new system. That lack of faith saved our lives.

Near dawn on the third day, as I moved beside a trail, I heard a voice say in English, "Stop. Who are you and what do you want?"

"It's me, Colonel John Williamson, the Commander, and I've got Colonel John Rivers with me and he's been wounded. I think his wound is getting infected. I need your help."

"Move forward six steps, lay your weapons on the log and then place your arms over your head. Then, lace your fingers together behind your head. For your safety and ours, you'll be secured and escorted onto the base. Move too quickly and I'll blow you a new butt-hole. I am Corporal Silvers and I'm your guide on this trip in the scenic mountains of Washington state. You either do as I've asked, or I'll kill you now."

We moved forward and placed our weapons on the log and my hands immediately went up and into the air. I was tired, dirty, and not feeling well. I'd had very little to eat for four days, not sure if our drinking water was good so I'd drank little, which meant I was probably dehydrated, and feeling feverish. John was just plain out of it and the last mile or so he'd been either praying or talking to himself. I found out later he'd been talking to his long dead wife.

We were made to sit and our injuries were cared for. Besides his head wound, John also had cut up legs from walking through briers and brush, small cuts and bruises all over his body, just as I did. When you're covered with small injuries, they can take a lot of energy out of a person.

"Good job, Silvers." I said, and meant it.

"Thank you, sir."

"If I'd not listened to you, would you have really killed us?"

"Yes, sir, and never batted an eye doing it either."

"Good man." I replied.

He grinned.

Once in camp, cleaned up a little, given some hot soup and some coffee, we relaxed a little. I wanted a shower, but was just too tired and worn out to do that. Of all things, we needed sleep the most, followed by a shave and shower. Then a doctor visited us, declared us both human, and we were told to rest. We moved to my room and I opened my booze. We both had a double and I left the cap off the thing. I knew it would take more than just one double to bring us back down to earth. My adrenaline was all that was keeping my ass from dragging in the dirt. I also knew we didn't need more than two or three drinks, or we'd sleep for days.

"Well, what now?" River asked and then downed his whiskey in one gulp.

"Andy? You in your office?" I knocked my drink back and poured us another one.

"Uh, yes sir. Do you need me?"

"Care for an adult beverage, First Sergeant?" I asked as I re-filled our glasses.

"Sir, I'll pass, since it's not 0700 yet. I'll take you up on the invitation this evening if it's still open."

"The invitation will still be open. Listen, contact base, let them know that Colonel Rivers and I are both safe and here now. Make sure we are removed from any casualty listings or MIA listings. We are both healthy, weak as hell, and ready to serve. We just need a few hours of sleep."

"Aye, sir, and I'll speak with them on the horn myself. Glad to see you both back safely, sir. While we took one hell of a beating, the Russians lost more gear, material and lives, but since we withdrew they consider it a win."

"Let them call it what they wish. I am going to bed. See that I'm up at noon."

"Yes, sir." he replied and then left.

"I'm off to my tent and bed. If you need me, just let me know. I won't be back up though, because I was given a sleeping pill and told to go to bed." Rivers said.

He extended his hand and as we shook, he said, "You're one hell of a fine man, Colonel."

I replied, "So are you, Colonel. Get some rest."

I'd been handed a sleeping pill too, but tossed it to the weeds on the way to my tent. I didn't like drugs and the only ones I usually took at all were pain pills when in the field and seriously injured. Other than that, I passed on all medications if I could. We surely didn't drink much, not if a person wanted to stay alive. Plus, the booze was just not available like it once was. Oh, we had some guys who made booze, but it was rough stuff and mainly used by our medical clinic for pain.

As I lay in bed, I read the report on our recent battle at the saw mill and our casualties were much less than I suspected. Numbers were still being adjusted, because some troops continued to straggle in like Rivers and I. We'd lost some gear and had captured some Russian arms and ammunition. I fell asleep with the report in my hands and sitting up in bed, but just before I went to sleep, I thought of a way to hurt the Russians. I would hurt them enough to bring tears.

"Yuliy, this is General Anatolievich, and I am ordering your return to Russia. It seems there are those here who are not pleased with your work in America. So, you have been asked to return to explain your progress in the war."

My God, they will have me shot! Bykov thought, but said, "I am sorry to hear this, General. I have tried my best while assigned here."

"Your best has many angered and they are calling for your head. Our dead are backlogged at the airports in America because we do not have enough aircraft to bring them all home. I want you on the first flight home in the morning. I will try to help you, as I always have, but I can only do so much. I think you are facing a gulag at least, and for a good number of years."

"I have failed you and Mother Russia."

"Perhaps I can talk to the Generals Counsel and get you assigned here working with me. I can promise nothing but it beats the options. I must go now, I have a meeting, but catch the first plane back home."

"Yes, of course, sir. I will let you know by phone when I arrive in Moscow."

"Good, and I will send my private car for you then. Good-bye."

The phone went dead in Bykov's ear and he panicked. A few minutes later, he pulled his pistol, flipped the safety off and sat holding the loaded weapon. Placing it on his desk, he opened the top left drawer and pulled out a bottle of vodka. He picked up the glass on his desk, filled it with the strong drink, and gulped it down. He sat crying, like a child.

He picked up the phone, "Base Operations? I need the next flight back to Russia."

"What city, sir?" The Sergeant asked.

"Mos . . . Moscow."

"I have one leaving here at 1800 and —"

"I will take it."

"Yes, sir."

Aircraft tail number zero, eight, niner, four, one, three, or call sign Blue Goose was powered up and the ground generators were doing their job as Colonel Yuliy Bykov boarded and was shown to a first class seat. The gentle hum of the ground equipment usually calmed him, but this early evening he was drunk. He'd spent the afternoon drinking and scared to death of returning. Now he dropped into the seat and mumbled to himself about the bastards in Moscow not knowing anything about a combat unit.

"Sir, please buckle your seat belt." The stewardess said as she past his seat.

"Ladies and Gentlemen, this is your Captain, Foma Aleskeevich, and our flight time from here to Moscow is sixteen hours and five minutes. Both the co-pilot and I would like to thank you for flying with us and if you need anything during our flight, contact a stewardess. Crew to take off positions, please."

Near the fence outside the base, a man on a bicycle stopped moving and decided to watch this airplane take off. He worked for the airlines, as a local hire, and he was a landing gear specialist and his pay was much better than average.

The big beast taxied to the end of the runway and then it stopped. Then, more power was heard being applied by the pilot, but the brakes held the aircraft in place. Finally the aircraft was freed and it gave a giant shudder just before it began to roll down the runway.

The General always grew nervous during take offs and landings. He'd read somewhere that was when 90% of all aircraft crashes occurred. After what seemed like a very long time to him, the aircraft nose came up, and he heard the wheels whirling into the wheel wells. They gave a loud thump when they locked up and the doors closed. The aircraft began a gentle turn to the left with the nose slightly up. He pulled his bottle from his coat and took a long snort. Replacing the bottle, he fell back into his seat a defeated man.

Some bells sounded and the pilot said, "This is your pilot speaking and we've just passed through 20,000 feet and will continue to climb until we reach our cruising altitude of —"

Colonel Bykov heard a loud explosion and the aircraft began to shudder violently.

Not realizing his microphone was still hot and on 'cabin', the pilot asked, "What in the hell was that and look at the dash. Tower this is Blue Goose and I am declaring an in-flight emergency."

The man standing at the fence had seen the explosion and now watched as the aircraft made an attempt to return to the base. He smiled, mounted his bicycle and rode toward home. He would report the results to the resistance as soon as he knew the status of the plane. He was sure it would all be reported on the television.

"Captain to crew, please assume crash landing positions. The aircraft is still under my control, but once we land, evacuate the aircraft immediately." the Captain's voice was still calm and collected.

The aircraft began to bounce around and shiver as they gently moved into position to land at Seattle. He sat watching outside the window and saw them fly over the perimeter fence.

When the co-pilot flipped the landing gear switch, and the gear started down, they pulled a cord attached to the detonator inserted in a block of C-4. When the cord was fully extended it detonated, blowing the nose landing gear from the aircraft and creating a second hole in the aircraft. Hydraulics and electrical systems were damaged.

"Uh tower, I've just had a second explosion in the nose wheel well area and I've no choice but to land now."

"Go around, Blue Goose, and we'll look you over."

"Negative on the go around, because my instrument panel is lit up like a Christmas tree. Be advised, I am putting her down now."

At the word *now* the rear landing gear screeched as rubber met the concrete, and the pilot began to slowly reduce power. The wings began to wobble as the co-pilot read off their air speed.

Without notice, the left wing struck the ground, the aircraft cartwheeled twice and began to break apart. The main body landed upside down hard on the runway and continued to slide. There was a loud explosion as the fuel stored in both wings went up in flames. Burning fuel soon began to leak into the cabin.

It was then the cabin began to break apart and into sections. A giant wall of flames moved through the section that Colonel Bykov sat and his screams of pain and fear joined the others. The broken shell rolled to a stop about halfway down the runway.

From where the wheels first touched down to the ditch the dead crew finally struck, the runway was littered with aircraft parts and pieces of human bodies. Emergency response personnel ran from their vehicles and pulled people from the flames and broken parts of the aircraft.

One man ran from the fire, his clothing aflame, and he stumbled around as he burned. He gave a hideous scream as his slacks melted to his legs. Finally, he fell to the ground and after jerking a few times, he stopped moving. He was dead.

The Colonel was in deep pain with burns over 85% of his body. He had a nasty gash to his forehead and his left arm was missing at the elbow. He shivered and moaned as he attempted to breathe in all the smoke. Minutes later, his world faded from full light through various stages of gray until it turned black and finally he lost consciousness.

The doctor approached Master Sergeant Kovarov and when near he said, "I am sorry Master Sergeant, but Colonel Bykov passed away about ten minutes ago. He was too badly burned to survive and in a great deal of pain. Do they know what happened?"

"Sabotage is all I know, and apparently with two bombs."

"I must return to my work. The resistance killed over 200 this day and I have a hospital full of injured, of which many will die if I don't do my share. I am sorry about your commander." He turned and walked back down the pea green hallway and the through the double doors.

Kovarov stood, straightened his posture and walked from the hospital like the top enlisted dog he was and while he was hurting inside, he kept it to himself. He went back to his quarters, showered, and had a breakfast of cold-cuts, soup and bread. He then dressed in a fresh uniform and went to his duty section, even though it was late evening, because there would be phone calls and visitors, all high ranking, wanting to know what had happened.

An hour later, after he'd answered the calls from Generals in Moscow and other bases in America, he opened his locker and pulled out a bottle of top shelf vodka. Usually a man who never drank alone, he poured a triple and took a sip. There was a loud clap of thunder and he realized it was rare to hear that sound in this part of the United States. Soon rain was beating against the widow panes. He decided right then to spend the night in his office, because he had a small twin bed in a back store room and he wanted to be alone.

The Colonel's death didn't really bother him, but the many deaths of people he had known over the years were beginning to take a toll on him. He'd known when first assigned here they were locked in a war they could not win. Russia had over 48,000 deaths already and they were no closer to winning the war now than the first day they arrived. Partisan wars were never won, because there were no front lines. The enemy could bring the war to any spot they chose and then melt into the population. They also fought efficiently, usually losing only one or two people for every ten or more they killed. Kovarov was no coward, but all had been quiet here until Williamson showed up.

He watched the rain beat on the glass panes and thought, *If I can remove the head, the rest of the snake will die. Williamson is the brains behind the partisans here, and their leader. He took another sip of his drink. There must be a way to kill him. Obviously the one million dollars reward is not working. Kill Williamson*, he thought again.

He watched a single raindrop strike the pane and began to run down the glass. He took a drink.

Kill Williamson and make him pay for making mother Russia look like a fool. He's only one man and you'd think it would be easy to kill just one man. But, I will do it one day. One day soon, I will stand here in this office with his severed head on my desk. Then, and only then, can I return to Russia to retire and rest. I must kill him, or he kills me.

Raising the glass, he said, "To Colonel John Williamson, wherever you are, know that one of us will soon die."

The End

BE SURE TO WATCH FOR BOOK 8

OF THE FALL OF AMERICA SERIES,

AN AMAZON BEST SELLING SERIES.

ABOUT THE AUTHOR

W.R. Benton was born on his grandfather's farm, delivered by his grandmother, near Vida, Missouri, down in the Ozark Mountains. He attended public schools in the local area and graduated from Rolla Senior High, Rolla, Missouri, in 1971. After graduation, he joined the United States Air Force and began a career that would span over 26 years. He has an Associate's Degree in Search and Rescue, Survival Operations, a Bachelors Degree in Occupational Safety and Health, and a Masters Degree in Clinical Psychology completed, except for his thesis. His first Book released was *"Silently Beats the Drum,"* and over 40 more books have followed, along with 9 Audio Editions of his work. Many of his stories are available in paperbacks as well. His book, *"War Paint,"* will soon be a feature movie.

W. R. Benton is popular among readers who love hard continuous action and adventure. As a young reader, he would often turn pages to find more excitement. So, when he turned to writing, he decided his readers should be entertained, made to think, and feel the emotions of his characters. Many readers say his work grasps them in the first paragraph and maintains their interest until the last paragraph, which is exactly what W. R. strives for when writing.

Mister Benton lives in Mississippi, with his wife, dogs, and cats, on an imaginary ranch with thousands of make-believe cows and horses.

www.wrbenton.net

www.facebook.com/wrbenton01

On a trip to the Lake Clark area of the Alaskan bush, a sudden arctic weather system forces down the small plane of Dr. Jim Wade, and his son David. Both have survived the crash, but not unscathed. Food, fire and shelter are all a priority. Following the death of his father, now it is up to David to figure out what to do next, and how to survive, on a remote Alaskan mountain—in winter!

This is a fictional story of survival, resilience and of the spirit to live. It is both authentic and accurate, having been written by a former Air Force life support survival instructor. For ages 10 and up

Both are available at Amazon and other online bookstores

Set adrift, a family of three are cast out to sea in a rubber raft, where they must find a way to conquer one terrifying tragedy after another or die in the process.

In this gripping story of survival everyone will be tested to their limits. Christian faith and hope are hallmarks of this tale that will touch your heart..

The NEW WORLD ORDER series
'A political-thriller uncomfortably close to today's headlines'

As the rich and elite of the world move to put the new world order in place across the globe, they understand they must move quickly. At times just as rich and exciting in content as real American history — this is a series of heroism, valor, patriotism, greed, blackmail, sex, traitors, and death, as normal day-to-day Americans make a valiant stand against the takeover.

Available at Amazon

Mark of the Beast, Vol. 1 - the rich and elite move quickly to take complete control of the world and all governments. They attempt to place the whole world under the control of one leader, unidentified, with a totalitarian world government. They hope to have one world bank, one currency, one government, and they promise comfortable lives for all citizens of the world. Countries are invaded by UN troops and martial law is declared, a few weapons are gathered, food is suddenly strictly rationed, no cars, no gas, and no utilities for anyone who is not wealthy and a part of the New World Order.

California Invasion, Vol. 2 - In Volume 2 of the New World Order series, the Order shows a new U.S. President what will happen if he doesn't do their bidding. These shadowy puppet-masters will sacrifice anyone, even elites in the upper circles of power, and they prove that to the new President in vivid detail. Individual lives mean nothing when their objective is so close they can taste it.

COWBOYS AND ZOMBIES

A bone gnawing tale of western horror

Exhausted from his long vision quest, a young warrior falls prey to the lies of the Sioux demon "Double Face". He is tricked into accepting the gift of eternal life, but immortality comes at a terrible price; he will need to feast on the flesh of the living to survive and his bite will turn all men into his army of unspeakable undead creatures.

Available for the Kindle
..and in Paperback Feb. 2018

9 781944 476618